I COULD BE FAMOUS

I COULD BE FAMOUS

SYDNEY RENDE

FLEET

FLEET

First published in the United States by Bloomsbury Publishing in 2026
First published in Great Britain in 2026 by Fleet

1 3 5 7 9 10 8 6 4 2

Copyright © Sydney Rende, 2026

The moral right of the author has been asserted.

All characters and events in this publication, other than those
clearly in the public domain, are fictitious and any resemblance
to real persons, living or dead, is purely coincidental.

A CIP catalogue record for this book
is available from the British Library.

ISBN 978-0-349-72528-4

Typeset by Westchester Publishing Services
Printed and bound in Great Britain by Clays Ltd, Elcograf S.p.A.

Papers used by Fleet are from well-managed forests
and other responsible sources.

MIX
Paper | Supporting
responsible forestry
FSC
www.fsc.org   FSC® C104740

Fleet
An imprint of
Little, Brown Book Group
Carmelite House
50 Victoria Embankment
London EC4Y 0DZ

The authorised representative
in the EEA is
Hachette Ireland
8 Castlecourt Centre
Dublin 15, D15 XTP3, Ireland
(email: info@hbgi.ie)

An Hachette UK Company
www.hachette.co.uk

www.littlebrown.co.uk

For Scar

How should a person be? I sometimes wonder about it, and I can't help answering like this: a celebrity.

—SHEILA HETI, *HOW SHOULD A PERSON BE?*

CONTENTS

CONTENTS

Nothing Special

I sent a message to a celebrity on the internet. It said, *I think we'd make a good match*. I added my phone number at the end.

I didn't expect him to respond. Still, now that the message had been sent, I was checking my phone constantly—scrolling my thumb down to refresh the screen almost twenty, thirty times a day. Three days passed like this: me unlocking my phone, opening the message, closing it, then opening it again. On the third day, I typed out, *never mind*. I let the words sit in the text box for a few hours to gather some heat. Then I went back and deleted them. I felt like a loser. My boyfriend didn't seem to notice.

"I'm being ignored," I said. He was standing at the stove, making vegetable curry for dinner. I was sitting at his kitchen table, waiting to eat. We'd met at a potluck thrown by a mutual friend who needed Tupperware. To the friend's disappointment, most people had brought raw, whole foods—pineapples, eggplant, heads of broccoli. I had brought pizza bagels. They were not A Hit.

"Lots of sodium," my boyfriend had said, before he was my boyfriend. Now we'd been together for almost a year. He had this messy, shoulder-length hair—bleached blond from a life in the sun—that he combed through with his fingers in the mornings. Sometimes I watched him tug at the knots and thought I could love him. Other times I thought about how relieved I would feel if he died—or better yet, if he had never existed. We didn't have a lot in common. He made his own chili garlic paste, grew cilantro in his backyard. He was in graduate school for social work and used terms like "relationship coefficient" and "primitive midbrain." Once, after I'd posted a video of myself organizing my refrigerator, we'd gotten into a fight about my inability to activate my "prefrontal cortex." I was always at a disadvantage during our fights because I never had any idea what we were talking about.

"That sounds like a car part," I'd told him. Then he called me shallow and naive, said I was "chasing fame's elusive fart," or something like that, and I said, "Oh, yes, please, all-knowing Man God, Decider of Destinies, please tell me more about myself."

After that we didn't talk for a few hours, and later that night I snuck into his backyard and sprayed his cilantro with Febreze.

"Who's ignoring you?" he asked me now. He adjusted the heat on the stove and stirred. "Smell that?"

Veganism was our newest Thing. It had something to do with the testosterone levels in red meat contributing to the volatility of arguments, apparently. Over the last few weeks of nuts, root vegetables, and milk substitutes, my boyfriend had become lean and hyperaware of his surroundings, all his senses operating at full speed. But as far as I could tell, the diet was only making me gassy.

"Arlo Banks," I said.

"The actor?" The curry bubbled and splattered against his white shirt. He looked down at the mess and then kept stirring.

"Yes, the actor."

Arlo Banks had been a teen star. Back then, he was known for his falsetto on a musical show about Catholic school boys. Also his icy-blue eyes and the way he flipped his hair off his forehead. Now he had short hair. According to his profile, he was traveling a lot. He'd been to Antarctica to take photos with people who studied ice, to the Amazon to take photos with people who'd never heard of photos. He was a very active person. I liked to watch him travel. This video of him riding a dirt bike through a jungle was particularly inspiring. And another of him climbing a tall, flat rock. He looked like someone who did whatever he wanted, executed his life plans with great zeal. If he did end up calling me like I'd asked, that would mean he was also reliable. That's not something you see often in a famous actor.

"Why would he be ignoring you?" my boyfriend said. "Ow, fuck." He turned the heat down. "Do you know him? I'm confused."

I stared at my phone, at the unanswered message.

"I sent him a message and he didn't respond."

"Are you talking about the guy from that Christian show? The one who sings and dances?"

My boyfriend was confused but not upset. He seemed more concerned about the curry than my sadness. "Here," he said, "try this."

He dipped a spoon into the sauce and then held his hand under the spoon while he walked it over to the kitchen table. He held the spoon to my mouth. "It's hot."

It smelled spicy. I licked the spoon and started to cough. "He doesn't really do that kind of thing anymore."

"Did you expect him to respond? Does it need more salt?"

"I guess so."

He went back to the stove and added salt.

"I guess I thought he would want to know me."

My boyfriend plated the food and brought the plates to the table, then sat down next to me. "Forks," he said. He stood up and got two forks and brought them to the table. "Napkins." He got up again and got two napkins.

"This looks delicious," I said. It looked sloppy and a little gray, like it had been cooked for too long. I stared at it and thought it looked exactly like me in the form of food.

"No offense," he said, "but why would Arlo Banks want to know you?"

It wasn't as crazy an idea as it sounded. I was five foot seven, 116 pounds, with olive skin, hazel eyes, and long brown hair that shimmered all on its own. I could have been a model. When I was a kid, a man in a suit at a Nordstrom department store confronted me and my mother, asked if I wanted to be in an upcoming shoot for pajamas. I started crying. Maybe I was scared. I certainly hadn't known that I'd just been offered a career path. Whenever my mother told the story, she said that I'd grabbed onto her leg and buried my face behind her knee, that she had to pick me up and carry me out of the store. I had a lot of regret about this, about how stupid and scared I'd been in the face of something so propelling. Often, I wondered where I'd be if I had said yes. Maybe I'd already be dating Arlo Banks, or someone like Arlo Banks. I had once heard him say in an interview that he was lonely even though he had so many friends. His fame isolated him. He wanted a partner, someone to collaborate with, to be inspired by—a muse. The more I thought about it, the less invested I felt in my current relationship and the more certain I was that Arlo Banks and I belonged together.

"Every time you start a sentence with 'no offense' you end up saying something offensive." I nudged my plate away. My boyfriend shoveled the curry into his mouth, leaning over his plate so that any food that fell from his fork would land back in the slop pile to be scooped up again.

"I guess I'm just confused about your motive. Like, what's the goal?" my boyfriend asked, showing off his new plant-based reasonability.

"The goal is maybe he would want to take me sailing or jet skiing. Maybe he'd want to take me to the Amazon."

My boyfriend chewed on the slop, swallowed, coughed it back up, then re-swallowed. "You don't want to go to the Amazon."

He was right, actually. I had no interest in exploring the Amazon. But if Arlo Banks wanted to fly me there first-class, I would not complain.

"You have no idea what I want," I said.

"I have *some* idea."

The spices in the curry were making him sweat. He wiped his forehead with his napkin and stared out the window. "It was hot today. Maybe I should buy a window unit."

"Maybe." I was so sad I could have died.

★ ★ ★

Over the next few days my message to Arlo Banks remained unanswered. His most recent post was a video of himself in a canoe in some vast, unnamed body of water. His arms were raised in the air and he was wearing a blue-green shirt that matched the color of the water. I thought maybe he didn't have good service. That could have been it. Still, whenever my phone buzzed, my heart dropped into my stomach, and I'd rush to see if it was him. It was never him, but it was often my boyfriend.

Are you at In-N-Out? My phone says you are.

Are you really eating a cheeseburger?

Your passive aggression is not charming.

I ate the cheeseburger and ignored my boyfriend. I didn't like him very much. I scrolled through my profile to a time-lapse video I'd posted of him, digging a hole in the wet sand of the Venice Beach shoreline in front of the setting sun. I had no idea why I'd posted it. Most of the people I followed—girls I'd gone to high school or college with, girls I'd met in the bathroom at parties—were engaged or having babies. Some were buying homes or fostering kittens. They posted photos of themselves with their fiancés beneath the fall foliage, of their babies in bathtubs, of the pinto–bean–size diamonds on their fingers. I was jealous of how content they seemed in their lives, how everything seemed to be working out for them. In my stupid video of the sunset, my boyfriend had a stain on his shirt—a big yellowish splotch that looked like dried urine. It was probably some kind of plant juice. Disgusting. I couldn't understand why he insisted on wearing the same old T-shirts, as if he were making a statement against consumer capitalism, the absurdity of appearances. I didn't care about any of that. I wanted a boyfriend who had specific outfits for air travel. I watched the video a few more times and then deleted it.

Later that night my friend Jude invited me to a party. It wasn't a potluck, it was a real party. Jude—who'd hosted the potluck, and whom I blamed for getting me into this whole mess with the vegan social worker—knew someone who knew the host. The party was at a luxury apartment complex in Hollywood that was known for housing beautiful people who hosted extravagant parties. It had a rooftop pool with a pool bar, a DJ, and cabanas all around the perimeter for people to post photos of themselves lounging on. I wore a tight black dress with long sleeves. I wanted to look impressive, even though I was pretty sure Arlo Banks wouldn't be there. I went straight to the open bar and ordered a vodka and water. Everyone at the party looked like a model, or like someone who hung around models in the hopes of soaking up glamour.

"It's like a roof full of glass giraffes," Jude said, once I found her. She pointed to a blonde giraffe who was standing by the DJ, dancing with only the top half of her body, moving her arms in a little jig.

"That's Ramona. I do spin with her. She's the hottest person I've ever seen."

I suddenly felt defensive, like I had to prove that I belonged at this party with the world's hottest people.

"Is she a model?"

"Influencer. She has, like, four hundred thousand followers."

"What does she post?"

"Herself, obviously."

The hot girl turned and pointed at Jude, then dance-shuffled across the patio toward us.

"Do you guys want to dance?"

She hadn't stopped dancing. I wondered if she was on some sort of drug. Her hairline was a little damp with sweat and she didn't look capable of blinking. Still, she had the attitude of someone who had never been rejected by anyone or excluded from anything. Jude and I followed her out to the dance floor like obedient pets. She interlaced her fingers with mine, raised our arms in the air, and smiled at me like we were already close friends. I thought I might be in love with her. Or maybe I wanted to be her—I didn't see the difference. I didn't want to sleep with her, although I wouldn't have minded sleeping next to her, waking up to the coconutty smell of her hair, watching her try on all the outfits she'd gotten for free.

"Do you want another drink?" I said, jerking my hips.

"I have to pee." She started walking and I followed her.

There was a line outside the bathroom, but the hot girl pranced past everyone and into the building's interior. She led me down a long hallway and opened the door to an apartment. Inside looked like a stock photo of a luxury apartment, with floor-to-ceiling windows, gray vinyl floors, and a long white leather couch. She led us into the bathroom and closed the door, then leaned over the toilet and threw up.

"Sorry," she said to the toilet. She held back her hair at the nape of her neck. I hovered above her, feeling useless and a little creepy for staring. She threw up again, then stood, flushed the toilet, turned on the tap of the sink, and stuck her mouth under the faucet. She spat the water down the drain.

"Are you okay?" It was a stupid thing to say. Obviously, she was fine. She would always be fine, no matter the circumstances. The building could blow up, incinerate us, splatter our guts all over the street, and she'd walk out of the ash with nothing worse than a chipped toenail.

"I'm good." She combed through her hair in the mirror. There was a men's razor on the counter and a bottle of two-in-one shampoo on the ledge of the bathtub.

"Do you live here?"

"God, no. Everyone who lives here is a try-hard. It's like, I don't need to shit where I eat, you know?"

"Totally." I had no idea what she was talking about. She opened the medicine cabinet and took out the Vaseline, dabbed some on her lips and her cheekbones. She made eye contact with me through the mirror.

"You have the best skin I've ever seen." She turned around, touched my cheek with the greasy pads of her fingers. "Do you even wear makeup?"

"Not really," I said proudly.

"You could be an influencer." She pursed her lips and examined my face, then reached up and tousled my hair. "Give me your phone."

I gave her my phone.

"Get in the tub."

I climbed over the rim of the tub and sat down with my knees to my chest, waiting for more instructions.

"Not like that." She held the phone up and tested the angle. "Put one leg over."

I leaned back against the tub and put my leg over the rim in what felt like a birthing position. Maybe the alcohol had gone to my head, or the position of my legs in the tub had sparked some sense of new life in me, but I felt like something important was about to happen.

"No." She shook her head. "Put the other foot up by the faucet. And don't smile. And lift that arm over your head."

I did everything she said and stared at the phone. It was difficult not to smile. My chest tingled and I fought the urge to laugh. "This feels weird."

"I know, right?" She looked at the phone. "Got it. This is hot."

I got out of the tub and stood beside her and looked at the photo. I could smell the alcohol on her breath and the coconut in her hair. She was right—I did look hot. A little uncomfortable, maybe, but definitely hot. I stared at my face in the photo and felt sad, suddenly, at the thought of my wasted potential. I could have been this person, but I wasn't. I didn't know what I was.

"You should post this," she said.

"I don't know."

"Why?" She almost looked offended, like not posting the photo would be an insult to her specifically. She clicked out of the photo and opened the app. I felt my face get hot. The last thing I'd been looking at was my message to Arlo Banks. I watched her eyes scan the message, then I sat down on the rim of the tub, feeling defeated. She probably thought I was a stalker, that I had come to this party specifically to find her and hold her hand and smell her hair. I was too plagued with desperation to be her friend. She glanced at me, then back at the phone. She moved her thumbs around on the screen and then handed the phone back to me.

"I posted it."

She had cut out the shampoo bottle on the corner ledge of the tub and enhanced the shadows, with the caption *scrub-a-dub in the tub.*

"I don't have that many followers," I said.

She turned to the mirror to look at herself, wiped the black from the corner of her eye.

"I put my number in there, too. I'm Ramona."

She leaned over and kissed me on the lips—not in a sexual way. In the way you might kiss a baby. Her lips tasted like apple, not at all like puke. Then she grabbed my hand and led me back to the dance floor.

★ ★ ★

The next morning, I woke up to a text.

Brunch at joans?

I jumped out of bed and put on the coolest outfit I owned—a sleeveless, mustard-colored jumpsuit with buttons down the front and cuffed ankles. I paired it with my white leather high-tops and stared at myself in the mirror. I looked like somebody, but I wasn't sure who. I texted Ramona back and left for the restaurant.

I sat at a table on the patio for almost twenty minutes, wondering if the whole thing had been a delusion. I was about thirty seconds away from sending a pathetic follow-up text when Ramona seemed to appear out of nowhere in loose jeans and a hooded sweatshirt, towering above me like a supermodel.

"God, am I hungover," she said. She sat down across from me and pulled her hair back into a ponytail. She didn't look hungover or even tired. I suddenly felt embarrassed about my lack of hangover and also the sophistication of my outfit.

"Did you order?"

"Oh, no," I said. "I just got here."

Ramona looked down at the menu then tossed it to the side. "All I want is, like, an entire confetti cake. You know?"

In the twenty minutes I'd been sitting alone, I'd scoured the menu in an effort to find the perfect brunch order. I'd been between the yogurt parfait (a cute food) and the kale salad with an added poached egg (a classy food). Now I thought both of these were garbage orders and I'd probably just ask for whatever Ramona was having.

"Can I just have two brownies?" she said, when the server came over to take our order. She giggled at herself. "And a black coffee."

"Me, too," I said.

"I have to show you something," Ramona said, when the server walked away. She talked as though we'd been friends for years and this were just another morning we were spending together, hungover and sharing secrets. She reached into her bag, pulled out a small velvet box, and put it on the table.

"Open it. I just got them."

I reached across the table and opened the box. Inside was a pair of diamond earrings. They caught the sunlight and shot it into my eyes.

"Whoa," I said. They must have cost thousands of dollars.

"Yeah, I know. But there's one problem." She pulled on her earlobes, which were conspicuously unpierced.

"Oh, that's easy," I said. And Ramona smiled like she'd discovered something new about me that she liked or could at least make use of.

When our brownies arrived, Ramona pulled hers apart and stuck the pieces into her mouth one at a time, sucking the gooey bits off her fingers. If she had been anyone else, I would have thought her eating habits were gross. But somehow she made the whole thing look good—sexy, even.

"So you'll come with me?" she said, her thumb in her mouth as she licked the chocolate off her nail. She pulled on her ear again with her clean hand.

"Yes," I said confidently.

She pulled a fifty from her wallet and tossed it on the table. "Let's go now."

★   ★   ★

Ramona quickly became my best friend. I had no idea if I was also her best friend, but based on the amount of time she spent on her phone, I assumed I wasn't. Still, she brought me with her to parties at the apartment complex, introduced me to other hot people as if I were a gem she'd found while digging through a pile of trash.

"This is Jane," she'd say, nudging me forward to put me on display. "Isn't she perfect?"

I felt good when I was around her, like as long as she was with me, I was a successful person. I broke up with my boyfriend via text (Ramona's words), and he sent back a long paragraph criticizing my primordial Horcrux, or whatever. Ramona laughed at it. She laughed like she was on camera: tossing her head back and opening her mouth to the sky, her hair draping down her back like a shiny curtain. I learned to laugh like she laughed and talk the way she talked and throw my shoulders back the way she did when she walked into a room. Somehow, I even grew an inch taller. The parties she brought me to were packed with more perfect people—influencers, YouTube stars, reality TV contestants, but nobody I had seen before or recognized. Still, they were stars, famous for being themselves in virtual places. I met a guy who was known for eating all types of cake on camera, and a couple who'd met on a reality show that stranded hot singles on an island. Now they were brand ambassadors for weight-loss tea and blackhead erasers. There were wellness influencers who posted photos of their broccoli and their abs, mom influencers who'd erased their stretch marks, ASMR creators who scratched their scalps into microphones. I even met a girl who'd gotten her own TV show after she filmed herself smashing loaves of sourdough bread with her face. Everyone had money and shimmery skin. Their eyelashes were surgically elongated, their clothes limited edition. But nobody compared to Ramona. She was the person everyone wanted to be—effortlessly mysterious, a geode among river stones. Being tied to her had turned me into a person people wanted to look at. She posted photos of us together at these parties, in swimming pools, on deep, plush couches. Before I met her, I had three hundred followers. Now I had nearly three thousand followers, and Ramona made sure I posted at least once a day. If I skipped a day, she'd text me, *Where are you?* Then she'd send me a photo of myself that she'd edited. *This one.*

★   ★   ★

When Ramona finally invited me to her house, she told me to pack a bag.

"You're staying the weekend," she said. "You don't need a toothbrush or any of that stuff. I have it all. Just bring options. We're having people over."

I felt like I had been invited to the Met Gala. I packed two suitcases, the first with dresses, jumpers, leotards, silk tops, flare jeans, boyfriend jeans, leather leggings—all clothes I'd gotten from Ramona, or because of Ramona, or with Ramona since my life with her had begun. I loaded the second suitcase with shoes. Ramona texted me her address: 68 Paradise Cove Road, which sounded exactly right. I couldn't imagine her living somewhere other than paradise. She would look out of place anywhere else. I hadn't dared invite her to my stupid little studio, which was just a converted garage that belonged to the house in front of it. It was a sad, soggy room, paid for by my equally sad receptionist job, both of which I had come to believe I was too good for.

When I plugged the directions to Ramona's into my phone, I saw the house was in Malibu. Arlo Banks lived in Malibu. At least, I assumed he did. In strapping myself to Ramona, I had all but forgotten about my original dream to date Arlo Banks, travel the world with him, and move into his home. I opened the message I'd sent him, months ago, which had gone unseen and unanswered. It looked even more pathetic now. I felt the urge to laugh at it, as if someone else had written it. I clicked out of the message and opened the map and drove to Malibu, where my new life was waiting for me.

Ramona's bungalow was small but spacious, with one open wall that revealed a backyard with a pool, plush patio furniture, and a small outdoor bar. The view from the yard overlooked the houses below and, farther out, the ocean—all of it decorated with palm trees and flowering cacti, yellow dirt and smooth rocks. Inside, the living room couch looked lived-in, a little worn, but in a soft, homey way, and Ramona had hung up all these Technicolor prints on the walls. I thought the house must have been worth a couple million dollars, which now felt attainable. I wanted to take a picture of the whole thing and send it to the social worker as proof that my way had been the right way. My way had landed me here, while he was still cooking plant-based slop in his dishwasher-less kitchen. I was proud of myself. Even though none of this belonged to me, I felt like I had a right to it.

In the kitchen, Ramona had set out wineglasses and a few bottles of red wine. She uncorked one and poured a glass for herself and one for me.

"Tonight is going to be special." She held her glass in the air to meet mine. "There's someone I want you to meet."

"Who?"

"Just a friend of my boyfriend's."

"You have a boyfriend?"

I had never seen or heard Ramona talk about her boyfriend. He hadn't been at any of the parties she'd taken me to, and he wasn't in any of her photos. I felt disappointed at the thought of all Ramona's magnificent energy being channeled into a stupid boy. It didn't seem right that someone so perfect still had to put up with the mundane rituals of a relationship. I couldn't picture her cleaning the shaven hair off the bathroom sink, or burying her head into a pillow to muffle the sound of snoring. She was too good for all of that.

"Sort of," she said.

I thought her boyfriend must have been someone high-profile, someone who didn't like his photo taken and didn't want to stand out in a crowd. Suddenly I couldn't think about anything other than who he might be, and who his friend might be, and who I might become as a result of meeting them.

"Let's get dressed," Ramona said. She helped me carry my suitcases to her bedroom, then opened them and dumped all the clothes on the floor.

"Not this," she said, flinging a pair of jeans into the corner. She held up a silver slip dress and shook it out. "Can I wear this? It looks better on you, but I love it so much." She held the dress to her chest.

"Of course." I would have let her wear my skin if she asked for it. I watched her undress in front of her mirror. She kicked off her sweatpants and threw her shirt and bra to the floor and stared at herself. I could see the blue veins that crept up her chest and the faint outline of her rib cage between her breasts. I had never noticed that space on my own body, but her breasts were so small and her ribs so prominent that I couldn't look anywhere else.

Ramona met my eyes through the mirror and smiled. I wasn't even embarrassed. She was so used to people staring at her this way, and I wasn't any different from everyone else. Ramona slid the dress over her head and smoothed it out along her stomach.

"I'm a little nervous," she said. "I don't have my boyfriend over very much. Usually we go to his place."

I got up from her bed and walked to the mirror and put my arms around her waist. I stuffed my face into her hair and breathed in. I couldn't help myself. I felt so comfortable, so at home, there in her expensive house among her shimmery belongings. Everything smelled like her—sweet and raw, like something new to earth. I wanted to smell like that, too.

"I love you," I said. The words slipped out easy, almost by mistake.

Ramona reached back and petted my head. "I love you, too," she said, but it sounded too sweet, too light, as if she were talking to a puppy she'd just met. This was how Ramona talked to everyone, no matter the circumstances. Her voice was cute and high, always curling up at the ends of her sentences. I wanted her to know that I *loved* her loved her, in a way that I was pretty sure was unconditional. I slipped my hand under her dress and rested it against her hip. I felt the tiny hairs on her skin prick up. She placed her hand on top of mine and slowly pulled it off her body, then turned around and pressed her forehead against mine.

"You should wear the sequined dress. It makes your ass look huge."

She walked over to her closet and sifted through her clothes, then pulled out a short sequined dress with spaghetti straps and a pair of black boots and tossed them at me. I didn't ask questions. I got undressed and put them on. Ramona didn't watch me. Instead, she walked into her bathroom and sat at the vanity and glued on fake eyelashes. I wondered who else had loved her the way that I did, if her boyfriend felt something similar to what I felt. From Ramona's bed I held my phone up and captured her through the doorframe, leaning in toward the mirror and fixing a false eyelash to her eye with a pair of tweezers. Her lips were tucked into her mouth and her hair fell long down her back. I adjusted the photo's brightness, applied a hazy filter that made it look as though it were from another time. I captioned it *my best friend*, with a twinkly star, then posted it. Ramona came out of the bathroom a few minutes later, her face done, her hair full and parted down the middle. The doorbell rang. She reached for my hands and squeezed them.

"You're going to do great," she said. She fluffed up my hair, flicked my cheeks to give them some color. I felt like I was being prepped for an audition. An audition for what? I had no idea, but I guessed she wanted this mystery man to fall in love with me so that we could both be dating celebrities, which would really heighten our platform and look great in photos.

We walked out of the bedroom and through the kitchen and dining room, where I stopped and poured myself more wine. Ramona went through the living room and opened the front door.

"I missed you," I heard her say in a tone I didn't recognize. It was low, breathy, the way you might sound when you've just woken up. She closed the door and I heard sets of footsteps coming toward me. I took a big gulp of wine and wiped my mouth with my arm. I felt on the cusp of something huge. Everything I'd done until now—my stint with the social worker, that first night with Ramona in the bathroom, even my stupid message to Arlo Banks—was merely preparation for this moment.

Ramona entered the room followed by two men in suits. I immediately noticed their feet: their leather loafers, the way the hems of their pants sagged and brushed the ground as they walked. Both of their suits looked a size too big, as were their fat ties, knotted tightly at their necks. And they were old. One man was entirely bald, with a neck that looked like a rooster's wattle and puffy cheeks, pink with rosacea. He reached out his fat hand and tucked Ramona's hair behind her ear, revealing one glistening diamond, and whispered something into her neck. She giggled and play-fully smacked his hand away. The other man was just as old, maybe 65 or 150, with wispy white hair. One of his ears was pierced with a gold stud, and he was holding a bouquet of dyed-orange roses. He held the roses out in my direction.

"I brought these for you." His voice was croaky and used up. "Although they aren't nearly as beautiful as you are."

I took the roses. Ramona was smiling at me like whatever was happening was exactly right. I jerked my head in the direction of her bedroom and blinked in an effort to send some kind of telepathic message.

"We'll be right back," she said. She kissed the bald man on the cheek. "Pour yourselves some wine."

I followed Ramona to her bedroom and closed the door behind us. She paced across the room, her eyes wide with anger, like I'd already ruined the night.

"What is going on?" I put the flowers on her dresser. "Is that your boyfriend?"

"You're blowing it. You haven't smiled once."

I felt dizzy and sat down on her bed. "What are you talking about?"

"Bill is a really nice guy." She sat down beside me. "He'll buy you whatever you want, take you wherever you want to go. Do you want to go to Bali? He'll take you there. Do you want a new apartment, nice things?"

"I don't want to go to Bali with *him*. He's, like, one hundred years old. Who even is he?"

"He does something with insurance or computers. Who cares? He's rich and he wants to spend his money on you. You don't even have to have sex with him."

I felt my face get hot. My armpits were beginning to itch. "Do *you* have sex with *that man*?"

"That's not really any of your business." Ramona got up and straightened her dress in the mirror. I stared at her reflection and wanted to cry. My chest ached, like a wire had been twisted around my heart.

"I can't believe you're being so judgmental," she said. "A rich guy wants to buy you things and take you places. A lot of people would kill for that. And I picked him out specifically for you. He's vetted. He's not a creep. He's just lonely. His wife is dead and he, like, collects trains or something."

"Trains?"

"Yeah, like toy trains."

"Oh, great. That makes me feel better."

"Fine, whatever. I'll send him home."

She walked toward the door and I began to panic. I was upset, maybe even angry at her, but I couldn't stand the thought of her leaving me.

"I'm afraid" was the only thing I could think to say. It was true. I was afraid of the men standing in her dining room, afraid of what they might do to us. I wanted to scoop Ramona up in my arms and carry her out of the house, somewhere safe where we could live without consequences. But I was afraid of her, too. She had tricked me, or was in the process of tricking me. I could feel it all over my body, a million needles pricking my skin alert.

Ramona let go of the doorknob and walked over to me. She knelt between my legs. "I'm not trying to scare you." She rested her hands on my knees. "I thought this was what you wanted."

She looked so small and harmless. I didn't want to disappoint her, to blow up some idea she'd had of our future.

"Just give me a minute."

Ramona kissed my knee and stood up. "Oh, and your name is Sasha. And don't call me Ramona, okay? Call me Randy."

She looked, suddenly, like an entirely different person. I wanted to put her in the bathtub and scrub everything off her—the fake eyelashes, fake name, the cigar-smoky smell of that man's breath on her neck—until she was recognizable again. I didn't know how to say any of this to her. She reached for my hand and I grabbed it, let her pull me to my feet and lead me out of the room.

"I'm sorry," I said to the old men. "I didn't feel well."

"You look well, now," Bill said. He was beaming at me. He looked like a retired talk show host. He handed me a new glass of wine and we followed Ramona and the bald man out to the patio. Bill put his hand on my lower back as we walked, gently nudging me forward.

"Watch your step there," he said, like a grandpa.

We sat down on the patio furniture—a deep L-shaped couch with a matching ottoman—and Ramona put her hand on the bald man's thigh and said, "Isn't this furniture beautiful? It's new. Pigskin suede. Wendel has the best sense of style. I always say he should have been an interior decorator."

Wendel?

"Randy has expensive taste," he said, stroking her shoulder. "We had it handmade in Italy."

Randy and Wendel? Together they sounded like cartoon zoo animals who danced the alphabet: *The Great Adventures of Randy and Wendel*! I hated it. They kissed—Ramona's glossed lips pursed far from her face in a way that suggested she didn't want to make too much contact. Wendel's lips were pale and thin, a little dry. I couldn't look at them. I turned toward Bill.

"So you like trains."

"Oh sure, sure. There's just something so romantic about them. The old ones, anyway."

I nodded. Bill nodded.

"I suppose we should discuss . . ." He wagged his hand in between his body and mine.

"Oh, um." I had no idea what to say, or how a typical arrangement like this worked. Ramona stood up and led Wendel toward the pool, where she slipped the straps of my dress off her shoulders and let it fall to the pavement. She stepped out of it and dove into the water. Wendel unbuckled his belt. I didn't want to watch him undress, but I heard the heavy plop of his body as it hit the water, the light splashing as she made her way to him, the giggling as he wrapped his fat body around hers.

"One thousand dollars a week," I said.

Bill laughed. His laugh sounded like an old elf's.

"Okay, sure, but I was thinking more about gifts. Clothing. Isn't there something you want?"

"What do you want?" The words came out harsh and snipped.

"Just some company," he said, his eyes glassy. "My wife died five years ago. We used to go to this steak house downtown. It's decorated like the dining car of an old train. Velvet curtains, brass luggage rails. It's very intimate. Maybe I could take you there."

I imagined him and his wife—a curly-haired woman with hot-pink lipstick and silvery eye shadow—sitting at a candlelit table, spooning cottage cheese out of cantaloupe halves into each other's mouth.

"I want to go to the Amazon," I said. "I want to fly first-class."

He reached out and patted me on the head. "I admire a girl with ambition. Well, why not? The sky is the limit."

He began to talk about his favorite train cars, and I curled up against the cushions and listened to the sound of swishing water.

Later, Ramona poured us shots, and the bald man told some story about John Travolta, how he'd ripped him off over a real estate investment out in the Mojave Desert and blah blah, and Ramona laughed like it was the funniest thing she'd ever heard. I drank a bottle of wine while Bill talked to me about his favorite airline (Delta, he said, had the best executive lounge), then I passed out on the handmade Italian couch. A few hours later I woke up to find Bill asleep on the opposite side of the couch, still in his suit, his tie undone, his hand clinging to my left foot. I tried to shake him off, but his grip was too tight. I sat up and pried his hand away, one finger at a time, so as not to wake him. Then I stood up and walked into the house.

Ramona and Wendel weren't in the living room. They weren't in the kitchen or the dining room, either. I walked down the hallway toward Ramona's bedroom door and held my ear to it. I stayed that way for a while, holding my breath, listening for a sign. But I didn't hear anything. Eventually my head started to ache, and I turned around and left through the front door, with nothing but Ramona's sequined dress.

★   ★   ★

I didn't go to the Amazon with Bill. I didn't fly anywhere first-class or move to Malibu. I never even went back to Ramona's to get my clothes. After that night, she stopped texting me. I didn't wonder why. I saw her here and there for a while—at a party at the apartment complex, at a rooftop in West Hollywood. I'd wave and she'd wave back or nod, then carry on tossing her head back so her diamond earrings caught the light, laughing with whatever new person she'd become invested in. She posted more photos and videos, documenting her skin-care routine, trying on shoes, floating on pink rafts in pools with girls I'd never seen, girls who looked sort of like me. I still had her sequined dress, and sometimes I'd put it on and stare at myself in the mirror and wonder if I'd made a mistake—if I'd gone through with it, with Bill, maybe I could have had everything I ever wanted. But I didn't think that was likely. I didn't want to be a person who liked Bill, or whatever Bill had to offer.

Whenever I wore Ramona's sequined dress for too long, my skin began to itch. And I developed a small coconut allergy. The smell of coconut made my throat scratchy, like something was clawing at it, trying to escape.

One day, at work, I read online that Arlo Banks had grown tired of Hollywood. On a whim he'd picked up and moved to Ibiza or Tasmania or some other fairy-tale land. He ordered a bowl of soup from a waitress at a café and fell in love with her. This was public knowledge, all over the internet. There was only one photo of the waitress online, in her black pants and black T-shirt, black shoes, black apron. She was smiling and holding her fingers in a peace sign, her eyes squinted so you couldn't even see what color they were, a shadow creating a weird dark spot on her neck. Then, almost overnight, there were more photos. Photos of her and Arlo Banks on camels, beside waterfalls, smudged with desert dirt on ATVs. There were photos of them in the Mediterranean Sea, his arms wrapped around her waist, fingers toying with her hair. She had long brown hair and hazel eyes and olive skin. She looked exactly like me. Other than that, there was nothing special about her.

The Hole in Your
Heart Is Mine

Duke had a tattoo of his dead mom on his upper thigh. I found it the first time I took his pants off. His mom was young and smiling politely at me, etched into the soft spot of his leg like fine art. I could tell that her hair had been blonde. She was wearing a turtleneck and she was prettier than me.

"It's an old picture."

No shit, I wanted to say, but I didn't want to hurt his feelings.

"Cancer," he said. "The quick kind."

Then he kissed me.

Duke was a sailor, a biker, a jet skier—the sort of man who spent a lot of time wearing short shorts in a squatting position. He kept his kayak leaned against the wall beside the refrigerator of his four-hundred-square-foot studio. His bike hung by its front wheel on the opposite wall. He was training for the New York City Triathlon. When he ran, he strapped miniature beanbags to his running shoes, and his mom peeked out from under his tiny shorts, smiling. On weekends he'd bike along the Hudson until the concrete faded to forest, park the bike beside the river, dive in, and let the current drift him down. Then he'd swim back upstream, like a salmon, every once in a while ducking down for an underwater somersault. I wondered if he was trying to outrun the cancer in his bloodline. It didn't matter to me. I made him my boyfriend anyway. He was the first guy I'd been with who didn't act like he had something to teach me.

"What's the word for when you learn things best by doing them?" he asked one morning as he strapped on a pair of Rollerblades. He'd gotten them on sale at Modell's and had decided that from now on he would blade around the city. That's what he called it—blading.

"*Kinesthetic.*" I was smarter than him. Or at least I had a better vocabulary.

"I think that's what I have," he said, like it was a disease. "I have to *feel* it. I have to go through the motions, you know? Just watch. This time tomorrow, I'll be blading backwards."

I had been planning to leave New York before I met him. My lease was almost up and I'd been fired from my job as a hostess at a Midtown restaurant for being too unlikable. I have a face that's hard to look at. I'm not ugly, but something doesn't sit right. It's more of a feeling than a physical trait you could point to. I'm often jealous of people whose noses are a ripple too long or whose gums are too gummy.

For those people it's a quick fix. My issue is vague—my face sometimes made people at the restaurant wince. "What's wrong?" they'd say, staring. And I'd have to tell them nothing was wrong, that I just had a difficult face. Then for the rest of the conversation they'd look at me funny, like at any moment I might lean over and try to lick their eyeballs.

Duke didn't look at me like that. He didn't look at me in any particular way, and I couldn't tell if he liked me or if he just didn't mind having me around in a take-it-or-leave-it sort of way. But in everything else, he was emphatic. He could get worked up about almost anything: climate change, time travel, blood scabbing over on a wound. ("Isn't it crazy how the human body just *heals itself*?" he'd say, tapping the scab with the pad of his finger.) Whenever he got excited, his eyes bulged and glowed extra green. They were beautiful. But a little off. A little creepy. I liked staring into them.

Duke sat down on the floor and adjusted his feet in the Rollerblades. As his shorts scrunched up around his crotch, his mom smiled at me. She had one of those faces you smiled back at without thinking. Her eyelashes were long, her cheeks freckled. Her skin was actually hairy, given its place-ment in the ambiguous zone where Duke's pubic hair turned to leg hair, but I imagined her as someone who'd never had wrinkles, whose freckles made her look like a girl, even in middle age.

"What's so funny?" Duke asked. He stretched his legs straight and tried to touch his toes. I shook the smile off my face. Even if I had been laughing at him—his feet splayed outward in the Rollerblades made him look like an awkward ballerina—he wouldn't have caught on. He was incapable of embarrassment, missing whatever gene it was that kept people from doing their private stuff in public places. He hummed loudly on the subway, slurped water from his hydration pack at restaurants. He wore Velcro sneakers because he thought laces were hazardous.

"Nothing," I said. I offered him my hand and he waved it away. He sprang to his feet and jerked back and forth on the Rollerblades. Then he flung his arms wide, bent his knees, and steadied himself. He stood tall with his shoulders back and put his fists on his hips.

"Superman," he said.

"Blade Boy."

He puffed his chest out even more, which really made him look like a cartoon.

"Dope."

★　★　★

Duke worked for a bike-tour company in Central Park. He led tourists around the park as they wobbled behind him on tandem bikes. He held their cameras. He tightened their helmets. He taught them when to switch gears, how to raise a hand for assistance versus how to raise a hand to signal a turn. He'd written himself a whole script and liked to practice on me whenever we were together.

"Okey dokey, folks! Let's start by making sure everyone's helmets are good and tight," he'd say, eyes wide, his voice an octave higher than usual. "You'll notice two buckles on the straps, one on the left and one on the right. Make sure you hear both buckles click. Repeat after me: These helmets are so nice, we buckle them twice!"

Sometimes he said this in an Australian accent for no reason at all. And he had notes for each landmark—every tunnel where a dead body had been found, every bridge where something romantic had occurred. "You are standing in the exact spot where the Prep School Killer strangled a schoolgirl!" and "If you look to the left, you'll see Bow Bridge. Justin Bieber once said he wanted to propose there."

"Where *is* the best place to propose?" someone always asked, eyebrows raised.

"I tell them the East Meadow, since it's close to the public restrooms," he'd explained to me, nodding in agreement with himself. Duke didn't pretend to know anything about romance. I liked this most about him. He thought holding hands while walking only slowed you down, that anniversaries should be saved for massive international events, like the Olympics, or a 6.5 magnitude earthquake. A bouquet of flowers didn't make sense, biologically.

"Why would you give someone a handful of dying plants and challenge them to keep them alive?" he asked me once. He genuinely wanted to know. His apartment was stuffed with scraggly green plants, potted in empty bean cans.

"Actually, for my birthday, buy me flowers. I bet I can keep those fuckers alive for weeks," he said.

I liked when he made these small references to our future together. I felt secure with him. I didn't need gifts or public displays of affection. I had a boyfriend who could, in a pickle, throw me over one shoulder and his kayak over the other, jump into the water, and paddle us both to safety. When my lease was up, I decided to move into his apartment and see if he could change my life.

"I ran out of beans. Can you bring beans?" was all he said. So I brought beans and little else. He lived in one of those massive mirrored-glass buildings overlooking the Hudson, surrounded by car dealerships and indoor-sports complexes. Everything oversize and glistening. Like Duke, the building exuded self-sufficiency. Solar panels lined the roof, along with some other futuristic contraption that Duke said was "harnessing wind like a windmill" but in a "less invasive way." Trees were growing—real, rooted trees—in a glass-enclosed terrace he referred to as "the Atrium." I liked the sparkly newness of it all, the way it felt like a separate ecosystem within the city. I never asked how he afforded it. The apartment itself was mostly empty, except for a mattress tucked in the corner of the room and all the adventure gear hanging from the walls. I knew Duke had moved around a lot before we met, that he saw no use in furniture that required one to sit still. He had a hard time sitting still, which was especially evident now that we lived together in a building made almost entirely out of glass.

"After my mom died, I thought there was something wrong with me," he told me one night as he arranged himself into a wall sit against the floor-to-ceiling window. It was the first time he'd mentioned his mom since the night we met. I wondered if my moving in had unlocked some special chamber of his brain, one that held all his honest feelings.

"You know, like a hole?" He pointed to his chest. "Turns out it's normal. I just needed salt water."

He'd grown up in Iowa or Kansas, somewhere without salt water. The first time he saw the ocean, he said, he drank it.

"I knew I wasn't supposed to," he assured me. "But I needed to drink it in order to heal the hole. And look, it worked." He pushed himself off the window and posed with his feet spread wide, as if I were supposed to know from looking at him that the ocean had patched his moth-eaten heart.

"Which ocean?" I asked.

He pointed to the window.

"You drank the Hudson River?"

"Coney Island. I figure they all connect." He slowly interlaced his fingers. I imagined him squatting on the Coney Island shoreline, surrounded by empty Big Gulp cups and broken beer bottles, cigarette butts and used napkins, oversize men wading into the water to piss.

In his own way, he was sort of magical.

"You should market that strategy," I said.

"Yeah, babe. Maybe I will."

Often my jokes whooshed right past him. He pulled out his phone and made a note, then showed it to me. It read *Ocean water. Add to smoothies?*

He loved adding things to smoothies. Most recently, he'd gotten into these supplements called Alpha Male, which came in a stainless steel bottle and contained something called cat-claw extract. He'd toss two in the blender with milk and a banana or sometimes swallow them dry. They were supposed to "stimulate dormant brain cells," he explained. He wanted every organ in his body to be functioning at full throttle. Nothing about him bothered me.

Every once in a while—like, when I was watching him brush his teeth with baking soda, lips peeled back like an angry dog—I was completely overcome by his mere existence. I'd strip off my clothes and beg him (not in a pathetic way) to get on top of me. Sex was exactly fine. Duke was a quick learner, after all. But he only ever lasted a few seconds in one position before needing to change it up, exercise a new muscle group.

"Get on top."

"No."

We were fully naked under the sheet, and his mom's face was smashed up against my thigh, sticky with sweat. He lifted his chest off mine and examined me for signs of injury. "Why not?"

I'm not going to sit on your mom's face, I wanted to say. My bare ass would suffocate her sweet smile like some sort of blubbery alien force. I'd be killing her all over again.

"We have to talk about your mom," I said.

"Babe, this is not the best time for me to be thinking about my mom."

"Why do you have that tattoo?"

"Which tattoo?"

It occurred to me then that he had others—I'd just never considered them before.

"Obviously the one of your mom."

He looked confused. "It's my mom."

"It's just—it's so lifelike."

"That's the whole point."

"It is?"

Now he looked agitated. "You don't get it. I love my mom. Your mom is, like, on a yacht somewhere."

I had no idea what he was talking about. My mom lived in Delaware. I had never even brought her up.

"My mom died of *cancer*." Then, more slowly, like he was teaching me the word for the first time: "*Cancer.*"

I didn't like his tone. "What does cancer have to do with it? If she had died of something totally ridiculous, like being hit by a tour bus or whatever, you still would have gotten that tattoo."

He thought about this. Then he said, "There are no tour buses in Kansas."

I wanted to poke a little hole in him, to squeeze out some molecular explanation for his behavior, but he was made of concrete.

"Has anybody ever asked you about it?" I asked.

The green in his eyes whirled with tears. "My mom isn't an 'it.' She's a person."

"Was a person."

He was still inside me, and I locked my ankles around his waist. I would lie there and make him stare down at my difficult face until he admitted that he hated me. His eyes glowed. I was sure he was going to explode. Then, out of nowhere, he forced my ankles apart, got out of bed, and stood over me. From this angle, I was face to face with his mom, but her gaze seemed to have shifted toward Duke's dick.

"Do you want a Muscle Milk?"

I shook my head. He got down on the floor and did twenty push-ups. I watched his balls skim the ground then pop back up in time with his breath.

"Ah," he said, when he was finished, "I feel better."

But later I heard him crying in the bathroom. It was more like a whimper, just loud enough to hear from the other side of the door. I listened as he turned on the shower and let the water run, trying, unsuccessfully, to muffle himself.

"Everything okay?" I knocked.

"All good."

"What's wrong?" I asked, in my sweetest voice. "You can tell me."

He took some deep breaths.

"It's just . . . we're not going to be able to stop it. You know what I mean? Not *really*. In the end, the earth is so much more powerful than we are."

"Stop what?"

I thought his Alpha pills might have been making him more emotional. Recently, he had gotten upset about a range of topics: GMOs (anti), euthanasia (pro), vitamin D–blocking sunscreen (anti), dog collars (anti), GMOs again (pro).

He sniffled. "Climate change. It's going to hit us like a tsunami. Literally, a tsunami is coming. No matter how hard I try, I'll never be as strong as a current. I'll never have as much energy as a storm. The earth is a giant, pulsing muscle. It's, like, magic."

"Are you happy or sad?" I couldn't tell.

"Don't you see?" He was sobbing now. He blew his nose into something. "How I feel is irrelevant. *We* are irrelevant."

I had never heard him say the word *irrelevant* before. I felt proud of him and ashamed of myself. The sound of his sobs suddenly made me feel helpless, unsafe. After a few minutes we were both in tears, curled into ourselves on opposite sides of the bathroom door.

Eventually Duke came out, eyes bloodshot, the skin around them puffy and wet. He bent down and scooped me off the floor and cradled me in his arms.

"I didn't mean to scare you," he said. "It's just—the hole. I'm starting to feel it again."

I tucked my face into his neck. "Should we go to Coney Island?"

I wanted to watch him drink the ocean. I wanted to see the murky scum dribble down his chin as it healed him.

He thought about it. "I think this is a different kind of hole. It feels so vast this time. Like a black hole."

"Or a sinkhole."

"Exactly, babe."

He carried me to the bed and laid me down. I felt like a corpse, but in a sexy way. I kissed him. He slipped my shirt off, then his own. I unbuttoned my pants and pushed them down to my feet. He went for his.

"Hold on," I said, stopping him. I held his face in my hands. If his mom got involved, I'd lose everything. "Can we just make this about me?"

He paused. Something flickered in his eyes, like a glitch. Then he shrugged, scooched himself down, down, down.

★　★　★

In the morning, I woke to Duke doing burpees on the carpet. He burst upward, his feet springing from the floor, his arms stretched high above him.

"I have an idea. Do you want to hear it?"

"Sure." I yawned.

He smiled at me knowingly, like the idea was already underway, working its charm through his hollowing insides.

"I know how to win the triathlon."

His eyes were beaming. He ducked under the bed in search of something. "The trick is to let Mother Earth guide you. Use her power to thrust you forward. You see, I've been doing it all wrong! You have to swim *with* the current, not against it. You have to *seek* her power, not fight it! I've been so far removed from her, up here in my ivory tower."

He yanked a large hiking backpack out from under the bed.

"Where are you going with that?"

"The woods. I need to harness the earth's energy, you know? Refuel. That's the only way I'll be able to win." He bounced up and down on his feet like he was holding an invisible jump rope. "Think of it as a rebirth."

I watched his hands jitter as he spoke. The triathlon was only ten days away. Professional athletes would be competing. Olympians. Duke was durable and determined—more firefighter than Olympian. His mom peeked out at me from beneath his shorts. I wondered how many rebirths he would need to find the right replacement.

"But what am I supposed to do?" I said. We hadn't spent a night apart since I moved in.

"I'll need someone to drive me out there." He transitioned to jumping jacks. "And water the plants while I'm gone."

I nodded sort of absently. Duke shot his fist into the air. "Dope."

He bladed to REI for supplies. I felt strange and out of place, alone in the apartment. I had gotten used to navigating around his sharp, forceful movements, and now I was suddenly unsure of what to do with my hands. I tried to make the bed, but the fitted sheet was actually a flat sheet, and the flat sheet was the wrong size. I hadn't noticed before. It was the bed of someone who'd grown up without a mother, who never had anyone to teach him how to make it. I tried folding the clothes on the floor, but all his clothes were made of spandex or nylon and slipped right out of a fold. Eventually I sat down and held my knees to my chest, listening for the sound of the door.

Duke came home carrying two giant shopping bags filled with brand-new camping gear. I sprang from the floor and reached my arms around his neck and interlaced my fingers. I hung from him like a baby chimpanzee, and he bent his knees to keep from toppling over.

"Let me come with you." I loved him and I didn't know what would happen to me when he left.

"With me?"

"Sure. I can help. I can build a fire."

"You can't build a fire." He dropped his bags and peeled me off him. "You can barely ride a bike. Besides, I only have one sleeping bag."

"I'll buy one."

"No," he said, more forceful than I was prepared for. I sat down on the bed, curled my body around a pillow.

"I'm sorry." He put his hand on his chest to signify that the hole was to blame for his outburst. "It only works if I go alone."

★   ★   ★

Duke insisted on renting a Jeep Wrangler to drive north. The next morning, he tossed his backpack on the back seat and hopped into the passenger side.

"This way we can breathe the air," he said, waving his arms through the empty space where the car door should have been.

"Do you have enough food?"

He pulled a butterfly knife from his pocket and fanned it out in front of his face. "I brought some beans. And this bad boy is for filleting fish."

There was traffic on the West Side Highway. Exhaust from the cement truck in front of us plumed in our faces. Duke unwrapped the bandana from around his neck, then reached over and tied it around my nose and mouth.

"You can keep that. I have another."

I suddenly wanted to cry. My bottom lip puffed out and I was grateful that Duke couldn't see the lower half of my face. "And you know how to pitch a tent?"

I thought he was going to roll his eyes. Instead he leaned over and kissed my cheek.

About an hour north of the city, the wind picked up. It blew through the car's empty doorframes and flipped the bandana up and into my eyes. I forced it back down. On the radio, a man was saying that heavy winds were to be expected throughout the night.

"This is a bad idea," I said.

"Babe, I lived on a sailboat for three months." News to me. "I know wind. This isn't wind."

We drove in silence for about another hour. Duke kept his eyes on the road. I wondered what he was thinking about, or whether he was thinking at all. Was this the hole taking over, draining him of all his magnificent energy? I wanted to reach over and shake him, but I kept both hands on the wheel, worried he might tumble out of the car with only a nudge. We passed a few exits for camping grounds and a handful of rest stops. The air began to feel thinner and cooler. It smelled like pine. We drove and drove until we heard the sound of rushing water.

"Here's good," Duke said.

I stopped the car in the middle of the road. There was nobody around, no signs nearby. Duke hopped out, hoisted his backpack onto his shoulder, and walked around to my side. He was calmer than I'd ever seen him. He wasn't bouncing on his toes. His hands weren't fluttering at his sides. Even his eyes focused steadily on the ground. He was still—stoic, almost—and I was scared.

"Okay, I'm off." He reached for my hands and held them in his. He smiled.

Tears pricked the backs of my eyes. "Should I come pick you up here? In a few days?"

Duke leaned into the car and kissed the top of my head. "Don't worry about it. I know what I'm doing."

He turned and walked behind the car and into the woods. I watched him in the rearview mirror. A few steps in, he knelt down and touched the ground with his hands. He stayed that way for about a minute, feeling the dirt. Then he stood up, looked around, and walked out of sight.

★   ★   ★

When I got back to the apartment, I put on a pair of Duke's running shorts and one of his slippery nylon tank tops. They smelled like sweat. I breathed them in. I got down on the floor and did one push-up. Then another, and another. The push-ups weren't making me feel any stronger, just more tired. I did five total, then lay on the floor, face down, and tried not to cry. I listened for anything—a creak in the door, the click of the air-conditioning. But I heard nothing at all. I watered the plants, popped two of Duke's man pills, then got into bed and pulled the sheet over my head for the rest of the day.

The next morning, I woke up to an empty bed, an empty apartment. Sharp sunlight reflected off the mirrored building

next door and beamed through the windows. I held my
hands over my eyes. Without Duke forcing me up and out of
bed, I was not motivated to move. I had sweated through the
sheets overnight and my scalp was damp, which felt close
enough to exercise. I stood up slowly, went to the bathroom,
and sat on the toilet. Everything seemed to fall out of me at
once. I blamed the pills. I grabbed a Muscle Milk from the
refrigerator and got back into bed, cradling it like a baby.
I slept through the day and night, waking up every few hours
with a rumbling in my stomach. I'd crawl to the bathroom,
drink another Muscle Milk, and get back into bed, feeling
like I'd been carved out.

Finally, after an indeterminable amount of time, I woke
up to the sound of Duke vomiting in the toilet. I knew what
had happened almost immediately: He had eaten something
poisonous—a berry, a mushroom, a dead squirrel—and had
made himself sick. He'd hitched a ride back to the city to be
sick in his own home. I still felt rotten, but I wanted to take
care of him. I wanted to show him what I could do for him,
why he needed me. I grabbed a Muscle Milk from the fridge
and knocked on the bathroom door.

"Are you okay?" I was almost in tears. "I'm so happy
you're home."

The vomiting got more violent.

"I can make you some broth."

I opened the bathroom door to give him the drink.

The person hovering over the toilet was frail and thin and
wearing a hospital gown that opened in the back, so I could
see a spine and hip bones protruding above a small, deflated
ass. I could tell from the dimpled thighs that it was a woman.

When she lifted her head out of the bowl, it was shiny and bald, almost reflective. She leaned over and flushed, then turned to face me.

"Sorry," she said, wiping her mouth with the back of her hand. "It's the chemo. You need this?" She pointed to the toilet.

Her face was swollen and round. It looked like a balloon, her neck the measly string attaching it to her body. Because her face was so puffed up, I couldn't determine her age, but I knew who she was. She wasn't beautiful at all, but sickly and weak, barely human. Her eyes looked permanently wide. They were seafoam green, like Duke's, and I could see in them the person she had been.

I tiptoed backward and closed the door. I stood there for a moment on my toes, my knees bent like suspecting prey. There was more gagging, then the sound of the toilet flushing. I nudged the door open a crack and peered through.

She was looking right at me. She leaned against the toilet and gulped in air.

"Can you make tea?"

I blinked furiously. I clenched my entire face. When I unclenched, she was still there, staring. I opened the door a little wider.

"Pow!" I screamed. I waved my hands in her face. "Hoo-rah!"

She just sat there. I stood back and pointed at her.

"Be gone!"

She glanced around the bathroom, as if admiring its decor. I was out of ideas. I walked backward to the kitchen to make tea.

We didn't have any tea, so I poured the Muscle Milk into a mug and stuck it in the microwave for thirty seconds. I went back to the bathroom and handed it to her. I hovered over her, a little wobbly, but I didn't want to lose the high ground.

"You're hogging my toilet."

"It's my toilet." She swished the hot milk around in her mouth. "I'm the one paying for it."

It had never occurred to me that her death was the source of Duke's financial stability. I was suddenly annoyed with him for not sharing this information with me. Then I had another idea. I ran my hand under the sink faucet and sprinkled water on top of her puffy head. I said, "You may now go with God."

She put her hands on the toilet seat and hoisted herself up. Once she got to her feet, I saw how short she was: tiny, like a kid but with all the fully formed features of an adult. I could have knocked her out in one punch. She reached out and touched the tips of my hair.

"Are you really going to kick a sick woman out of her own home?"

"Dead woman."

She swayed a bit, then gagged and vomited down her hospital gown. The smell of her was making me nauseous. I walked out of the bathroom and closed the door behind me, got back into bed, and pulled the covers over my head.

★　★　★

When I woke later, Duke's mom was standing over the stove, boiling an egg.

"It's weird," she said, stirring the water. She looked more alive, less gray. "You'd think the smell would bother me, but actually, they're the only thing I can eat these days."

I stared at her from beneath the sheet, just my eyes peeking out.

"Does the smell bother you?"

I didn't answer her. My stomach rumbled, but I felt safe in bed and didn't want to move. I had no idea what she might do. I watched her dip a bare hand into the boiling water and remove the egg. She didn't wince. She lifted the egg to her dried-out lips and bit into it, shell and all. As she chewed, I heard the shell crunch and grind between her teeth. A stream of warm yolk dripped down her chin. She didn't look like a mom at all.

"I should do some spring cleaning."

"I can do that," I said, trying to sound professional, or at least capable. I was angry at her for so many reasons—for not teaching Duke how to make a bed, for breaking off a piece of him and swallowing it, for lurking above us all this time, dangling out of reach, just high enough for him to know something was there.

She laughed and it sounded like a hiccup. A bit of shell got stuck in her throat and she coughed it up onto the floor.

"Are you going to pay the rent, too? You don't have any money. You don't have a job. You can't even fold his clothes." She walked over to the bed and sat down on its edge, felt the sheet with her hand. "What kind of bedding is this? Polyester? This will give me a rash."

I didn't think she had any right to be critical. She should have been grateful that I was there in the first place. Morning

45

sunlight bounced off her head and into my eyes. I yanked the sheet away from her and covered my face with it.

"You're the one who took a chunk of him with you," I said. "Now I have this stupid hole to deal with."

For a while she didn't say anything. I wondered briefly if she had died, sitting upright, head slumped over her neck. But then I felt her nails scratch my scalp.

"Do you want to hear the story I used to tell Duke when he was little?"

"Not really."

She chewed on her egg. "I would tell him that when he was born, just like all other babies, the doctor snipped his umbilical cord with a pair of scissors. And I'd reach down and pinch his belly button, like this."

She pinched my stomach through the sheet. I squirmed.

"Part of the cord remained attached to him, and the other half stayed attached to me, and after a while both halves dried out, shriveled up, and fell off, because they couldn't survive without one another. 'This happens to all mommies and their babies,' I'd say. Then I'd lean over like I had a secret."

She leaned over so her dry, flaky lips were right next to my ear.

"My doctor made a mistake," she whispered. "The scissors he used were dull, and they didn't cut through the cord all the way. They left behind one thin strand, so thin he couldn't even see it."

She sat up, bit the egg.

"His eyes would glow. He'd say, 'So we're still connected?' And I told him that no matter where he went, our souls would always be connected by the invisible cord. I'd point to his eyes and say, 'Your soul is the thing that keeps you from disappearing. It floats just behind your eyes, like a little cloud.'"

She peeled the sheets off my head and pointed at my eyes. Really stared into them. I stared back at hers and saw the sea. I blinked.

"Duke is my son. I know him better than anyone else could. He isn't thinking about you. And he isn't coming back here."

I was burning beneath the sheets, sweating all over. Who did she think she was, plopping into my life, clouding it with her stink? She was a sneaky sort of evil, the kind who slit your throat while combing your hair.

"All of this is perfectly logical and sound," I said.

"You should start thinking about where you'll go."

"Right. I can't wait to tell Duke about this. I can't wait to see the look on his face when I tell him his dead mom tried to throw me out on the street. He's going to hate you. He's going to laser off that stupid tattoo."

She stuffed the last bits of egg into her mouth, then patted me once, twice on the head. Her throat gurgled. She stood up, walked to the bathroom, and closed the door behind her. I knew exactly what to do. I threw the covers off and ran to the stove, grabbed the pot of steaming egg water. I would open the door and dump the hot water on her head as she hovered over the toilet bowl. Probably, she would begin to melt. Then I'd lift her stick legs into the air and push her face-first down the toilet. Once she was fully smushed inside the bowl, fetus-like, I'd flush her down. Good riddance.

I closed my eyes and burst into the bathroom, feeling a little like a superhero. I lifted the pot over my head and screamed as loud as I could, which wasn't very loud since I hadn't eaten in days. But when I opened my eyes, she was gone. The water in the toilet rippled.

★ ★ ★

Duke didn't come home the next day, or the next. After four days, his plants began to wither and dry out. I took this as a sign that something terrible had happened to him and decided to go looking for him.

I bladed to Columbus Circle. When I got there, a few guys who looked like Duke were standing around in bike shorts and sunglasses. A group of tourists straddled their bikes, waiting for someone to guide them. I approached the man who looked most in charge.

"Excuse me, I'm looking for Duke. Have you heard from him recently?"

"Duke, Duke, Duke," the man said, like he was trying to imagine his face. "I'm pretty sure he doesn't work here anymore."

"What do you mean? Did he quit?"

"About a week ago, I think."

"Did he say where he was going?"

"I didn't know him too well." The man adjusted his sunglasses. "I think he said he was headed west."

"West? West where?"

"No idea. Maybe Buffalo?"

"I'm his girlfriend." I hated this man. "He never said anything about going to Buffalo."

"Oh, shit." The man hopped onto a bike and adjusted the gears. "Well, if he comes back, tell him to get his ass over here. We need that enthusiasm." Then he turned to the tour group and said in a much louder, more excited tone, "All right, all right! Who's ready to explore the glorious pit of the Big Apple?"

I was disappointed in myself. I had been entrusted to look after a motherless child and lost him. A smarter person wouldn't have put so much faith in Duke. A smarter person would have known he was delusional. I went home and did all the things you're supposed to do when you're looking for a missing person. I called Duke's phone, which was also dead or missing. Then I called the police and explained the situation.

"Did he say when he was coming back?" the woman on the other end of the phone asked.

"No. He doesn't really do that kind of thing."

"So as far as you know, he's either on a camping trip, or in Buffalo?"

"I have no idea where he is. He could be anywhere."

"I'm sorry. But I can't file your boyfriend as a missing person just because he left you."

"He hasn't left *me*. He just left."

"Okay, ma'am. Have a good day."

I began to come undone. I spent the next few days pacing around the apartment. I couldn't eat and I had to concentrate hard on breathing. A constant ache in my chest kept me up at night. Whenever I heard the toilet running, I ran to it and knelt beside it. I stuck my face in the bowl and begged it to tell me where Duke had gone. I knew I was going insane. I felt like I'd been shredded to pieces, and all the scraps of me had been picked up by the wind and scattered to meaningless places.

By the morning of the triathlon, it was clear that Duke wasn't coming back. His bike still hung on the kitchen wall, unprepared. I bladed north along the river to the starting line anyway, a little apathetically. I leaned over the railing and stared out at the rubber-capped heads along the river. It was impossible to tell who was an Olympian and who was a regular person just trying to accomplish one thing. And it was impossible to tell if any of them was Duke. I watched them dive into the water and swim south. I bladed alongside them, pushing through the crowds and looking for signs of my boyfriend. I watched as the swimmers scurried out of the water over to the transition area, where they threw off their goggles and became bikers. Some of them didn't even change out of their swim clothes. Some bikes had pedals with shoes already attached, so the bikers only had to slip their wet feet into the shoes and start pedaling. The one thing they all did was put on a helmet. I whispered, "These helmets are so nice, we buckle them twice!" And as if I'd just cast a spell, Duke seemed to appear, bent over a bike in tiny spandex shorts and a matching tank top, tinkering with the chain. But when he stood up straight, I could see that his neck was too narrow. And he didn't have the tattoo.

That night, back at Duke's apartment, I read online that a Brazilian man had won the race. I didn't care who he was. I did wonder, briefly, if Duke was disappointed in himself, wherever he was, for not trying harder. I wondered if he missed me. I hoped that he did. For a while after that, I'd lie awake in Duke's bed at night and fantasize about his return: He'd burst through the door in tears, his skin torn and scabbing over, his face dark with dirt and sweat. He'd scoop me off the bed and cradle me in his arms.

"I'm so sorry," he'd say. "I love you and I'll never leave you again." And I'd stare straight through his crazy eyes, into his soul, and know that he meant it.

★   ★   ★

A few years later, long after I'd pulled myself together and moved out of Duke's apartment, bought a MetroCard, landed another job as a hostess at a West Village restaurant and eventually quit because I hated it, hated contorting my face to greet strangers, I flew to L.A. for a job interview at a casting agency in need of an assistant. I liked the idea of assigning faces to things: deciding which cheeks looked best with certain soap brands, which set of shoulders suited a Subaru commercial. I thought I would be good at it, and it was a good enough reason to leave New York. I got a hotel room in Santa Monica by the pier where they'd filmed over one hundred romantic comedies. It was one of the hotel concierge's main talking points.

"If you want more fun facts, you should do the bus tour," he said.

I told him thank you, but I was only there for one day and one night. I told him about the job interview, that I was nervous because I had never been to L.A. before. I had no idea how people behaved on this side of the country.

"Like normal," he said. He thought about it. "A little flaky. Probably from all the sun exposure."

At the interview, they asked me questions like "How do you answer a phone?" and "Which movie star would you buy this eucalyptus perfume from?" They nodded at my answers and jotted down notes.

"Thank you," they said, when it was over. "You'll hear from us in a few weeks. Or maybe not at all, depending."

They all looked like they spent too much time in the sun. I left feeling okay, not great. I wasn't sure if L.A. was a dependable place to start over. When I got back to the hotel, I had the rest of the day to kill, so I walked to the corner and hopped on the tour bus. I went to the top deck and sat in the back row. The people up there looked bored—they looked like they were being forced to sit there. The sun pounded my face and I squinted to keep from going blind.

After a few minutes a guide popped up from the stairs near the front. He had a microphone attached to the collar of his tank top and he was wearing a pair of sunglasses that wrapped around his head like goggles. There were some tattoos on his arms that I couldn't make out. He looked excited and tan.

"Okey dokey, folks! Who's ready to reach for the stars?" His tone was high-pitched and rehearsed. "I'm kidding, you can't touch the stars," he said, laughing at himself. One person in front of me sighed loudly. "They don't like when you get too close. It's a touchy subject." He used air quotes when he said *touchy subject*.

"If you look in the seat pocket in front of you, you'll see a pair of binoculars. You'll be able to see every pimple with those bad boys." He laughed and laughed, like he was the funniest person he'd ever heard. I grabbed the binoculars from the seat pocket in front of me, held them to my face, and stared at him through the lenses. The tattoo on his shoulder was a bicycle, and down the opposite arm was the phrase LIVE FREE OR DIE TRYING. I moved down his body toward his shorts. They were khaki, mid-length. I tried to see through them, which didn't work. I moved up to his face and looked at every feature. The magnifier made his teeth look like giant, frosty ice cubes. The pores on his cheeks were sprouting small hairs. A bead of sweat dripped from his hairline down the side of his face. And another one on the other side. He lifted his sunglasses to his forehead and I focused on his eyes. They stared right at me. They were green, and a little dead inside.

Smart Girl

My ex-boyfriend calls me from Florida to talk about his pubes.

"Are they weird?" he asks.

We go to schools in different time zones. Over the summer he broke up with me on the patio furniture in his backyard. I cried into his lap. He carried me to my car, then went inside to eat dinner with his family.

Now he plays lacrosse on scholarship at a school with palm trees and a rape problem.

"Why would your pubes be weird?" I say. My roommate, Jenny, shuts her laptop and listens from her bed.

"You tell me." He's angry with me for not telling him about the strangeness of his pubic hair. Why would I care about his pubic hair? One time he shaved the peachy space between his eyebrows with a disposable razor. I thought that was weird, but I never told him.

"The guys on the team are saying my pubes are weird," he says. "Like I have too many."

"Did you tell them you're from New Jersey?"

Jenny moves to my bed, holds her ear to the phone. She covers her mouth so he can't hear her breathing. I want to tell her that her breath is the last thing on his mind. His pubes take precedence over her breath or my breath or even his own breath, and he needs to sort out the pube situation before he asphyxiates.

"Tell them how cold it gets at home," I say, "how you need all the hair you can get to stay warm in the winter."

Jenny snorts into my ear. We're only a couple weeks into our first semester, but we're already close friends. Our sheets are the same shade of pale gray. We wear the same size shoe. It's easy to make one close friend, especially when the only other option is to be alone. Jenny is from Iowa and knows a lot about tornadoes. She taught me about storm cellars and state fairs and I taught her about boardwalks and pork roll. Our school also has a rape problem. They gave us whistles to wear around our necks. We are not supposed to go anywhere without each other.

"Whatever," he says. "I don't give a shit."

"Obviously you do, or you wouldn't be calling."

I can hear him moving around, trying to take up space and color in the silence. "I want to make sure it isn't something you thought about but never told me."

We dated for one year. There were a lot of things I'd thought but never told him. I thought it was strange that his parents let him smoke pot in his bedroom, which was in the attic. I thought it was irresponsible to have a bedroom in an attic. I didn't like the cartoons he watched when he was high, but I watched them anyway and laughed in all the right places. I thought sex was boring and sometimes painful—I was always stinging or burning after sex. To avoid it, I often pretended to fall asleep on his bed while watching boring cartoons.

I never told him about that. I never told him that when he dumped me, I'd just gone on the pill, and that I only cried so hard because my hormones were waking up, trying to orient themselves.

The pill is one yellow, chalky lentil every morning, except for the one week per month when the lentils are white and made of sugar instead of yellow and made of hormones. When I started taking them over the summer, I cried about everything. I cried when the fuel light on my dashboard blinked orange. I cried when the water in the shower was too hot and cried harder when I adjusted the knob and made it too cold. I cried with the losers of game shows and weight-loss commercials. "You're crying over spilled milk," my mom said, which also made me cry.

Since I've been at school, the pill has made my hormones less wet and droopy. As far as I can tell, they have dried up.

"I've never given any thought to your pubes," I say. His are the only boy's pubes I've seen. Now that they're on my mind, I remember them as wiry and scratchy. I don't have anything to compare them to, other than maybe a Brillo pad.

"I have to go," he says, and hangs up.

Jenny snorts again then makes a face like she feels bad about it. Jenny is always concerned with everyone else's feelings. She answers the phone in the shower, or while brushing her teeth, so whoever is calling doesn't think she's ignoring them. If she's late to a lecture, she stands on the other side of the closed door and watches through the small plexiglass window, so she doesn't disrupt anything or distract anybody. She wants everyone to feel comfortable all the time, for all their problems to be solvable with a high five and a smile. In Iowa, this is how they teach you to be.

"I feel bad for laughing," she says. "Is he okay?"

"I think he misses me." It feels good to be missed. It feels like winning.

★　★　★

I take all the right steps to forget my ex-boyfriend. I delete the pictures of us from my phone. I don't call him. Whenever I think about calling him, I go to a party instead. I bring Jenny and we drink beer until I forget. I make out with a boy I don't know against the basement wall of a house I don't know. I major in women's studies. I cut an inch off my hair. When the boy I made out with texts me, I decide not to reply until I am finished with all the steps. I delete more pictures. Still, like sabotage, my face breaks out into tiny clear pimples, my forehead a shiny braille.

"It's because you're taking birth control," my mom says. She and my dad come for Parents' Weekend. I bring them to the only restaurant on campus with white tablecloths. They don't ask me about my ex-boyfriend, about whether we are together or apart, or how he and his pubic hair are adjusting to the Florida climate. *Better to be concerned with the now* is something my mom likes to say. Also, *Better to be in the know than in the dark* and *Better to be safe than sorry.*

"Your hormones are rebelling against you," she says, like it's something she heard once and liked and can now be applied to any scenario. "But better to be pimply than pregnant."

"Why would hormones do that?" I ask. I've noticed the hormone uprising inside other girls who live in my hall—weight gains, unexplained sobs, cystic acne in places previously presumed poreless. Has everybody started taking birth control at once? Jenny has gained six pounds since the start of the semester. Once she got drunk and sobbed that her body had betrayed her. The worst part, she said, is that all the weight has gone straight to her armpits. Three pounds to each pit. She threw out all her tank tops. She threw out her bras and bought new, roomier ones to hold in the armpit blubber. "Time to start fresh," she said, staring at the bag of trash bras. Now, she eats iceberg lettuce and goes for long runs around campus. *You're taking all the right steps*, I tell her, over and over. I don't say, *You must be doing something wrong.*

"They're hormones." My mom shrugs, as if no further explanation is required. I'm worried my hormones will develop the temperament of a bad dog—that I'll wake up one day and my body will be gnawed to shreds, unrecognizable. "They don't like change."

I cover my forehead with my hand. It's about as smooth as a gravel driveway. I rub the pads of my fingers across the bumps, trying to understand them.

"Don't pick," my mom says. "You'll bleed all over your dinner."

"Veal parm," says my dad, and hands his menu to the waiter.

My parents pay for dinner. We go to Target and they pay for a body pillow, a bottle of benzoyl peroxide face wash, and a coffee machine that brews exactly one cup of coffee at a time, on a timer. I tell them I need AA batteries and tampons and they pay for those, too.

As we pile all my stuff onto the conveyor belt, my mom slips three packs of ultrathin condoms behind the tampons. She sent me to school with a bulky box of the exact same condoms, which she'd made my dad pick up at Costco. I wonder what she thinks I've been doing in the time I've been away, if she assumes I've already used up a box of one hundred condoms. Or does she think I'm sharing them, slipping them under the heavy wooden doors of all the girls' rooms in my building—an elusive condom fairy?

"Maybe you'll meet a boy," she says. "Someone like Zac Efron." She taps her nail on one pack of condoms as it slides down the conveyor belt. "Also, STDs."

My dad glares at the gum selection. He reaches for a pack of Trident, flips it over, and holds it up to his eyes so he can read the ingredients on the back.

"It's important to talk about this stuff," says my mom, staring at the condoms. She pats my dad's back.

My dad throws the gum behind the condoms. "Christ," he says. But he still pays. Later, he'll check his credit card statement and see how many travel points he earned for buying me condoms at Target compared to the amount he earned for buying me condoms at Costco. Buy your daughter enough condoms and you can fly to London or Hong Kong or Barcelona. Buy her the normal amount of condoms and you can fly to Newark.

I show my parents the library. I show them the big lawn where students hang hammocks and tightropes in between trees. I show them the outside of the football stadium and the blue-lit emergency poles that you're supposed to run to if you're being mugged or raped. During orientation, we each had to take a quiz to certify that we understood the circumstances in which we should use the emergency poles. The quiz went something like:

I will run to the emergency pole if I feel:

A) Angry, because my parents won't send me more money.
B) Depressed, because I miss my real friends.
C) Afraid, because I am alone for the first time and there is something strange in the air.
D) Afraid, because I am being followed by a stranger who could be carrying something sharp or heavy.

The correct answer was *(D) Afraid, because I am being followed by a stranger who could be carrying something sharp or heavy.* Although *(B) Depressed* was also considered an acceptable answer, after a boy in the back row argued that being *(B) Depressed* could be just as dangerous as something sharp or heavy.

My dad takes a photo of the stadium. He presses his hand against a blue emergency pole. He leans his weight into it, testing its strength. He knocks on it, hovers his finger over the emergency button.

"This calls the real cops?" he asks.

"Sure," I say, but I have no idea who it calls.

"And suppose you can't make it in time?" my mom says.

"In time for what?"

"Don't be smart."

★   ★   ★

My parents fly home on condom points. Back at my dorm room, Jenny is eating from a plastic to-go container of iceberg lettuce and balsamic vinegar that she concocted at the dining hall.

"Vinegar is good for your skin," she says.

"What is that supposed to mean?" I say.

Jenny moves to my bed. She dips her pinkie into a pool of vinegar and rubs it on my forehead like she's blessing me. "It helps. It's, like, acid or something."

"I have no idea what you're talking about." I wipe my forehead with my sleeve. "And now my face smells like a salad."

I glare at her and she stares back at me like a baby bird.

"I'm only trying to help," she says.

I don't talk to her for the next hour. I sit on my bed and look at photos I didn't delete. I haven't seen my ex-boyfriend since the night he made my hormones cry. I wonder if he would recognize me, now that the tears have burned off and the pimples have popped up like tiny graves in their place. I wonder what he's doing right now and who he's doing it with. His parents probably didn't give him a box of condoms before he left because they were high or just thinking about something else, like dinner.

I text the boy I kissed in someone's basement. The last message he sent me reads, *Jared from saturday night.*

What are you doing tonight?

He responds almost immediately. *Paint party. 1245 Gerard Ave.*

I type, *Should I come?* Then I delete it. I get up and stand in front of the closet I share with Jenny and put on a dress and cork wedges. The shoes belong to her, but I've already worn them three times and they are now considered a shared item, like the hair dryer and the full-length mirror and the toothpaste.

"Where are you going?" Jenny asks from her bed. One of us is always in bed.

"The library."

"You're wearing heels to the library?"

"I'll be back late."

★   ★   ★

At the party, I look for Jared From Saturday Night. The room glows in the dark and everybody's faces are smeared with paint. Paint splats against the walls. It splats into drinks. The air is thick and hot. It tastes like stale beer. When I push through the crowd, sweat from arms and shoulders and backs sticks to my body. I can't find Jared, but I meet another boy whose face is entirely painted blue. I have no idea what he looks like, other than blue. He gives me a beer and tells me he lives in Harrison Hall, same as me. We dance and he gets me three more beers and then we walk back from the party together. When we reach our building, we both go to his room.

"Are you going to wash your face?" I ask. He's sitting up in his bed, on top of the covers. His sheets are silky and yellow. His mom picked them out, I'm sure. If he lies down, he'll get blue paint all over his mom's yellow sheets.

"Are you?" he asks. My face is mostly unpainted, but I smeared a green glob across my forehead to hide the pimples.

"No." I'm standing above him, waiting for something— permission, a clue.

He points to his door, to the gray towel that hangs from a hook. "Grab that."

I take the towel off the hook and hand it to him. I watch him lay it over his pillows and smooth it down with his hands. I think, *Why didn't I think of that?* I think, *This guy is a problem solver.* He's probably a math or engineering major, somebody who studies how to solve problems. I'm attracted to him even though I can't see his face.

"Can you turn off the light, too?"

I flick the switch and the room goes black. I can only see the beady blue light from his phone as he clutches it in bed.

"Do you want to see my pool?"

"Sure," I say. I get into the bed beside him and he pulls up a photo on his phone. There's nothing interesting about the pool—just a rectangular cement pool filled with bluish water and surrounded by mowed grass and a patio with lawn chairs. There's nobody in the pool. He must have taken the photo on his way out the door to baseball practice or the SAT or to break up with his girlfriend. A photo of his empty pool that he planned to show to his next girlfriend.

"Cool," I say. I also have a pool. We are kids with pools. We are those types of kids. We could guess anything about each other and we would probably guess right. I guess he has two chocolate Labradors and a mom who likes to cook seafood. A mom who irons sheets. A dad who chews loudly and a younger brother with ADHD. Either that, or he is the younger brother with ADHD, and his older sister plays lacrosse or field hockey and will work in HR for a few years before getting married and having her own pool, cooking her own seafood. I guess he once had a girlfriend who he dumped for another girlfriend because the new girlfriend had migraines or acid reflux or some problem worse than ADHD, and being around her made him feel better about himself.

I keep my guesses to myself. I want to make sure he keeps his guesses to himself, too.

"Here's my dog." He swipes his finger to move to the next picture. It's a picture of a chocolate Labrador chewing the soft cotton head of a toy moose. "We had another one, but she died."

"I'm sorry." I also have a dead dog. We are exactly the same. Somehow, disguised, we found each other.

"Her name was Sandy," he says, and he shows me another picture of another Labrador, this one yellow with a white face and drooping eyes. This dog is lying on a slick wood floor, not chewing on anything, waiting to die.

After he shows me his pool and his dog and his dead dog, he takes off his shirt. He looks like a shadow in the vacant darkness that hugs our bodies. I take my dress off but leave my bra on. He stares at me in the dark, stares at nothing, and then pulls me close to him and kisses me. The kiss is just okay. His lips are chapped and taste like paint. His tongue is dry, like winter skin.

Until now, I have only had sex with my ex-boyfriend. In my experience, sex goes like kiss for a while, lie down, wait, flip over (maybe), wait more, and, finally, go to the bathroom. It isn't anything special. It doesn't make me cry. I've heard of girls crying during sex, like it's some sort of religious experience, like it unlocks some secret part of themselves, and they fall in love in one moment, there on their backs like Popsicles. Is that love? I don't want to fall in love like that.

I start to do what I have always done with the one person I've done it with. I kiss him. I run my hands along his chest. I kiss his neck. I wait for him to kiss my neck.

He doesn't kiss my neck. Instead he says, "Can I have a blow job?"

I stop kissing him. "What?"

"Blow job."

"You mean, right now? You want a blow job right now?" I have only ever given one blow job, to my ex-boyfriend. He stopped me after ten seconds because he was afraid of my teeth. Now, I can feel flecks of blue paint stuck to my teeth. I want to spit them out but I don't know where they'll land, and I don't want to ruin the sheets.

"Uh, yeah," he says. "If you want to."

I blink at him. I don't know what the right answer is. I feel betrayed, like he's sprung this big secret on me, a secret I was supposed to have known all along but had never been told. But I also feel stupid for not knowing what I want, for taking too much time to make a decision. Also, I have forgotten his name.

"Sure," I say finally. "I want to."

He leans back on his mom's sheets and slides out of his shorts. The room feels blacker, farther away. I can't see anything other than an outline of his body. I crawl back on my knees and feel around. I feel short, prickly hairs and small bumps and heat. He must be from some place warm, some place where hair is problematic. Then I remember he said he's from Annapolis. His dad is in the Navy. In the Navy, hair is problematic. I lean over and open my mouth.

While I'm down here, I'm trying to remember his name. He has a small name, the kind of name you can say with a clenched jaw. Ben? I wonder who else has done this for him, and if they'd known his name when they did it. I wonder if the girlfriend with acid reflux did this for him. Or maybe they broke up because she had acid reflux and couldn't do this for him. But mostly I wonder how much time has gone by and how much more time will go by before I can stop. I bob up and down. My neck begins to ache. My arms burn from holding myself up. I keep my eyes closed. Tim?

How long have I been down here? I start counting. I count to sixty and wonder if this is normal—the amount of time passed. Are people everywhere doing this, beneath sheets, or behind shower curtains, or in restaurant alleyways? Is someone doing this for my ex-boyfriend, right now, lifting her head up and down and up and down in tune with mine? Does she remember his name? Maybe she's more concerned about the volume of his pubes. Did he tell her he was from New Jersey? Also, did he ask for this? And were either of them prepared for how long it might take? I wonder how long is too long, and if I should say something to let this guy know that I'm growing weary. Something like *Are you concentrating?* Or *Is there any way to make this taste better?* I wonder if Jenny is asleep or if she's up in bed, worrying about where I am and what I'm doing. If I called her right now, she would answer. We are not supposed to go anywhere without each other.

I've lost track of the time. It has been a while. It has been hours, a day—or maybe three days. Three days spent on one blow job. The sun rose and set and rose and set and rose and set and I'm still here, bobbing up and down, shifting my weight from one arm to the other, wiggling my toes to keep the blood flowing in my feet. Rick? Nobody is named Rick. I wonder if my parents have tried to call. If they don't hear from me soon, they might call the school, or the police, who will no doubt ask around and find out where I am, who I'm with, what I'm doing. I didn't tell anybody where I was going. It could take them days to find me. They'll kick down the doors of every room in the building until they find me here, one week into the world's longest blow job.

What will my parents say? *Better off finishing what you started.* I push the question away. Concentrate on—Dean? His legs are tense. I glance up at his face and his eyes are narrowed toward the ceiling. We are both concentrating. I close my eyes again and more time passes. One week, one month, a year. One year crouched over the crotch of a guy whose name I don't know. I have blown a whole year away. *Everyone was so worried,* people will say. *You left without saying goodbye.* I didn't mean to disappear. I didn't mean to get trapped down here for so long. My back is sore and hunched. My mouth will be stuck in a permanent circle shape. I'll need physical therapy to learn how to speak again. Scientists will study me. They'll stick wires to my scalp and ask me what I was thinking. What was I thinking? How did I get here? What time is it? I need to wash my face.

Out of nowhere I feel something on top of my head. A hand. He lets it rest there like a dead fish on a table. His fingers splay around my scalp. I'm disgusted, suddenly, by this dead thing on my head. How dare this hand sit on top of me, with all its dead weight, while I work so hard to keep bobbing and remembering, my lips numb.

I gently smack the hand away. It comes back, seconds later, with another hand. Both hands spread out on top of my head, this time with more pressure. The hands push my head down. I push up against them. We struggle this way for a moment, my head pushing against the hands, the hands shoving me back down. Up, down, up, down, like a song.

A sharp pain pricks my throat. I feel a lump rising and I cough it back down. A hot tear leaks from the corner of my eye and slides down my cheek toward my mouth.

Using both my arms, I push the hands away and sit up on my knees. My back cracks. My mouth feels like a hole in a wall.

"I'm tired," I say. "Can we do something else?"

He puts his dead hands over his face. "I was, like, almost there."

"Sorry." I do feel sorry, having done all that work for nothing.

"Can you just go a little longer?"

The sun will come up soon. Silvery light seeps through the blinds. I see his face. It looks bluer in the light. Bluer and younger, the entire year I spent in his crotch only having made him smoother, more beautiful. I reach up and touch my forehead. The pimples feel bigger and angrier. They're angry at me. Everyone in the room is angry at me.

"I don't think so," I say. "Sorry."

He sighs. He reaches down to his feet and pulls his shorts up.

I want to cry—not in a hormonal way. I want to cry in a way that comes from my stomach and makes my head feel like it's floating away from my neck. I squint my eyes but nothing else comes out.

"I'm going back to my room." I scan the bed for my dress and find it crumpled under his shoulder. I tug, but he doesn't move. I look at him. His eyes are closed. His body is as stiff as a toothpick. His hand is stuffed into his shorts, moving up and down, up and down, making a tent out of them.

I remember his name is Ian.

I don't know what to do, so I sit beside him on my knees and watch, feeling stupid about everything. I count the seconds. Ten seconds, twenty seconds. All of a sudden he shudders and yelps like a puppy, then melts into the bed. It only took him twenty-three seconds. I yank my dress from under him, throw it over my neck, and run out of the room barefoot.

I walk down the hallway and into the girls' bathroom. Somebody left a small bottle of grapefruit-scented face wash on the sink, and I squirt some into my hand and rub it all over my forehead. I press down hard, trying to force the bumps to burrow under my skin. But when I wash the soap away and dry my face, they peer back at me through the mirror like a costume.

They don't tell you what to do if you feel *(C) Afraid, because I am alone and there is something strange in the air.* They don't tell you who to talk to or which button to press. I walk out of the bathroom and dial my ex-boyfriend's number.

"Hello?" His voice is slow and raspy, as if he's been dreaming.

"Do you think any of your friends are rapists?"

"Huh?"

"On the lacrosse team. Are they rapists?"

"What are you talking about? Are you okay?"

"What do you think?"

For a while he doesn't say anything. Then he says, "I don't know."

"But they're your friends?"

"Yeah, I guess they're my friends."

I understand now that all the boys I'll ever know will either become rapists or friends of rapists, or friends of friends of rapists, or friends of friends who might become rapists, under the right circumstances. It will be like that now.

Back in my room, Jenny is asleep with her back turned to me. Everyone has their backs turned to something. Everyone in the world is keeping secrets. I stare at the jumbo box of Costco condoms on my desk. It's unopened, unhelpful. I open it and take out one condom. It doesn't look like a weapon of self-defense. It looks like a packet of soy sauce. I grab a handful of condoms to keep in my desk drawer, then another handful for Jenny. I hold the box of remaining condoms under my arm and tiptoe out of the room. I want to be a problem solver.

It's barely morning and the hallway is quiet. I walk up to the room next to ours and take a condom from the box. I crouch down and slip it under the door. Then I slip another, and another. When I stand up, I feel my heels lift off the ground, then the balls of my feet. I push gently off my toes and hover for a moment, then float through the air to the next door, feeling heavier than I should. I grab another handful and slide them under the door, one by one. I slide condoms under the door of every room in the hallway until the box is empty. Nobody wakes up. Nobody asks questions. I hang in the silence, suspended in the air with all that I know. Behind me, I feel wings.

★ ★ ★

You are not supposed to be alone in the first place. But if you find yourself alone, against better judgment, you blow the whistle first, then run to the blue emergency pole. While you're running to the blue emergency pole, you're supposed to continue blowing the whistle at a quick pace. The speed at which you blow the whistle and the speed at which you run to the emergency pole should be equally panicked, equally berserk. Otherwise, someone might see you and think you're playing a game. *Look at that girl blowing her whistle alone in the dark*, they might say. *Perhaps she is writing a song.*

Trick

Arlo and Dan sit outside in the courtyard at the Chateau Marmont, shaded by a white canopy, their faces shrouded by potted monsteras and lush ferns. But not too shrouded. For instance, that woman at the corner table with her elderly mother is staring at them. Or rather, she's staring at Arlo. Her face is frozen with that particular flavor of aloofness associated with a celebrity sighting, as if she suddenly believes in her own invisibility. Arlo's seen it a million times before. He stares back at the woman, but she doesn't budge. He can't tell if she's a fan or if she wants to stick her fork in his eyeball. It's the same look, regardless.

"These fucking pickles," Dan says, peeling the top layer of bread off his club sandwich. He tosses the pickle slices to the side, then dabs the sandwich with his napkin to soak up the juice. "It's like, I'm paying thirty dollars for a sandwich that will send me into anaphylactic shock. I hate this fucking place. Next time I want a meeting, remind me that I hate this fucking place."

"What's up?" Arlo asks absently. He's still staring at the woman, waiting to see what she'll do next. He could smile at her or stick his tongue out. But he knows better than that. He blinks, and the woman's eyes dart to her lap. She digs her phone from her bag and starts furiously texting. Her mother, or whoever the older woman is, picks at a Caesar salad with her fingers.

"How'd it go with *Elite Design* last week?" Dan says as he reexamines the sandwich.

"Fine, whatever. They're a little intrusive. Like, who cares what my house looks like? I don't understand why I have to show everyone every inch of my personal life, you know? I'm an actor, not a circus freak. I'm a private person."

"The fuck you are." Dan bites the sandwich and winces like it's assaulted him. "People would kill to see the inside of your house." He pauses and winces again, this time at his own words. "I mean, fuck. Sorry, you know what I mean. Here's the bright side: they probably won't even air the episode now."

One month ago, Arlo was lounging on the yellow sands of Majorca with Carmen, steps away from the beachside restaurant where they'd met, where she'd served him a bowl of gazpacho that fateful day a year earlier, and the rest was history. Or at least, it should have been. He'd gone to Majorca to disappear. Not permanently, or anything like that. He just needed a break. There was no one particular reason why. He'd been in the spotlight since his seventeenth birthday, when the *Choir Boys* pilot aired and the world—or at least the world's teenage girls—saw what Arlo Banks could do.

It wasn't that he was especially talented. The dance moves were simple enough, and they'd dubbed all his songs with the voice of some Canadian kid who'd just landed a Broadway musical. It was more about how Arlo looked on-screen—perfectly symmetrical face, his golden hair swooped across his forehead, the tiny gap between his two front teeth on display. Every time his icy-blue eyes made contact with the camera, somewhere, in some living room, splayed out on a tweed couch, a teenage girl's heart sank straight through to her butt.

After six perfect seasons, *Choir Boys* wrapped, leaving Arlo with millions of fans and that Good Christian Boy reputation he'd come to embody so well. But by then, he was twenty-five years old. He'd slept with over forty women, had toyed with almost every drug, including something called Rhyzofedromol, which had, on more than one occasion, sent him into a dingy, self-hating hole. Dan had said, back then, that Arlo was in need of a rebranding. Or rather, an *un*branding.

"Rid yourself of that virgin ballerina bitch boy" was how Dan had put it, just after he'd nailed Arlo a role in a *Baywatch* film revival.

Arlo did *Baywatch*. He did *Beasts of Eden, Rodeo King, Wiseguy, Dudes of the Ranch, Truck Stop, The Night DJ, Limo Driver, Kill Mountain, Hercules, The Don Quixote Trip,* and *Pyramid Scheme.* He hired a trainer, got a six-pack and defined shoulders, bought an ATV and filmed himself in the dirt, jumping off cliffs, reeling in a sixty-pound tuna—manly things. He slept with more women. Still, some of them asked him to sing to them.

"I can't sing," he'd tell them, sprawled naked on his bed. "But I can do this." And then he'd flip onto his stomach and stick his dick between his legs so it poked through his butt cheeks like a tail.

Yes, it was that big. And, yes, most of the women were impressed.

But he was more drawn to the women who weren't impressed. He hadn't thought too deeply about it, but he was never as turned-on as when a woman called him talentless trash. Or when he did the dick-tail trick and a woman shrieked about what a freak he was, a dirty little creep.

"You can touch it," he'd say.

Usually, they did.

"You're disgusting," some of them said. Sometimes he got so turned on he'd black out and come to hours later, alone and naked on top of his sheets, his dick shriveled and limp as roadkill on his thigh.

For the record, Arlo never made anyone do anything they didn't want to do. He could usually tell, when he did the trick, if the woman was into it or not. The ones who weren't got out of there pretty quickly. Faked an emergency, suddenly remembered a dentist appointment. He didn't care. He got off on the insults, more than anything, and the fucked-up backwardness of his dick poking out behind him—stiff as a branch as some woman gawked at it—felt a little bit like magic.

Despite the strangeness of the whole thing, and the sheer number of women who'd seen the dick-tail trick, nobody ever leaked it to the press. Eventually, Arlo just got bored. The world didn't want to think of him as anything other than a squawking, preppy virgin, no matter the extremes he took to redefine himself. He lost interest in all the topless, comical roles in big-budget, low-grade movies. The sexy cowboy, the pirate hero, the hot orphan astronaut. None of it felt real or true to him. And while he had aged, his fans hadn't. Most of the girls pining after him online were teen-agers, watching *Choir Boys* for the first time commercial-free on Netflix. Everyone else, everyone who mattered, thought he was a complete joke.

So, yeah, he left. It wasn't "giving up." It was starting over. Turning a new leaf. Whatever you want to call it. He hadn't been in Majorca for more than a week when he met Carmen and fell in love with her.

★   ★   ★

"Nobody wants to come anywhere near the inside of my house now," Arlo says, turning his attention back to the staring woman. She's holding her phone in her lap, beneath the table, its camera pointed in his direction. What does she want, anyway? What can she do with a blurry video of him talking to his agent over a garden salad? Sell it? There are way more incriminating videos of him out there. He reaches over and plucks a pickle off Dan's plate and eats it.

"I didn't come here to drive the nail in the coffin," Dan says. He takes a massive bite of his club sandwich, and a glob of mayo smears the corner of his mouth. Arlo stares at it, disgusted. "In fact, I have good news."

"Oh yeah?"

Earlier that morning, Arlo had read the headlines and laughed: ARLO BANKS ACCUSED OF CANNIBALISM. ARLO BANKS LIKES TO DRINK WOMEN'S BLOOD. ARLO BANKS: VEGETARIAN OR CANNIBAL? CANNIBAL OR NOT, ARLO BANKS IS STILL HOT.

Apparently, a woman is talking. She has direct messages, she says. She has proof. Proof of what? Arlo wonders. As he glares at the glob of mayo on Dan's face, Arlo tries to understand why this woman would make up something so outrageous, so unbelievable, when she has real tabloid gold in the palm of her sweaty little hand. Then again, maybe Arlo didn't do the dick-tail trick with this one. Maybe he hadn't even slept with her.

"Yeah," Dan says. "Brent wants to meet with you."

Brent directed *Dudes of the Ranch*, which was terrible at the time and still is, but over the years has gathered somewhat of a cult following.

"About what?" Arlo looks back at the woman, who's finally slurping her carrot soup.

"*Dracula.*"

"You're joking," Arlo says, trying not to laugh.

But Dan can't help himself. He cracks up, mouth open, and Arlo watches the mash of chewed meat jiggle on his tongue.

"I wish I was, kid. Look, when I first saw the headlines, I thought you were in deep shit. We've got actors going down left and right. It's a fucking war zone out here. But this? This is just too good to be bad. Brent called *me*. He thinks we should capitalize. I agree with him."

"Brent's a terrible filmmaker." Arlo wishes, momentarily, that Carmen were here to listen to this. Then it occurs to him that, wherever she is, she might have seen the headlines, too. Maybe she'll call. Surely, if she knew about the tsunami of shit he was swimming in, she'd call.

"No shit," Dan says. "That's sort of his thing. It works. And *you* work in his shitty films. I can't explain why. What I'm saying is, you have to embrace your God-given role. Look at Tobey Maguire. He's not complaining."

"Tobey was Spider-Man."

"Exactly. And you're Dracula." Dan bites into his sandwich.

Arlo stares at his plate. *It's not the worst idea*, he thinks. Maybe, after everything, this one rumor—and its subsequent starring role—will be the thing to put *Choir Boys* behind him. Not to mention, it will take his mind off Carmen, who could still call, any day now. Where was she? She hadn't left a note. She had, however, left behind most of her clothes, her makeup, even the little coin purse where she kept all the stones she'd collected from the places they'd traveled together. It was as if she'd run out to grab a coffee and decided, on a whim, not to come home.

At first, Arlo hadn't thought much of it. They had gotten into a fight the night before she left. Something stupid. And Carmen was a flake by design. She went wherever she wanted, executed whatever new, shiny idea popped into her head regardless of the plan. After all, it had been her idea to come back to L.A., and not even twenty-four hours later they were splitting a bottle of wine in the Delta Sky Club, awaiting the flight to their new life together.

But now she's been gone for over a week, and Arlo still hasn't heard from her. He briefly considered calling her family in Spain, only to realize he didn't know how to reach them. In fact, he doesn't know them at all. He doesn't even know if she *has* a family, or if she does, if they're the people she would choose to go back to. They never talked about each other's past, which, now that Arlo is thinking about it, is probably not normal. But what does he know about normal? Maybe the best thing for him to do, at this point, is listen to Dan and bury himself in work until the rest sorts itself out.

"All right," Arlo says, "I'll meet with him."

"Fantastic." Dan takes another bite of his sandwich and makes a face like it's suddenly rancid. He pulls his phone from his pocket and holds the speaker to his mouth. "Hey, Siri, text Dayna Assistant: 'I hate this fucking place.'"

Arlo feels something moving toward him—an invisible force field, a strong gust of wind. He looks up from his plate and sees the woman who's been staring him down stomping across the patio, her mother in tow, her eyes narrowed in on a specific thought.

"Fuck me," Arlo mumbles.

Dan looks up from his phone and follows Arlo's gaze. "This fucking place."

And then, both suddenly and in slow motion, the woman is upon them. She stands with her hands on her hips and sort of wobbles back and forth on her feet. Up close, Arlo notices how tall and lanky she is, her limbs like unruly branches. Also, she has bad acne on her face. She can't be more than twenty-one years old.

"I just wanted to let you know that I think it's really inappropriate for you to be here right now." She says it all in one breath, like she's been holding the sentence in the pocket of space behind her front teeth this whole time. Beside her, the old woman—whom Arlo now assumes to be her grandmother—stares off at a distant table where a couple shares a shrimp cocktail.

"Okay," Arlo says calmly. "Thank you."

Her face flushes red, which makes her whiteheads flare up like night stars. Arlo gets the urge to reach over and squeeze the massive one between her eyebrows.

"You're welcome," she sort of screams. She hesitates, like she doesn't know whether she should keep talking or proudly walk away.

"Anything else?" Arlo sticks his fork into a radish and eats it.

The woman's face is so red it's nearly purple. She stares hazily at Arlo's salad in revelation. "I used to like you."

Arlo nods. This isn't the first time he's been confronted by a flustered fan. Although, usually the situation isn't so hostile. The last time a fan approached him, she told him that she'd had a crush on him her whole life, but now she was suddenly having stronger feelings for Chris Hemsworth, and she was sorry about that. She was sorry she couldn't bring the feelings back.

Dan leans back in his chair, wipes the mayo from his mouth with a napkin. "We're sorry for your loss. Now get the fuck out of here."

The woman's eyes grow wide and crazed with anger. She glances from Arlo to Dan, then back to Arlo, then turns and stomps off.

"I fucking hate Hollywood," she screams, at nobody in particular.

"Me, too, sweetie," says Dan.

The grandmother, or whoever the fuck she is, turns to follow the angry woman. As she passes by Arlo's chair, she reaches out and pats him on the head. Her hand lingers on his hair for a moment, and Arlo can't tell if she's trying to comfort him or regain her balance. Dan watches with lazy eyes until the woman removes her hand and walks away.

"She's going to make a voodoo doll out of that piece of hair she just snuck from your head," Dan says, laughing. "What a dump this place is."

Arlo finishes his salad, thinking about Carmen, about what she might have said to that woman. Since Carmen's disappearance, he's become fabulously depressed. He hasn't shaved his face in over a week, and he's been wearing the same gray Gucci sweatshirt everywhere. He can't help that his eyes still twinkle, that the tears give the turquoise in his irises a chemical glow. A few days ago, the paparazzi noticed him walking about solo, and so there were a few headlines speculating about a breakup. But now that this woman is running with the whole cannibalism thing, nobody seems to care anymore that Arlo is, in fact, newly heartbroken.

Carmen is the only person Arlo has ever loved. When they met, she'd never even heard of *Choir Boys*. She vaguely recognized him from a Calvin Klein underwear ad he'd done while promoting *Kill Mountain*. She worked at the restaurant where Arlo was eating alone at a table overlooking the Mediterranean, wondering what the rest of his life was going to be about.

"You didn't look so good on the billboard," she said in her thick Catalan accent. "You looked like you were going to poop on everyone."

The best thing about Carmen was her total imperviousness to Arlo's fame. She was unbothered by the paparazzi, thought American TV was stupid and culturally irrelevant. Her favorite movie was some Italian film from the forties about a kid and his dad searching for a stolen bicycle. She didn't even speak Italian, she just liked the way each scene offered up a new secret every time she watched it. Arlo had never heard of the film and, if he was being honest, didn't have any interest (he couldn't read subtitles without feeling tired), but he liked watching Carmen watch the movie, her eyes big and glossy as if in a trance.

"Look." She'd point. "Look how sad he is this time. Have you ever seen anyone look so beautifully sad?"

★　★　★

Dan flags down their server, who trots over to the table. He's young, maybe twenty, and has been eagerly waiting on the perimeter of the patio for this moment.

"What the fuck was that?" Dan says.

The server freezes in place, terrified. "I'm so sorry. I didn't see."

"It's okay," Arlo says, not wanting to cause any more of a scene. "We'll just take the check."

Dan gestures around the table. "I thought this was supposed to be a—what the fuck's it called? A safe space? You guys just let anyone eat here now?"

"Sorry," the server says again. He takes Arlo's plate and stumbles away, then comes back seconds later with the check and a bottle of champagne.

"On the house." He rests the champagne in front of Arlo and the check in front of Dan and runs away again.

Dan stares at the check. Arlo reaches over and grabs it.

"All of this will blow over," Dan says. "Look at Franco. People still love him."

"I know." Arlo takes three one-hundred-dollar bills from his wallet and sticks them into the folder without looking at the total.

Dan stands up, secures the button on his pants that he'd unhooked when he started eating.

"You hear from Carmen?"

"No."

"She'll regret it," Dan says matter-of-factly. "At least you aren't married." He squeezes Arlo's shoulder. "Brent wants to see you Wednesday."

Arlo nods, and Dan walks away, past the scared server, who watches from behind a table of rolled napkins. Dan points at the server and keeps walking until he's out of sight.

Arlo pulls his phone from his pocket and googles himself. He's done this three times today, already, and knows no good can come of it. But he can't help himself.

NO COMMENT FROM ARLO BANKS ON CANNIBALISM is the first headline he sees. It's new. He clicks it.

Arlo Banks has yet to address the cannibalism rumors being circulated about him. In an exclusive interview with Page Six, his accuser, who wishes to remain anonymous, has admitted that their sexual encounter was consensual until the moment he tried to gnaw off her pinkie toe.

Arlo concentrates on the champagne bottle, trying to recall if he's ever tried to gnaw off a woman's toe, but nothing comes up. He can't remember every woman he's slept with, but various details flash across his mind—a freckle on an upper lip, a lace bra, a high-pitched gasp. He remembers some of their faces, their voices, the words they called him. And he remembers the thrill of the dick-tail trick, which he's done too many times to count. Now that trick seems so innocent compared to what he's being accused of. Who is this woman, and what has he done to make her hate him this much? As he scans his mind for the women he's been with, only a few experiences stand out. Sure, there was the PA who wanted him to bite off her nails (which was *her* idea, by the way), and that bartender who broke down in tears, which Arlo assumed had more to do with her father's MS diagnosis than anything Arlo had done. There was one woman whose lip bled pretty badly after he bit it, but there's nothing cannibalistic about a lip bite, and besides, afterward *she* apologized to *him*. Something about a blood-clotting disorder, though it was difficult to understand what she was saying, her mouth so full of blood.

But this was all years ago, before Carmen. She had taught him how to love, how to enjoy loving someone. He hadn't needed any tricks with her. Love and sex had happened hand in hand, softly, each trying not to break the other. Even thinking about Carmen now, despite how angry he is with her, he can't help but miss the way she'd touch him gently, as if he were a precious doll, how at night she'd reach over and rub his earlobe with her thumb and forefinger until he was asleep.

He pulls another hundred-dollar bill from his wallet and places it on top of the bill folder. Then he slides on his baseball cap and keeps his eyes on the ground as he walks out of the restaurant.

★　★　★

The next morning, Arlo is on his deck overlooking the Malibu bluffs, which are especially green this time of year and speckled with bright yellow poppies, reminding him of a surreal Dr. Seuss illustration, when he reads the newest headline:

SECOND WOMAN COMES FORWARD, SAYS ARLO BANKS TRIED TO CUT OFF HER EAR AND FRY IT IN OIL. Again, he laughs.

He's almost impressed by the creativity. Who would want to eat a fried ear? He finds himself staring foggily at the horizon, imagining what a fried ear would taste like. Gummy, probably, and tough—like beef fat. He doesn't even eat beef.

Unsurprisingly, this woman also wants to remain anonymous. Still, she's discussed in great detail the events of their alleged encounter. Apparently, they met at an after-party for some charity event in the Hills. Arlo was charming, sweet. She described his eyes as "warm and sad, not at all like a sociopath's." Which is why she was so surprised when, back at his house, he held a pair of kitchen scissors to her face and told her he wanted to feel the resistance of her flesh as the blade snipped through it.

"He said he was hungry," she told the magazine. "And then talked about battering my ears and deep-frying them like pickle slices." Needless to say, she called herself an Uber and snuck out while he was in the bathroom, probably sharpening his razor blade or crushing up some ketamine to sneak into her drink.

Arlo has no recollection of any of this. He can't remember the last charity event he went to, and he doesn't even know if he owns kitchen scissors. He takes out his phone and dials Carmen's number, almost by reflex. She won't answer, but he wants to leave her a message anyway. He wants his side of the story out there, somewhere.

"I don't know if you've been reading the news," he says after the beep, "but there are some women talking. None of it is true, okay? It's all lies. I wish I knew where you were."

He hangs up, and as he stuffs his phone back into his pocket, it begins to vibrate. For a second, a wave of hope flips his stomach on its side, but when he looks at the caller ID, it's just Marc, his lawyer.

"I've seen the headlines," Marc says. "Don't talk to anyone."

"It's not true, Marc." Arlo lies down on the chaise lounge and lets the morning sun warm his forehead.

"True, not true, whatever. The only person you should be talking to is me, do you understand? The last thing we want is to blow this out of proportion."

"Right." For the first time, Arlo feels a little embarrassed.

"Okay." Marc is chewing on something on the other end of the phone. "Now, I have to ask. Do any of these women have proof?"

"Proof?"

"A photo, a video. Anything to back up what they're saying."

"A photo of what, Marc? Me chowing on their limbs? No, there are no photos of that, as far as I know."

"Okay." Marc's voice is muffled by whatever he's eating. "I had to ask. Just keep your mouth shut and let's hope no lawsuits come of this."

Arlo has only been involved in one lawsuit: some driver rear-ended him on the 405 and later sued for four thousand dollars in damages. It was no big deal. Arlo gave the guy the money, even though the incident wasn't his fault. It was all over the news at the time, with most articles praising Arlo for covering the costs, behaving like a gentleman throughout the whole ordeal. AMERICA'S CHOIRBOY PAYS IT FORWARD. GOD BLESS ARLO BANKS, THE GOOD SAMARITAN. Those are the headlines Arlo is accustomed to reading about his personal life.

Somehow, he knows that paying off women who have accused him of trying to eat their body parts won't garner the same positive publicity.

Marc swallows. "Have you heard from Carmen?"

"No."

"Well, try to get in touch with her if you can. Could be good publicity. Loyal Girlfriend, and all that."

"She's gone," Arlo says, his eyes closed and directed at the sun.

★   ★   ★

Throughout the morning, Arlo gets more calls. Kirk, his manager, calls to second Dan's suggestion that he take the *Dracula* role.

"Lean in," Kirk says. "It works for all the comedians."

Arlo gets a call from his publicist, who tells him to lie low and suggests hiring a PI to track down Carmen. "She won't be hard to find. The tricky part will be convincing her to come back."

"No shit," Arlo says.

His trainer calls with breathing exercises. His masseuse offers a hot-stone massage. Dan calls for no reason in particular, other than to say he's seen the new headlines but still isn't super-worried. Then he calls again, this time with Kirk, to discuss *Dracula* terms.

"I haven't even spoken to Brent yet," Arlo says.

"Just getting the ball rolling," one of them replies. "*Dracula*, starring Arlo Banks."

That each of these people has something to lose from an Arlo Banks Downfall doesn't escape him. Still, it feels good to have so many people rallying around him, to know that the support system is there, ready to defend him. If he didn't know any better, he would call it love.

★　★　★

At sunset, Arlo goes for a walk along the bluffs to clear his head. By now, three women have accused him of trying to eat them. This third woman has come out and said that he tried to chew her lips off, that he left her bloody and crying in her bedroom. It turns out her name is Cara and she does not care who knows it. The name Cara doesn't sound familiar, but Arlo recognizes her face as the girl with the blood-clot disease, and he chalks the whole thing up to a cry for attention. He googles her name and, once he scrolls past all the headlines, finds a video of her wearing black lingerie on a hotel bed, drinking a Budweiser in a can. "Budweiser," she says, "not just for the boys." Arlo closes the video and puts his phone away. *She wants more followers*, he tells himself. It couldn't be more obvious. And for the record, he didn't leave her bleeding out in her bedroom. She got embarrassed and kicked him out. Of course, that defense is moot now. But at least he understands where this girl is coming from. At least he isn't totally in the dark.

He walks down the dirt path that winds through the bluffs, kicking a sharp stone as he goes. The path is mostly empty, save for a few people walking dogs, pushing strollers. He doesn't need to worry about the people up here. To them, Arlo is more of a landmark than an actual person. They quietly congratulate themselves for being rich enough to live in his neighborhood while exercising their exclusive luxury to ignore him. He enjoys this quality in them—it reminds him a little of Carmen.

Still, today he avoids eye contact. His face is all over the internet, and it's obvious everyone has seen it. He feels their heads turn slightly as he passes, their eyes lingering on his back, waiting for him to turn around and bite their necks. He considers that he could do it—launch himself onto a suspecting mother and dig his teeth into her collarbone—and nobody would be surprised. What do you call that? Privilege? He knows by now he should feel more embarrassed, but the image still makes him want to laugh. The situation is so ridiculous, so over-the-top insane, he decides that Dan is right: It's too good to be bad. He should do *Dracula*. He should lean in, make a joke of the whole thing. He'll be this year's most popular Halloween costume. Maybe he'll even be invited to host *SNL*. He's got too much support, too much ahead of him, to let this be the thing that brings him down.

He kicks the stone into the brush and looks up to see two women approaching. They appear to be about his age, each wearing patterned leggings with a matching cropped tank. One of them is holding her phone out in front of them, filming herself as they walk and talk to each other. Her hair is pulled into a ponytail high on her head. The other's hair is twisted into two long braids that fall in front of her chest. They stop walking and pucker their lips at the camera, gaze cutely at their own reflections. They remind Arlo of the kind of women he used to sleep with before he met Carmen—women who craved attention, fame, whether it was their own or someone else's. He enjoyed their earnestness, their stark determination to have what he had.

Arlo narrows his eyes on the women. He tousles his hair, stiffens his shoulders. He wants them to see him and feel what all the women before them have felt: desire, envy, whatever you want to call it. He needs that right now.

The ponytailed woman looks up first. She sees Arlo, no more than ten feet away from her, and drops her arm. Her phone falls to the sand, but she doesn't bend down to pick it up. The woman with braids looks from her friend to Arlo. The three of them stand still, Arlo's eyes darting between the two women, their eyes steady on what he thinks might be the bridge of his nose. He examines them briefly. They are totally paralyzed, their mouths slightly parted, their eyes popped like marbles. Neither of them even blinks. Then, the ponytailed girl's lip begins to tremble.

"It's okay," he says, realizing this is not the starstruck reaction he was going for. He holds his hands up in front of his body and walks slowly toward them. "I'm not going to hurt you."

The girls step back. The braided one leans down and picks the phone out of the sand.

"We'll call the police," she says.

"There's no need for that," Arlo says, but he's still walking forward. With each step he takes, they take one step back. The ponytailed woman's eyes are wet with fear, and suddenly, Arlo recognizes her. Or at least, he thinks he does. Her face, or one like it, flashes across his mind—her lips painted pink, her sparkly eyeliner smudged at the corners of her eyes. He sees her hoisting a giant champagne bottle stuck with sparklers in the air, gliding toward him in a pair of stiletto heels. He sees her in his bed, tangled between the silky sheets, her ponytail loosened so some of her hair has fallen out around her cheeks. Then, as quickly as it came, the image is gone. He blinks, trying to remember where it came from.

The woman with the braids holds the phone up and points its camera at him. "I'm filming you. You won't get away with anything."

He's only a few feet from them now. His feet keep shuffling forward despite the alarm ringing in his ears. His brain has lost command of his body, each of his limbs functioning in a panicked, every-man-for-himself fashion. He has no control over what happens next. It feels a little bit like acting.

"I'm not trying to get away with anything," Arlo says, his hands now in his pockets. "I'm just trying to go for a walk."

Tears stream down the ponytailed woman's face, which is still frozen. *Get a grip*, Arlo wants to tell her. But as he opens his mouth, the woman with the braids thrusts her arm back and throws the phone at his head. It hits him in the temple, and he stumbles into the brush.

"Run!" the braided woman screams. She takes off, tugging on her friend's hand, but she remains still. Arlo stares at her, his forearms protecting his head, and tries again to recall her face from his memory.

"Julia!" the other one yells. And, as if startled from a dream, the woman jolts and runs away.

Arlo lowers his arms and watches them zigzag down the path and out of sight. His vision is fuzzy, his ears are still ringing. He touches his throbbing temple, then moves his hands to his chest, his stomach, unsure if he is really standing there in the flesh or if he's actually somewhere else, someone else, just tuning in momentarily to see what happens next.

He looks down and sees the phone at his feet, face up, still recording. He picks it up and presses stop. Then he plays it back.

As the video runs, Arlo stares directly into his own eyes. He hadn't realized that he'd been staring at the camera the whole time, slowly inching forward, his face poised at the lens. He does not look afraid or shocked. He looks determined, even a little intimidating. Maybe he is a good actor, after all. He watches the video a few times, each time recognizing himself less and less. Maybe he should show it to Brent. He doesn't know if he should feel ashamed or proud of this idea.

Instinctively, he deletes the video, then throws the phone into the bushes and walks onward.

★   ★   ★

The night before Carmen left Arlo, she'd found messages on his phone. They weren't that bad—just a few back-and-forths with a former costar he'd made out with once on-screen. He hadn't seen her in years, and they were only planning to catch up over dinner. Still, to prove his wrongdoing, Carmen decided to read the messages out loud to him in a kind of dramatic reenactment, which was made especially dramatic every time she rolled her *r*'s.

"'I've missed you, Arlo,'" Carmen said, her hands tense around his phone as they stood on opposite sides of their king bed. "'Hollywood hasn't been the same without you.'"

"'I've missed you, too. I can't wait to see you.'"

Carmen's eyes caught fire.

"'You're still my best on-screen kiss.'"

"'I'm even better off-screen.'"

Okay, so the messages were kind of bad. But Arlo had never intended to cheat on Carmen. He was just a flirt. He tried to explain this to her, that he couldn't help himself, that he wasn't sure how else to talk to a woman he'd once kissed, even if he was completely unattracted to her, which he was. Wasn't. What he meant was, he was only attracted to Carmen.

"Womanizer!" Carmen screamed. He didn't think they had that word in Spain, and he wondered where Carmen had learned it. She grabbed a glass bottle of lotion from her nightstand and threw it at his head, but her aim was terrible. The bottle smashed the wall behind him. Gooey bits of glass slid slowly down the wall.

"Are you crazy?" he said, which was the wrong thing to say.

"Garbage-weasel-dickhead!" Carmen screamed. He hadn't seen her this angry before. Even during the few minor fights they'd had, she'd never called him names. "What, you can't control yourself? You don't know how to talk to women? I never heard anything so idiotic in my life. You stupid piece of shit."

He watched the disgust creep across her face. Then, against his better judgment, a particular warmness began to throb in his dick. He hated to admit it, but her whole show was turning him on. The next thing he knew, he'd unbuttoned his pants and pushed them down to his ankles. Then he was lying face down on the bed, his dick stuffed through his legs. He felt it poking out behind him, his old magic trick.

Carmen fell silent. Arlo lay there, face down on the pillow, waiting for her to do something. His heart was thumping in his stomach, his body stuck with needles. Here he was, offering his whole self up to her—all his fucked-up freakiness, his insecurity, his uncontrollable desires. He'd never felt so vulnerable as he did then, knowing, for the first time, that if he was rejected, he would never recover.

He doesn't remember what happened after that. Whatever Carmen had done, whatever she'd said, was too painful for him to revisit. But in the morning, she was gone. Arlo knew she wasn't coming back.

★ ★ ★

Two days after Arlo's walk along the bluffs, a lawsuit is filed. One of the anonymous accusers is seeking justice. Arlo is drinking a cappuccino and preparing for his meeting with Brent when Marc calls with the news.

"If she's staying anonymous, she just wants money," he says. "We'll pay her off and have her sign an NDA."

"Okay," Arlo says, feeling, for some reason, a little guilty. "Does she want an apology?"

"The money is the apology."

"Do you think I'll get to see her?" Arlo wants to see her face, to scan her eyes for that same paralyzing fear he'd seen in the woman with the ponytail. He wants to know what they are so afraid of.

"Doubt it," Marc says. "Unless you want to fight. But I don't recommend that, at this point."

"I don't want to fight. Just give her whatever she wants."

"I'm sorry this is happening to you. This is a fucked-up time."

Arlo hangs up. He finishes his cappuccino, then heads into his bedroom to take a steam shower. He lets the steam seep into his nostrils and down his ear canals and fog his mind. He wants to give these women whatever they want. He means that. He wants to be the person who makes things better for them.

After the shower, he shaves his beard—steady, downward strokes. The shaving cream he uses smells like eucalyptus. He stares at himself in the mirror and runs the pads of his fingers along the soft skin of his cheeks. For the first time in weeks, he recognizes himself, and a little smirk of relief escapes through the corner of his lips. He puts on pants and a clean white T-shirt and slides into his leather loafers, which he bought with Carmen in Italy. He runs some salt spray through his hair to give it a little volume, then grabs his sunglasses and heads for the front door.

Morning light floods the foyer as he opens the door, and he holds his hands over his glasses to shield his eyes more. There's the sound of shuffling, scurrying, and a wave of voices shouting indiscriminately. He looks up and sees four news vans, reporters and paparazzi with microphones and cameras hoisted on their shoulders, approaching him from all angles. He tries to walk forward, toward his car, but he can't even see his car. Too many people are in the way. They rush up to him and stick their microphones in his face.

"Arlo, do you know about the lawsuit filed against you?" someone says.

"Arlo, are you a cannibal?"

"Did you hurt those women?"

"Do you think you'll go to jail?"

"How are you coping with the disappearance of your girlfriend?"

"Should women be afraid of you?"

Arlo keeps his head down and shuffles forward, trying not to panic. He has never been swarmed by so many hostile people at once. *Ants*, he thinks. *Like ants on a carcass.*

"Arlo," one of them says as he shoulders through the crowd. "Did you eat your girlfriend?"

Arlo stops, looks up at the man. He's wearing a golf shirt with a stain on the collar and his microphone has no label. Behind him, a man in a bucket hat holds a camera on his shoulder.

"Is it true you ate your girlfriend?" the pap says. The rest of the ants have fallen silent, awaiting Arlo's answer. Carmen's face flickers in his mind—her soft skin, her long, wavy hair, eyes that change color depending on the light. His chest tightens. He looks into the camera.

"No," he says. Though he doesn't know if his face tells a different story.

Monsters

A few weeks before we were set to film season eight, I made an account on a dating app. I had been dumped on national television at the beginning of the summer (they put the dumping in the season finale), and I thought it'd be a good idea to start off the new season with an exceptionally attractive and mature rebound.

Our show was called *Hotel California*. They called it that because for the first handful of seasons we all worked at the Hotel Bel-Air. I was in reception. Derek ran the bar. Riley and Maya were hostesses—although they both left the show after season three. (Maya met some billionaire who started a "voluntourism" business. He took her to Costa Rica to save the turtles, or whatever, and ended up buying the whole beach town and naming it after her. Riley went to Vegas. Last I heard she was waiting tables at the Ramsay's Kitchen in Harrah's.) There were eight of us in total. Around season five, we grew a little too recognizable, in certain circles, to continue working at the hotel. People—fans, crazy ones—started booking rooms just to be near us, and management wasn't psyched about that. Plus, we didn't need the minimum wage anymore. So production filtered a handful of new cast members in and out over the next few seasons, waiting to see who stuck.

By season six, Derek and I were the only original cast members left on the show. This gave us a lot of clout. We got paid more than everyone else. This was also because we had real chemistry—people liked to watch us. We'd met while working at the hotel, before the show started, and became instant friends. I'd pop into the bar when my shift was over at reception, and Derek would make me vodka sodas on the house while I gave him all the dirt on the guests. Once, when a certain newly single and extremely famous actress was staying at the hotel, I'd put in a good word for Derek at check-in. She came to the bar that night, got completely wasted on champagne and showed us her facelift scars and gave us each two hundred dollars and called us cute. Then she took Derek back to her room. They texted for a little while after that, but the fling fizzled when she went on location in London. I think she married some guy over there and then divorced him a few months later. Anyway, Derek and I always knew how to turn a normal, dumb day into a time.

I didn't meet Gemma until season six. We'd been filming at a bar on Sunset late into the night (Derek's birthday), and she came out of nowhere.

"I think I'm in love with you," she said. She was at least a full head taller than me, and she was kind of hovering over me in a way that would have looked desperate had she not been beautiful. Her face was perfectly angular, her skin smooth and lightly freckled. She looked glass blown. But she smelled like cigarettes. "We should make out."

The kiss made it into the episode. I never watched it, but I remember her running her hands through my hair. I remember she tasted like lime. And I remember my whole body going a little numb afterward. In the moment, I hadn't been thinking about the cameras, but Gemma had noticed them. She'd pop up occasionally wherever we were filming, usually at a bar or a restaurant in West Hollywood, and find her way to me. She didn't try to be coy about it. She said things like "I was hoping I'd find you here" and "I've been thinking about you," which would have sounded psychotic coming from anyone else, but she was so good at flirting, so comfortable in her clean, glossy skin, that it actually turned me on. I mean, it was like being hit on by a celebrity. Derek thought she was sketchy.

"I don't even think she's a real lesbian," he said one morning at my apartment. We were drinking mimosas and eating animal-style burgers to cure our hangovers. We did that a lot back then.

"So? I'm basically not a real lesbian."

"If you weren't completely gay, we would have fucked by now."

"Ew. Can you not?"

"I'm pretty sure I saw her making out with that asshole bouncer."

"When? Who?"

"Like, a few months ago, I don't know. The guy who kicked you out of the bar for stealing french fries."

Derek snorted, and I laughed. "I hid in the bathroom for like two hours."

"He literally held your hands behind your back like a criminal."

"You're just jealous she likes me instead of you."

"That's probably true." Derek's mouth was full of burger. "Even more reason not to trust her."

I knew Gemma wanted to get on TV, but that didn't bother me. Everyone in L.A. wants to get on TV. I was drawn to her. She had an aura that couldn't be ignored.

"That's the cigs," Derek said.

The first time Gemma and I got together alone, I invited her to go with me to the five-dollar psychic on La Cienega. It wasn't my idea—production wanted me to do it. The psychic read our palms and told us we were soulmates and said something about eating cantaloupe to strengthen our bond. She made us hold hands and gaze into each other's eyes. I remember feeling afraid to blink, like if I closed my eyes for even a split second, Gemma might disappear. I actually started crying, which made Gemma cry, and she somehow looked even more beautiful with tears streaming down her face. After that we were a couple, and she officially joined the cast a few weeks later.

That season, I became desperately obsessed with her. Everyone would mock me in their confessionals. *Gemma and I aren't eating sugar right now. Gemma says yellow makes my eyes pop. Gemma says if I spin in a circle three times while moaning her name, bubble gum will shoot out my ass.* Nobody could stomach me—not even Derek, who once referred to me, on-screen, as a "sickening, wide-eyed little Furby."

It went on like that for two seasons. Gemma moved into my apartment. We bought an expensive couch. We talked about eloping in Cabo. Sometimes, we shared a toothbrush. Until one random night after filming wrapped for season seven, I was home alone, and I got a call from Jimmy, our producer.

"We're going to film at your place tonight," he said. "Be there in thirty."

"What happened?" I assumed someone had been arrested. I was so stupid with love I couldn't see what was about to happen to me.

"Just buzz us in. I'll explain when we get there."

Moments after the cameras were up, Gemma and Derek walked through the door together, looking all solemn and pitiful. They sat down on the couch, legs flush against each other, hands intertwined, and told me that I was moving out.

★   ★   ★

So I spent the summer reinventing myself. I hired a personal trainer and started working out in an EMS suit. I stopped drinking on weeknights and tried to wean myself off Adderall. When that didn't work, I upped my dose and lost fifteen pounds. I got Botox in my neck, which made me look like a fairy princess. I hadn't heard from Gemma or Derek all summer. The last time I spoke to them was at the reunion. I was proud of the way I'd handled it.

"You two have a reckoning coming your way," I said. "The worst of your lives is yet to come."

Chilling, I know. Everyone loved it. They wanted more of me. They invited me onto their podcasts. They wrote articles about me, about the justice I deserved. They sent me messages begging for me-themed merch, so I put my face on sweatshirts and coffee mugs and sold it to them. A few months later, I had enough money for a down payment, and I bought a house in Beachwood Canyon. A new relationship would round me out nicely before we picked up cameras.

I didn't want someone to go out with me because they had seen me on TV. I wanted someone to go out with me because I was an extremely chill person, and if they had seen me on TV, they might have suspected the opposite. So I set my preferences to "men" in the hopes that most of them had never watched reality TV. Then I filled out my profile as plainly as I could.

Age: 28

Height: 5'6"

Location: Los Angeles

Occupation: Entertainment

Looking for:

I had no idea what I was looking for. Someone to die with, maybe, or at least someone who could fall in love with me immediately.

Looking for: Love, or equivalent

I started matching with people, but a lot of them knew me already. They sent me messages:

Are you as nuts as you seem on TV?

I bet you're hotter on TV than you are in person.

You seem like a fake bitch. I'll pass.

It's crazy, the things people will say to you. I ignored all of them, except for one: Cleo. I thought his name was sexy, and I liked his thick black hair, which he wore shaggy and tousled in a way that didn't seem strategic at all. I thought he was probably Italian or Spanish, and I'd always wanted to have a fling with a European.

Hey Mel, I'd love to take you to dinner sometime.

Adorable. I responded right away.

I'd like that.

We agreed to meet at a little martini bar that also served lamb souvlaki and shrimp scampi in Los Feliz. Derek and I had been there a few times together off-season when we wanted to get wasted extravagantly. It was a small, amber-lit space, its ceiling decorated with crystal chandeliers. Tiny candles lined the bar, and you had to hold them to the drink menu to read the cocktails. It was the perfect place to go if you didn't want to be noticed. I got there exactly seventeen minutes late, which was perfect timing. I saw Cleo sitting at the bar beyond the host stand. He hadn't noticed me walking in, so I pretended to fiddle with something in my bag for a few moments before looking up at him again. When I did, he was smiling at me. I smiled back. He waved me over.

"I almost thought you were going to make me drink alone." He stood up from the barstool and wrapped his arms around me. He was a lot taller than me, and his embrace was firm but not aggressive. His shirt smelled like laundry detergent. I made sure to pull away first.

"Who, me?" Gemma had turned me into a fantastic flirt. I knew when to talk, when to laugh, when to pause for effect. This also made for great TV. "What are you drinking?"

He sat back down, and I took the seat next to him.

"Bulleit on the rocks."

"Oh, not for me. Brown drinks make me crazy."

"Crazy how?"

"Hopefully you'll never know." I looked at the bartender, who was standing on the other side of the bar, watching us. "I'll have a vodka martini."

She nodded, and her eyes lingered on mine a little too long.

Cleo and I spent the next twenty minutes totally engrossed in each other. He was asking me questions I would never have answered had they come from some other, less magnetic person. *Who's your favorite family member? What's the weirdest thing you've ever done? Do you remember the best day of your life?* I mean really psychotic questions. I kept searching for clues that he knew who I was, but his eyes were too curious, too lasered in on mine, not bouncing around my face like he was distracted by some preconceived notion he'd had of me.

The bartender poured us our second round of drinks. She kept letting her eyes drift toward me, then snapping them away when I made eye contact with her. Cleo sipped his drink, then paused, the rim of the glass still in his mouth. He put the drink down.

"I have to ask—why are you single?"

I felt like I'd been caught. How had I not prepared an answer to this question?

"Honestly?"

"Yes, of course." He had this bashful smile that made me want to tell him everything.

"I haven't quite figured out what I want."

Cleo's gaze darted off to the side. I was worried that I was losing him.

"I mean, I know what I want now. I just didn't know *until* now."

He looked back at me, half distracted. "What's that?"

"Normalcy, I guess."

"Sorry," he said, his eyes trailing away again. "It's just . . ." He nodded toward the bartender. I turned to look at her. She was staring at me so awkwardly. She looked like she might cry.

"Is everything okay?" Cleo asked her. He cocked his head and furrowed his brow like a confused dog, which was a cute look for him.

She nodded, then scurried to the back of the house somewhere, embarrassed. I felt relieved to not feel her breathing so close to us.

"What was that?" Cleo said.

If he was going to be my season eight boyfriend, I'd have to tell him eventually.

"It's me. I swear this never happens. Barely anyone watches my show anymore." A lie, obviously, but I didn't want to scare him off.

"Your show?"

"It's not *my* show. I'm on a show."

"You're an actress?" He looked betrayed.

"Not exactly." I fiddled with the stem of my martini glass. "It's a reality show about me and my friends."

"Like one of those dating shows?"

I was almost impressed by how little he knew about reality TV.

"Sort of. But it's not a competition. The cameras just follow us around and document our lives."

Cleo looked around the room as if he were seeing it with new eyes. "Are there cameras here right now?"

"God, no." I didn't want to talk too much about the show. I wanted to talk about future vacations we'd take together to Nantucket, Amalfi, Marrakech—romantic places. I reached out and touched the top of his hand and felt comforted by its warmth. "We don't start filming again until next month. Look, you don't have anything to worry about. I don't let the show affect my real life."

"You said the show is about your life."

"It's about one part of my life. I'm actually looking to get out soon." It was a thought I'd never had before, and I was surprised by how easily the words escaped.

"Why?"

"The whole group is pretty toxic. We used to be close, but now everyone's turned into monsters. We fight a lot."

"Oh, man." He stared at my hand on his. "People watch you fight?"

After two drinks and a handful of olives, I was drunker than I wanted to be on a first date. I realized that I barely knew him, and I'd done a weird thing there with my hand. I removed it.

"Not me, specifically. But sure, I guess so. People love to watch you make a mess out of yourself. It makes them feel better about their own messes. It's all very scientific, very anthropological."

He thought about this. "You make it sound like a battleground."

"That's what it feels like, sometimes."

"Then why do it in the first place?"

Money. Fame. The high you get when a group of strangers screams your name with tears in their eyes. The ability to strut around L.A. like you really belong there (most people don't), like you landed in the exact right spot. That rush of adrenaline—a floating sensation, actually—that comes when the cameras start rolling. The bowling-ball-size sense of relief

you feel when you slap your ex across the face, and the vindi-
cation that comes with all the comments after the betrayal was
broadcast nationwide. *Gemma and Derek are snakes. Mel should
get her own show. Justice for Mel.* The tingling sense of accom-
plishment when you negotiate your contract up 200 percent.
I mean, it's really something.

"It seemed like a good idea at the time."

The bartender reemerged from the back of the house and
shuffled toward us with the expression of someone who'd
just been scolded. She leaned over the bar so her face was in
between ours.

"I'm so sorry," she whispered, looking at me. "My
manager says you have to leave."

"What?"

She gave me a pleading look. "I tried to explain, you
know, you're not the one to blame. It's the other guy who
caused a scene, but he didn't care. He's a dick, my manager.
He wanted to come out here and do it himself, but I told
him I'd handle it. I don't want to embarrass you."

Suddenly I couldn't breathe. I was too afraid to make eye
contact with Cleo, so I just stared down at my drink.

"I have no idea what you're talking about."

"Last time you guys were here . . ." She glanced at Cleo.
"Not you two, sorry, you and the other guy. And, uh,
remember, my manager asked you not to come back?"

"No, I don't remember that." I couldn't decide whether to
be apologetic or defensive. "Do you know who I am?"

I meant it genuinely, but it came out like a threat. I felt
Cleo's eyes on me.

"Oh, um. Yes? I know you've been here before. It's just
that last time, the guy you were with, he stole a bottle of

Casamigos. Or, I mean, he tried to. You were both pretty wasted."

"I don't think that was me."

"Well, it's just, I was here that night. Your hair was longer. You were ordering vodka martinis, remember?" She leaned in closer and whispered, "You had, like, six of them."

I held my hand up to stop her from further incriminating me in front of Cleo, who by now certainly never wanted to see me again. "Okay, thanks. I remember."

I still didn't remember, but I had ended so many of my nights out with Derek in the bathroom with my shirt off, wrapped around the toilet while he held back my hair. I would have lost more of those nights had it not been for the cameras, one cameraman in the bathroom with us, Jimmy on the other side of the door. Watching those episodes made me want to take a potato peeler to my skin. That's the thing about reality TV—most of the time you can't stand to look at yourself.

"I'm so sorry," she said.

"No, don't worry about it. It's fine. I'll go."

"Wait." She backstepped away from us toward her POS system. "One second."

She came back and handed me the bill. "Sorry."

I dug through my bag for my wallet. Cleo sat still beside me.

"Thanks," she said, after she ran my card. Then she looked at Cleo. "It really wasn't her fault."

"Just stop," I said. "I'm pretty sure he's already come to his own conclusion about that."

She stood there like a dumb little rodent, waiting. I tipped her one hundred dollars, then put the receipt down on the bar in front of Cleo. When I tried to make eye contact with him, he was staring blankly at the bill.

"I had a great time," I said.

"Oh, yeah. Me, too."

I felt him growing afraid of me.

"It'd be really great if you could not tell anybody about this."

Cleo exchanged glances with the bartender, the two of them sharing the same panicky thought. As I watched their eyes meet, I felt like I might throw up. I wondered how long he'd stay at the bar, if they'd share notes once I was gone, if they'd get drunk and go home together. I took out my phone to call myself a car. There were three texts and a missed call, all from Derek.

Can we meet before filming?

It's about Gemma.

Don't ignore me.

There had been one night, just before we filmed season seven, that Derek, Gemma, and I decided to go to the movies. We had wanted to do something wholesome before descending into the chaos of a new season. I don't remember what we saw, but I remember Gemma sat in the middle. We snuck in a bottle of wine to share and passed it back and forth during the previews. An older couple was sitting behind us, and the woman kept whispering loudly to her husband about the whole place reeking of alcohol, or something. Gemma turned around and got into it with her. The woman got so worked up she went and got the theater attendant, who asked us to leave and said he'd refund our tickets. I remember Gemma grabbing my hand, lacing her fingers into mine, and, cool as ever, telling the attendant that we weren't going anywhere. The older woman hadn't known that she was fighting a losing battle from the beginning. Gemma always got her way.

She held my hand throughout the movie, and I remember thinking I had everything I'd ever wanted. It was during those moments of affection when the cameras were down that I knew Gemma loved me. I hadn't been thinking about Derek on her left. I hadn't looked at her other hand.

Fuck off, I wrote.

★ ★ ★

My eyes were heavy on the drive home from the bar, which took all of five minutes. I fell asleep anyway and woke to the driver tapping me on the foot.

"This is the address, miss."

It was dark, and I was drunk, but when I opened my eyes, I could see my adorable Spanish-style home, tucked into the hill behind a pair of peppermint trees. It was so big. It was mine.

"I win," I said.

When I reached my front door, I realized my keys were gone. Maybe they had fallen out of my bag in the car, but the driver had sped away, so I walked around the side of my house and checked for open windows like an intruder. The guest bathroom window was unlocked. The soaking tub sat on the other side of it, and I climbed through the window and stepped into the tub. I thought briefly about sitting down and falling asleep there, curled up in the tub. There was a fresh towel hanging that I could use as a blanket. Instead, I got out of the tub and drank from the sink. I opened the medicine cabinet. There was a bottle of Adderall, some makeup wipes, and lip gloss. I dabbed some of the gloss onto my lips and stared at myself in the mirror. My face had responded well to the breakup. I was way more beautiful now than I was when I was dating Gemma. Mainly, all the weight I'd lost had hollowed out my cheeks in a very on-trend way. Plus, the Botox I'd been getting in my neck was slimming it down nicely. I looked like a ballerina.

"Drinks," I said. "We need drinks!"

I gave myself a little kiss on the mirror. Then I headed toward the kitchen for the half-empty bottle of wine that was in my refrigerator. But on my way there, I heard a knock on the front door—it spooked me, and I jumped. It was almost eleven at night, a totally unreasonable hour to be showing up at someone's door unannounced. It was probably the driver returning my keys. I pivoted toward the front door and made my way down the hall. He knocked again, and this time the knock sounded more desperate, more like a pound. It occurred to me, suddenly, that the person knocking might not be the driver. It was possible, after all the media attention I'd gotten lately, that the desperately knocking person was maybe, potentially, my first stalker. I felt both afraid of and excited by this alternative. I was the most famous I'd ever been and probably would ever be—it was important to take a moment to acknowledge and appreciate that. A stalker was a new milestone for me, and that was something to be proud of. But I also needed a weapon of self-defense. I ran to the kitchen and grabbed a knife from the knife block. Then I opened the refrigerator door and took a congratulatory swig from the bottle of wine. It tasted sour and stale. There was another pound on the door. I held the knife behind my back and tiptoed back toward the front door. The adrenaline made my legs and arms tremble.

"I am not afraid," I whispered. Then, louder, I said, "Who is it?"

Nobody answered. There was another pound on the door.

"I have a gun," I lied. I'd heard women say this in movies when they were about to be attacked. Usually in the movies the women still got attacked, or some hot actor came to save them in the nick of time. Nobody was coming to save me.

"Where the fuck did you get a gun?"

I recognized Derek's voice immediately. I let my hand with the knife fall to my side.

"I'm not opening the door for you."

"Mel, please. It's an emergency. I wouldn't be here if it wasn't."

"How did you get my address?"

"From Jimmy. Open the door. I have to piss."

"Definitely not."

"If you don't open the door, I'm going to piss on it."

He had a lisp that got worse when he was drunk, and I could hear it now. I knew he really would piss on my door if he'd been drinking, and that was not something I wanted to deal with in the morning. I opened the door.

"Jesus, thank you." Derek looked me up and down. His eyes landed on the knife. "That's not a gun."

"I thought you were a stalker."

"What was your plan? Saw me in half with a bread knife?"

I glanced down at my hand. It turned out I had, in fact, chosen the bread knife.

"What do you want?"

Derek shoved past me into the house. "First I need your bathroom."

I went back to the kitchen and let him wander around my house in search of the bathroom. I wanted him to take in all the rooms, all the furniture and art and taste I'd acquired since he blew up our friendship. There was a promotional photo of me, wearing a long black dress with cutouts on the sides and a high thigh slit, hanging above the mantel in the living room, and I wanted him to see it. A few minutes later he came sauntering into the kitchen.

"Thanks." He sat down on a stool at the kitchen island.

"So?"

"Can you put that down?" He pointed to the knife, still in my hand.

"No."

He rubbed his cheek with his hand, a move he used to do when he was trying to find someone to sleep with. *Girls love a jawline*, he once said.

"I haven't heard from Gemma in a week. Nobody has."

I got the wine from the fridge and took another swig. "I don't see what this has to do with me. She's your girlfriend."

"She's not my girlfriend."

"Oh, just your lover."

"Don't say *lover.*"

I gave him a good stare. I had expected him to look awful, but he didn't. He looked like he'd been starting his mornings with mushroom-infused teas. I realized he wasn't drunk after all, but his eyes were swollen and red as if he'd been crying. Or maybe he was ridiculously stoned. Above him hung a ceiling rack adorned with a bunch of pots and pans I'd never used, and I hoped one of them would fall on his head.

"Maybe she left you."

He was quiet for a moment in an introspective way that I'd come to understand as acting. He did this thing where he focused hard on one particular spot and tried to make himself cry. More often it would make one of the blood vessels under his left eye explode.

"It's been bad, Mel. She's still getting death threats. And now nobody has heard from her."

"She probably went to one of those wellness retreats. She was always talking about them. Or else she's in Cabo popping enough Klonopin to remain comatose until her call time next week."

"This is serious."

"I don't need *you* to tell *me* what is serious."

"Forget about me. I'm telling you Gemma is missing. She could have been kidnapped or killed."

"Or abducted by aliens."

I took a swig from the bottle and instinctively offered it to Derek. He shook his head.

"Oh, don't tell me you've gone sober?"

He giggled kind of sadly. "I've had paparazzi all over me for the last three months. The last thing I need is a bunch of photos of me drunk off my ass circulating. Do you have any idea how bad it's been for us?"

I drank the wine. "Frankly, I don't give a shit."

"I never wanted to hurt you," he said with the same solemn look he'd had in my apartment the night Gemma dumped me. "I miss you a lot."

I still hated him, I could feel it, but enough time had passed to dull the rage, and I had to imagine Derek's and Gemma's hands intertwined as they sat on my couch together to stand my ground.

"You ruined everything."

"I know."

With each swig of wine, I felt my shoulders relaxing. "I went on a date tonight."

His face perked up. "With who?"

"His name was Cleo."

"A dude?"

"Yeah, I don't know. I think I was looking for a friend."

I decided not to tell him how the date had ended, how humiliated I'd been. After all, I still wanted him to envy me. I wanted him to know I'd come out on top.

"I'm still your friend," he said.

I glared at him. "Did you see my living room?"

"Yeah." He shrugged. "Your house is cool."

His tone made it difficult to decipher if he was being genuine or just trying to placate me. But it felt good to hear the words. I reminded myself, again, not to trust him.

"I'm sure Gemma is okay," I said, in the same tone.

"Would you consider"—he took a dramatic breath in, then let it out slowly with his lips pursed, a move I was sure he learned in some discount acting class—"sending her a message? You might be the only person she'll respond to."

"You have to be joking."

"Mel, this is real. I need your help."

"I have no reason on earth to help you."

His eyes shrank into two tiny slits, a look he made whenever he was plotting something. Derek was always scheming. It was so obvious to me now. Everything he did was for the sake of entertainment, his own or everyone else's, and I felt stupid for never having seen it before.

"You aren't completely innocent, you know."

"I know one point seven million people who'd disagree with you."

"They don't know the whole story."

"Oh, and you do?"

We were trapped in some kind of sinister staring contest that I couldn't help but feel deserved to be on TV.

"I know more than you think."

"Yeah, right." I could feel the rage building in my chest. I was used to this feeling in the weeks before filming picked up. "Have you two been bonding over how crazy I am? How clingy and manipulative and poor, poor you?"

Derek broke eye contact with me and stared down at his feet. "I know you threatened her."

A dull numbness crept up my limbs toward my head, and I started to feel a floating sensation that I hadn't felt since the day Gemma dumped me.

"I didn't *threaten* her." My voice quivered with rage, and I tried to steady it. "Although I'm sure you two have spent the last few months perfecting that narrative for season eight."

"Mel, you totally lost yourself. You were possessed. You told her you'd kill her if she ever tried to leave you."

My legs went numb. I leaned back against the refrigerator to keep from falling over.

"I never said that."

"Yeah, you did. She recorded you. And the only reason she hasn't released it is because I told her not to, because I knew you didn't mean it, because despite your insane behavior, I know you're not insane, so you're welcome."

I wanted to speak but I couldn't feel my face. I looked at my hands. I was still holding the wine in one hand and the knife in the other.

I raised the knife in front of my face. "You need to leave."

Derek scoffed, "Oh, so you *are* going to stab me? Look at yourself."

"I mean it." My eyes were blurry with tears. I pointed the knife at him.

Derek sighed, then stood up and began backing away. "Just text her, will you? I'm doing a wellness check at her apartment tomorrow morning with her landlord. I'll be there at eight, if you care at all."

"Get fucked" was the only ridiculous thing I could think to say.

He turned and walked down the hallway and out of sight. I heard the front door close behind him. The knife fell from my hand and clanged against the tile floor. Tears slid down my cheeks and neck and soaked the neckline of my shirt. I was shaking.

Even in her absence, Gemma was still pulling all the strings. Wherever she was, she'd stay there long enough to build up public sympathy, and then, once everyone was good and worried, boom—she'd reappear in front of the camera, all thin and victim-y. I mean, she was remarkable. After seven seasons, I couldn't believe how naive I'd been. Had

I really thought I could go out on top and not come crashing down? Had I really thought Gemma would let me win? When I closed my eyes, Cleo's face, his eyes glazed with fear, flashed across my mind.

I took out my phone and typed out a message:

Gemma missing. Doing a wellness check tomorrow morning at my old place.

I got a response moments later.

Jimmy: *Time?*

8am

Jimmy: *Thx. We'll be there.*

★ ★ ★

I didn't sleep, my insides vibrating at a low enough frequency to keep me dizzily awake all night. I kept thinking about Cleo and the bartender—the look they exchanged, like they were two hostages plotting their escape, had felt so familiar.

In the morning, I drove to my old apartment from memory, changing lanes and making turns absentmindedly. I felt like I was driving back in time, like once I arrived, I'd see a former version of myself through the window, curled on the couch next to Gemma, our legs tangled like vines. Or maybe I'd see Derek, opening and closing all of our kitchen drawers as he searched for a bottle opener, eyeing the nape of Gemma's neck as she pulled her hair into a bun.

I parked the car in the lot and looked at myself in the rear-view mirror. I felt around for the mascara in my center console and flicked some onto my eyelashes. I blinked a few times and forced a smile. Beyond the mirror, Jimmy and a few cameramen were walking toward my car. Behind them, Derek sat on the ledge outside the building's front door, smoking a cigarette. We looked at each other briefly. He broke his gaze and spit onto the sidewalk. I steadied my breath.

Jimmy motioned for me to roll my window down. It was a beautiful day. "Let's get you mic'd up," he said. "We're rolling."

Party Favors

The morning of my birthday, Beau says he'll make me whatever cake I want.

"Coconut carrot cake," I say. "With raspberry jam and cream cheese frosting."

"I can't make that." He closes one eye and uses his thumbs and forefingers to frame my face. We are videographers. We do weddings and sweet sixteens and bar mitzvahs and vow renewals. Moments with good bits people want to remember and bad bits people want wiped out. We did the funeral for the guy who saved all those kids in the Delaware River. All the kids were there—in tiny suits, doll dresses, eyes glazed with confusion. The video went viral. We don't want our own kids yet. We are each waiting for something to happen to us first. Recognition, money. Either of those things.

"Make a bowl of brownie batter and I'll eat it over the sink," I say. Sometimes I stare at engagement rings the size of grapes on the internet all day long. Other days on the internet, I meet strangers, pretend I'm someone else.

"I'll just surprise you," he says, lowering his hands. He gets up and goes to the desk in the corner of the room and logs in to the computer. He's the better editor. He knows how each shot is supposed to look, how to splice them all together to make you feel the right way. This is sort of his superpower—creating scenes in his head out of nothing.

This morning, he's editing the wedding video we shot last weekend, trying to get the voice-over from the father of the bride's speech to line up with the moment he hands her off to the groom. Trying to jerk tears. I've seen this part a thousand times. *For you, sir, a gift.* The father doesn't say that, but everyone will think it when they watch Beau's edit.

"I can't listen to that anymore," I say. We're supposed to be doing whatever I want to do today—at least until the wedding, which starts at five. "Also, I have a session this morning."

"A session? *Today?*" Beau contemplates the floor for a moment, then in a more I've-taken-a-moment-to-think-about-this-and-yes-I-am-going-through-with-being-upset tone says, "You have a session today."

"Today is my day. This is what I want. It's just twenty minutes. Not even."

"Who's it with?"

"You know I can't tell you."

Beau always wants to know who, but the site is local, so I take the anonymity thing seriously. It's basically the only rule you have to follow if you want any credibility.

"Fine." He gets up from the desk and walks out of the room, leaving the door open behind him. I get out of bed and close it, then put on the pair of sparkly, strappy stilettos that I bought at the Halloween store. I take off the old pair of Beau's boxers that I wear to sleep, but I leave on his big T-shirt. The shirt is long enough that you can't tell if I'm wearing anything underneath, which is the point. I sit down at the desk and open the laptop, sign in.

UnsungHero is online already. He's an older man with white hair and bug eyes and rosacea. A machete and a tribal mask hang on the wall behind where he sits. I think I know where he lives, in that condo complex off the Beltway. I can see the Beltway in the window behind him, below the machete.

"It's my birthday," I tell him. "Can you tell me a birthday story?"

"Aren't you forgetting something?"

I open the desk drawer and pull out a red balloon. I stretch it out with my hands and then blow it up so it's about the size of my head, maybe a little bigger. I roll it around between my hands in front of the camera. Then I stand up, move the chair out of the way, and adjust the camera so it's pointed at the floor. I put the balloon on the floor and then sit on it gently, so most of my weight is in my feet and the balloon doesn't pop.

"There we go," he says. "Now, let me think."

UnsungHero gets off on his own stories. He battles rapists and sex traffickers, abusive fathers and boyfriends. Always, he is the hero. He likes to use props: knives, hammers, the unloaded handgun he keeps in his desk. Once, he used the machete.

The balloons are also a prop. I'm supposed to pop them with my ass as he pulls the trigger or bashes the rapist's head in. All I have to do is sit there and wait for my cue.

Occasionally he asks me to tie a dish towel around my mouth so I look more captured.

This time he tells me a story about an assassin. "Like James Bond," he says. "Or Brad Pitt from that movie."

He is Brad Pitt. He has been assigned to assassinate me—an interesting plot twist. Turns out I have killed a lot of people.

"Kids," he says. "Innocent children."

I wonder if he's been to our website, if he's seen the funeral video that went viral. Beau says that video makes him feel icky, that he can't appreciate the followers it earned us (two thousand of them) knowing that they came at the expense of the kids. But twice I've woken up in the middle of the night to find him lying with his back to me, watching the video on his phone.

Of course, I want UnsungHero to fuck me before he kills me. I want one final go at it. This final fuck will also be the best I've ever had. Or at least, I will appreciate it more than all the others. I sit on my balloon and appreciate. Unsung-Hero is holding what looks like a wooden crab mallet (the murder weapon), and his other hand is in his pants. I can't see the hand in his pants, but I know it's there from the way his rosacea flares up as he nears the end of the story.

"I'm going to fuck you to death," he says. Creative. I wonder about the crab mallet's purpose. Maybe he just needs something to hold on to.

"Not yet," I say. "I want the wide-angle lens." It's two hundred dollars. "And the electric kettle," I add, which is only forty dollars.

He nods, not wanting to break character. His eyes move around the screen and I hear his mouse click. I get a notification that reads, *You've received two new gifts! Click here to see who's spoiling you.* I bounce up and down on the balloon.

UnsungHero lifts the crab mallet over his head. His face is nearly purple—my cue. I bounce on the balloon sort of frantically, and on the fourth bounce it pops. My ass splats against the floor. UnsungHero drops the mallet and groans. I check the time.

★   ★   ★

In the kitchen, Beau is rifling through the cabinets to see if we have any baking supplies. He's pulled out some flour and olive oil and is staring at them like he's expecting them to tell him what to do. He hasn't addressed the standing mixer, which was a recent gift from a guy with an ear fetish.

"Good news," I say. "I got you the wide-angle lens." I stand behind him and put my arms around his waist and rest my head against his back.

"You did?"

"I got it for both of us. I want breakfast."

I let go of him and he kisses my head, meaning he's no longer upset. He walks to the refrigerator and takes out the eggs. They're the three-dollar kind that come in a Styrofoam container. Beau bought them at Rite Aid. Anyway, I don't want them.

"No," I say. "Never mind. Let's just sit here and talk about our future."

"You always do this." He puts the eggs away.

"I know."

"You always want to talk about our future instead of doing something simple like eating breakfast," he explains, as if I don't know myself.

"The problem is every time we talk about it we come to a different conclusion."

Beau keeps a list in his phone of all the things he wants to do for his kids, just in case he decides to want kids. He wants to put them in seersucker suits. He wants to teach them how to make homemade spaghetti, how to craft a coffee table out of pinewood. All of this sounds romantic to me, but in a misty, montage-y sort of way that feels more like a scene from a movie than real life.

"The problem is you can't make spaghetti," I say. "You can't even make a coconut carrot cake with raspberry jam and cream cheese frosting."

"I'm not the one giving virtual jerk-offs to creeps on the internet."

Sometimes I feel like we're living in two different realities. I'm here, in the world of actions and reactions, and Beau is off somewhere in his head, creating a whole different story of us.

"Don't give me that look," he says. "I'm right here."

* * *

In the end we decide to spend the morning at the zoo. It's Beau's idea at first, but I come around when he reminds me about the elephants.

"Their trunks are their hands," he says, and I agree that's something I would like to see today.

The zoo costs thirty-five dollars a person, but if you park in the lot for the ice-skating rink and walk a half mile through the woods, you can see the whole back perimeter of the zoo for free. Back here are the elephants, rhinos, and zebras, who live together in the desert, and one leopard, who lives alone in a jungle that's separated from the desert by a concrete wall. We sit down outside the desert area and wait.

Beau's camera is draped around his neck. He holds it up to his eyes and adjusts the lens.

"If you could be any animal, which would you be?" he says.

"You mean which would I want to be or which would I actually be?"

He thinks about this. "I guess both, if they're different."

"I want to be a giraffe. But I'm probably more like a groundhog."

"I can see you as a giraffe." He lowers the camera and looks me up and down. "Long limbs." He wiggles his arms to show me what my long limbs look like. "I'd be a panther."

"Every boy thinks they're a panther." This is true. I had a boyfriend in high school who used to call his dick "panther-like," which didn't mean anything. Another boy I slept with when I was twenty-one told me that he'd once communicated telepathically with a panther on an African safari. He'd read the message in the yellows of its eyes. *Fuck off*, the message said. Brilliant. This same boy also told me my vagina was "tight like a tiger," which was unrelated. What is it with boys and panthers and tightness? All of my boyfriends have had black hair, and that might have something to do with it.

"What's wrong with panthers?" Beau says. "They're sleek and smart and good climbers."

"Exactly. Have you ever met a boy who's all three of those things?"

He looks hurt. Beau is smart but not sleek. He's usually running fifteen minutes behind schedule, and when he finally shows up, he's forgotten his wallet or his passport or his sense of self. But he always knows which direction is north, which comes in handy more than you would think.

I would rather have a smart boyfriend than a sleek one. And I don't see the benefits of dating someone who's a good climber, other than their likely ability to pick me up and hold me over their head with ease, which is actually something to think about.

"Sometimes I think you hate men," he says.

"Sometimes I do."

There's a zebra standing in the tiny desert. It swats the flies on its ass with its tail. It stares at us and stands very still.

"Does it see us?" Beau says. He holds the camera up.

"I don't know. Sh."

We stare at the zebra and it stares back at us, startled. Like something is out of place. *It's us*, I want to say. *We are not where we're supposed to be. We're only passing through.* To communicate this, I stand up slowly and then bow my head. I've seen someone do this successfully in a movie about horses or dragons. But the zebra trots away, toward its paying customers.

"Damn it. I missed it." Beau turns the camera to me and it shutters.

We have thousands of photos of me. Me opening the refrigerator. Me brushing my teeth. Me on the toilet, in black and white. We don't do anything with them. One day, Beau says, he will turn them into a series. A still series of me, in motion.

Beau wants to play another hypothetical game: "If you knew you were going to die at the end of the year, what would you do?"

He likes these games because there are no consequences for talking this way. No plans to activate, no promises engraved in stone. If he tells me about something he actually wants—his own gallery, a billion dollars, a kid who can make a bow and arrow out of stuff he finds in the woods—I'll lock it in my brain and throw it at him whenever he does something stupid, like leave a full trash bag on the back stoop overnight for the raccoons to pick at. Every time we talk about our future, it crawls an inch farther away from us.

Beau blames it on my camming. He says it adds a "creep factor" to our relationship that he can't reconcile. Stop camming, he says, and he'll take our future more seriously. But I know this isn't true. I know he likes having something to point to that separates us from every other stupid couple, something a little grimy. I guess I feel the same way. When I'm on camera, doing what I do, I feel like I'm getting away with something, like I'm somehow evading all the societal norms I was supposed to succumb to while simultaneously enjoying the benefits of a secure relationship. I've never explained this to Beau. Instead, whenever we get into this argument, I tell him I'm in it for the gifts, which is mostly true. And then he huffs away, the same way he does before a session, pretending to be angrier than he is, because he also likes the gifts. These conversations make us dizzy. They're like swinging around a bag of bricks. The hypothetical conversations are lighter, made of fairy dust. Though usually I find a way to dampen them.

"The end of this year?" I ask. "It's August. That's not even five months."

Beau thinks about this. "A year from today, you are going to die. What do you do?"

"Is everyone going to die, or just me? If it's just me, do other people know that I'm going to die? Or, if it's everyone, do we all know that we're going to die? Or do only I know?"

"It's only you. You're going to die and you're the only one who knows it."

"If that's the case, I feel like the first thing I would do is tell everyone."

Beau shakes his head like I've misunderstood him. "You're supposed to say something like 'I'd buy a house in Milan,' or 'I'd pay off my family's mortgage.'"

"But I don't want a house in Milan." I know what I'm supposed to say, but I don't want to say it. What I want to say is *This is a stupid, make-believe game and it's a waste of everyone's time.* At least when I play make-believe with the creeps on the internet, I get real-life prizes.

"It doesn't have to be that." Beau's frustrated, rubbing his eyes with the palms of his hands.

"And if I paid off my family's mortgage, they'd wonder why. They'd ask questions until I finally had to tell them. And then everyone would know I was going to die, and we'd probably just spend the year preparing for my death. Planning the services, what to wear, what people will eat, who will give the speeches. You'd have to film it. By the time I died, nobody would even be that sad. The blow would be softened from all the preparing. Besides, I don't think my family even has a mortgage. But I can ask my dad about that, if you think it's important."

"Look." Beau points to the right side of the desert. "Elephant."

I look in the direction of his finger but see nothing. I can't tell if he's pointing far away or nearby.

"Where?"

"Over there, by the concrete wall." He holds the camera to his face.

I stare at the concrete wall and the elephant comes into focus. It's hard to see because it's the same color as the concrete. Plus its body is turned away from us, toward the concrete, so we're staring at its butt.

"Let's get closer," Beau says, and we stand up and walk along the fence. We turn the corner and stare at the elephant from the side. Its head is pressed up against the concrete like it's being punished. It stands perfectly still, looking prehistoric, made of stone. Its trunk hangs low and limp above the ground. I'm suddenly overcome with shame, like I'm peering into something private, something that wasn't meant for me.

"It's like it's praying," Beau says. He holds up his camera and gets the shot.

"It's depressed." I know this for a fact. I don't want to look at it anymore.

"You don't know that. It could be sleeping."

"It's trapped."

We watch the back of the zoo for another hour or so. We see one rhino go from standing to lying down, then we walk over to the leopard jungle and watch the leopard pace along the concrete wall.

"East to west," Beau says. "I wonder if that's primal."

"It's depression."

"You're ruining it."

Beau takes a photo of the leopard, then another photo of me while I bite the cuticle on my ring finger.

★   ★   ★

We have to get to the wedding early to do the bridal-party photos. The venue is a country club, and the ceremony site will overlook the golf course. Nobody is allowed to be playing golf during the ceremony, not even the most esteemed members. The groom tells us this proudly while we set up the tripod at the far end of the aisle. His family belongs to the club. So does hers. They met on the junior golf team, back during the summer after ninth grade.

"We almost beat Mount Royal," he says. "Their pool sucks."

"Plus their snack bar sucks," I say, pretending to be clued in to the country club scene. Beau gives me a weird look. The groom doesn't seem to notice or care. We follow him to the tennis courts and wait for the bride to come out of the clubhouse and show him herself.

"Turn around," I say. "She's coming."

The groom turns his back to the clubhouse and takes a few deep breaths, which Beau catches on video. The bride is wearing a dress that is actually a fancy silk tank top and a matching long silk skirt. A strip of her tanned skin separates the skirt from the top. This strikes me as a rebellious outfit to wear at a country club, and I instantly like her more than I like her fiancé.

I zoom in on the bride while Beau films the whole thing. Soon, they're both crying. Later Beau will overlay this scene with music that makes everyone else cry, too.

"Cry me a million dollars," Beau likes to say when he knows he's caught a golden moment. Nobody has ever paid us a million dollars, but sometimes they let us take home a floral arrangement.

Next are the bridesmaids. They line up and wait for the bride's instructions. The bride whispers to me that the girl with the red hair and the bigger arms should always be in the middle, one way or another, so her arms are hidden in the photos.

"Photoshop," I say, and the bride looks relieved, like she wasn't sure if I was the kind of photographer whose moral compass would ruin her wedding photos. I wink at her to emphasize that I have no morals, then grab the top of my own arm and squeeze. When I get married, I'll photoshop all of this away.

Beau goes to film the empty ceremony chairs and altar while I do the groomsmen. They're all wearing the same Nike sneakers, which I don't ask about, but I make sure to get their shoes in the photos.

"Pick him up," I say, feeling irrationally powerful in my T-shirt and jeans, my sweatshirt tied around my hips. I tell myself I'm immune to the dress code rather than unworthy of it. The tallest groomsman—a big, meaty guy who looms a full head above the rest—picks up the groom and cradles him like a baby. They both stare at the camera, looking lost. I get the shot.

"Not like that," I say. "Everyone hold him." They huddle together, confused at first, but they eventually decide who should hold what, and they line up with the groom in their arms like a prize fish. Everyone is fucked-up. I can tell from the way they wobble, the way their eyes water when they aren't even facing the sun.

"All done," I say after a few more positions, and they disperse to drink more liquor.

"Hey," says the tall, meaty guy. He stares at me with his head cocked. "Do I know you?"

"I don't think so." I replace the film and look around for something else to shoot.

I've only been recognized one other time. It happened at the movies. The college kid who tore our ticket stubs was greasier in person. Online he just liked to watch. He didn't want to put in any effort, which had always bothered me. When he came, he scowled, as if he were disappointed in me, specifically, for engaging with him. Then he immediately shut the camera off. When I gave him my ticket, his eyes grew terrified and glossy, and for a moment I thought he was going to cry. I realized this kid was a virgin, which I should probably have known already, but the camera is always a little fuzzy. He handed me my ripped ticket and I felt exactly like a pervert. I gave him a little curtsy in return. A little apology. Beau missed the whole exchange. I reminded myself to be grateful for that in the future.

The future came a few days later, one afternoon while Beau was out taking photos and I was doing a session with a guy who always made a point to remove his wedding ring on camera. He wanted me to see him go from married to unmarried, which was what would happen if his wife ever caught him, he assured me. I was pretty sure he was already divorced and living alone because the window behind him had vertical blinds. He wanted me topless. He wanted me to put on lipstick and lick my fingers. He wanted me to open my mouth around the camera while he came. That afternoon, I did it all for a silk pajama set and a new smart TV. I stood with my hands on the desk and my mouth open in front of the camera, tongue out. The guy came into his own camera and my view of him blurred. Beau walked into the bedroom then, just in time to see the guy wipe his camera dry. I looked at Beau, my tongue out, tits out, frozen in the position I'd been hired for. He stared back at me with a face as blank as bread. Then he lifted his camera up from around his neck, held it to his face, and got the shot.

★　★　★

The ceremony is what Beau refers to as "a layup" because the string quartet is playing "Somewhere over the Rainbow" and the groom is crying before the bride even walks down the aisle. A groomsman pulls a tissue from his pocket and hands it to him, but the groom waves it away and straightens his back. He blinks the tears back into his eye sockets. There's an empty chair up front where the bride's grandmother was meant to sit, with a sign that says RESERVED FOR NANA in fancy calligraphy. Beau zooms in on the chair, a shot he will later slow down and pair with some piano ballad about love and loss, or love lost. It doesn't matter. The ring bearer crawls down the aisle in a tuxedo-themed onesie, and his mom has to straighten him out when he crawls into a row and puts a rogue flower petal in his mouth. I stare at the kid and wonder if I want him, or some version of him, for myself. I zoom in on his face. *Yes*, I think, *definitely not*. The bride and groom read their personalized vows off their cell phones. Everyone cries silently. The kiss is about three seconds too long. On the other side of the aisle, Beau looks up at me from the monopod and tosses an imaginary basketball in the air.

At cocktail hour I get some pictures of the food while Beau films conversations, hugs, people laughing with dollops of pâté on their tongues. This is the kind of cocktail hour where you can get a made-to-order Cuban sandwich from a man in a chef's hat, then walk across the room and ask another man in another chef's hat to hand-roll you some spicy salmon. I take photos of the raw bar, elegantly on display in the center of the room, the king crab legs jutting out of the ice like zombies come alive. I swoop a glass of champagne off a caterer's tray, turn to face the window, and drink it in one gulp. Outside, the violinist is smoking a cigarette against the HVAC unit. I put the glass down and hold my camera to my eyes, focus. I won't put this one on the website, but maybe I'll submit it somewhere, if it's any good. Maybe I'll win a prize—a thousand dollars or a small gold plastic trophy. More likely it will end up among the stack of photos of me, shoved in the desk drawer in the corner of the bedroom.

The tall groomsman is squinting at me from behind the raw bar. He knows me, he's sure. He's seen me somewhere, or some other version of me. I point the camera at him and he looks away.

The groomsman's screen name is OceanHunter. I've met with him three times. He likes spearfishing and ice fishing and deep-sea fishing. He likes to watch me get dressed. That's it. The second time we met, as a bonus, I pretended to lose my underwear. I made a face like *Could it be under the bed?* Then I got on my hands and knees with my ass to the camera and searched. I reached far under the bed and felt around for a few seconds, then I found my underwear (finally!). I brought it over to the camera for him to examine for dust mites and then I put it on. The last time we met I pretended I had no idea I was on camera, and when I finished getting dressed, I looked back at him, horrified that I'd been caught. I'm really good at that face—my lips parted, eyes popping out with a sexy combination of embarrassment and terror. The face works every time.

★ ★ ★

In the bathroom, a girl is crying. Not a bridesmaid, but a friend of the bride's. This is not the kind of crying you want to get on camera. I wash my hands while she confesses to the bridesmaid whose big arms I'm going to photoshop because I have no morals.

"It's not the end of the world," says the big-armed woman. "People have sex with people they don't care about all the time."

I blow my nose into a paper towel. The crying girl watches me and does the same.

"You guys are really cute," she says to me in between heaving sighs. She hiccups. "You and the video man. He's so tall and you're so . . ." She starts to cry again.

"Oh, no," I say. "We're, like, totally broke."

They both stare at me like I've ruined something.

There's no seat reserved for Nana in the ballroom. They left her memory at the golf course. Everyone else sits at round tables with peony centerpieces and waits for the wedding party to make an entrance. Beau and I wait on opposite sides of the dance floor. One groomsman runs out and does a flip, lands on his feet. Another does a split, then gets up and stares at his ass theatrically, like he can't believe his pants are still intact. Acrobats, all of them. The Cirque du Soleil of wedding receptions. Later I'll suggest we add circus music to this scene, and Beau will say something like *The wedding industry is a circus*. He'll remind me that these are country club people, old money, and instead he'll pair the acrobatics with an acoustic version of something classic.

OceanHunter struts out to the dance floor with a small bridesmaid. He gets down on all fours and she sits on his back like she's riding a small horse. Clever. He glances at me, then blinks away. I lower the camera and watch him try to buck the bridesmaid off his back.

Eventually it's Mr. and Mrs. Whatever, and they're each wearing a flower crown as they run through the tables waving their hands in the air. The DJ blasts a song by a man who performs all of his ballads with a single guitar, and the two of them dance in their crowns. The crowns are meant to represent love, peace, money. Now that they're married, they have all these things in the form of dinnerware.

"Here with the woman of my dreams," sings the guitarist. They dance under a spotlight, King and Queen. We film them as all their dreams come true.

Beau and I move around the perimeter of the dance floor, following the dancing royals, until we're side by side. "They'll be divorced by next winter," Beau whispers. He squats behind the gimbal I got for popping a balloon with my tits. It was brilliant, how I did it. I fastened a safety pin to the knot at the end and stuck the balloon while UnsungHero was concentrating on my nipples.

"Probably," I say. But right now, as they mouth the words to this stupid song into each other's ears, they look happy.

★ ★ ★

We film the speeches, making sure to shoot from multiple angles. Everyone looks better at an angle, especially the bride's father. He stands in front of the table where all the royals sit and says the groom is the second son he never had. He already has a first son, who's sitting behind him, picking his fingernails. The father says the groom is the second son he'd always wanted, but instead he got his daughter, whom he loves regardless, just as much as he loves his first son. He loves everyone equally, to clarify. The only point he is trying to make here is that he loves the groom like a son. A son with a wicked golf swing. And, anyway, congratulations and enjoy the steak, which is actually Wagyu beef, by the way.

Beau will wipe most of this, except for the part about the golf swing.

In the men's bathroom they aren't crying, but they are snorting Adderall. I watch the groomsmen file out and wipe the powdery blue rings from around their nostrils. They miss some spots. They strut single file back to the dance floor, and OceanHunter makes eye contact with me again. I hold the camera to my face and again he looks away. I realize that we're playing a game. A little role reversal, if you will.

I follow the groomsmen out to the dance floor. The DJ is playing a song by another DJ. All the guests are clumped together in the center, jerking around like a panicked school of fish. I look for OceanHunter among the fish. I circle the dance floor with my camera at the ready. His head pops up above everyone else's. He sees me, then burrows back down. He pops up again and this time holds eye contact with me as he throws his suit jacket to a chair. The fish form a circle around him. He removes his belt from his pants and waves it in the air above him like a lasso. He loosens his bow tie, undoes the top buttons of his shirt. The fish cheer him on as he does a little dance—moving his hips from side to side while he tiptoes in a small circle. I hover my finger above the shutter button and wait. He turns his back to me and squats and shakes his ass. All the fish cheer louder, like this is the whole reason they came here tonight. The song picks up the pace. Everyone claps and bounces on their knees in anticipation of his big move. And then, on beat with the music, he drops to the floor, his legs spread into a split. I can't see him very well down there—his body is shrouded by legs—but everyone lets out a universal scream, impressed that a guy that large was able to perform such a nimble move.

My finger is still steady on the shutter button. Something else is coming—something just for me. The anticipation whirls in my gut. When OceanHunter stands up, he whips his head around to face me. He stares right into the camera with his lips slightly parted, his eyes wide with terror—my look. His mouth forms a perfect O, his hands clutch either side of his jaw. The message is brief, but clear: *You caught me!* I press the shutter release. I feel tingly all over, a rush of satisfaction, like I've won something. When I lower the camera, OceanHunter has returned to the crowd while another groomsman has swooped in and commanded everyone's attention. I look around for Beau and see him on the corner of the dance floor, capturing the moment from a different angle. He lowers his camera and stares at me.

★   ★   ★

All the Wagyu beef ends up back in the kitchen because everyone was too full of Cuban sandwiches and sushi rolls and miniature shrimp burritos to touch it. Once the party winds down, Beau and I sit in the kitchen and split a glass of champagne and pick at the unwanted dinners.

"Wagyu beef or chicken?" Beau holds each option in a hand and moves them up and down like they're on a scale.

"Hypothetically?"

He gives me a look that says my joke wasn't funny. I point to the beef plate and he hands it to me. We lean against a stainless steel table and eat our food. An annoying feeling rings in the air between us, a gnat we can't swat away.

"These weddings keep getting more and more ridiculous," he says, staring ahead at the kitchen wall.

"Painful."

"Ours won't be anything like this."

"Definitely not."

"We'll need a live band," he says. "And less food."

"No speeches." I feel like I'm going to cry.

One of the caterers wheels the half-eaten cake through the kitchen doors and leaves it next to us, all limp and crumbly. Beau sticks his fork in it.

"Fewer people, too," he says.

I nod. Too many theatrics, we agree. We get rid of the centerpieces, the acrobatics, the chairs for ghosts, the party favors. We chip away at our wedding until I can't see it anymore.

"In the end, I think it should just be the two of us," he says.

I close my eyes and try to picture it.

Home Videos

At *Elite Design*, we went into celebrities' homes and filmed them walking around, talking about their belongings, picking up stuff and putting it back down. Hilary Duff's home, for instance. And Kristen Stewart's home. I came to know a lot of celebrities this way—standing in their foyers and smelling their gardens and running my fingers along their wallpaper.

My job wasn't important. All I had to do was make sure nobody was thirsty. I took the morning coffee orders. I loaded the drinks cooler. I held Toby's seltzer while he was directing. That was basically it. They didn't pay me much.

Our celebrity home videos got millions of views on YouTube. Everyone wants to see the inside of a celebrity's home. They want to see the handmade soap in Angelina Jolie's powder room, what kind of milk is in Gwyneth Paltrow's refrigerator (which is goat's milk, by the way).

I didn't really care about any of it until we shot Candace Loon's home video. She had been a Playboy Bunny back in the nineties. She used to live in the Mansion, you know, with all the other girls, piled like tweens into pink-frosted bedrooms that reeked of vanilla perfume. I liked that about her. I liked that she had been broke once, that she did what she had to do, and now lived in Beverly Hills in this big white-brick colonial. She was forty-five, about twice my age, but you'd never have thought that. She'd been pretty vocal on social media about these facials she'd been getting in which blood from her ass was injected into her face with a thousand tiny needles. Apparently, this method works. Her boyfriend—some young hotshot director who'd grown up with Timothée Chalamet—was only twenty-eight.

Our first shot was always the entrance. Candace Loon's had this grand oak door, painted black, with a brushed-gold knob. When she opened it, a lemony scent wafted out from her foyer. Her skin was dewy and soft. She was wearing a silky, floral-patterned robe over a matching silk dress. Her vibe was very "Oh, you just caught me during my morning wellness routine," which the magazine was all about.

"*Elite Design!*" she said, sounding genuinely pumped, as if we were the celebrities. "Come on in."

"Let's get that one more time," Toby said. "But more casual. Actually, if you could sound a little annoyed, like we've interrupted something, our viewers like that."

Toby was all right. He was never impressed by any of the celebrities, or if he was, he never showed it. He liked to get in, get the take, and get out. I always got the impression he believed, deeply, that he had somewhere more important to be—like he should have been directing feature films, his name cast in a huge font on the silver screen, but had by some embarrassing accident landed here instead, filming celebrities in their pajamas. I didn't hold this against him. His homelife was pretty bleak. He'd had a wife and a daughter, at one point, but I was pretty sure he now had neither. Sometimes, after an extra-long shoot, he'd bring one of them up while I was loading the cooler into the van. *My ex-wife hated me drinking Diet Coke* or *My daughter would have loved this house.* He could ruin the whole mood of the day whenever he said stuff like that.

"More annoyed," Candace Loon said, staring up at her eyebrows like she was trying to calculate that feeling.

"Yeah," Toby said. "It's early. We've woken you up, but you're being a good sport about it."

"Got it." She nodded. Then she closed the door.

We did four takes at Candace Loon's front door, and then we were inside her home.

Right off the bat, she showed us her antique walnut credenza. Before the film crew arrived, the magazine had sent the design team in to "add accents"—that's what we called it. Their go-to move was to place giant vases with even more giant cherry-blossom branches in them throughout the house. Sometimes they used bowls of exotic fruit. On the back corner of the credenza, someone had placed this big decorative stone urn overflowing with green moss balls. Candace Loon ignored it. She pointed to the rings on the credenza's surface from the condensation on glasses that her kids had left there over the years, on their way to soccer practice or musical theater camp.

"Things can get really crazy in this house. But we love crazy." She ran her hand over the water rings. "I love looking at these rings as a reminder to live in whatever hectic moment is upon us."

She had four kids, two with one musician and two with another. One of the musicians was dead. The two kids that belonged to him were older now. They were also famous. Her daughter, who was something like seventeen, had an underwear line specifically for teenagers. It was extremely cool—everyone was all over it. Her son was in rehab, I was almost sure. He had tattoos on his neck. He posted these rambling videos on the internet about conspiracy theories he was working on. Anyway, it was obvious which of the older kids was the winner and which was the loser. I wondered if she ever thought about that.

"Oh, and this." Candace Loon pointed to the abstract painting above the credenza. "This was a gift from an artist friend in New Zealand. He's brilliant."

I didn't have any feelings about the credenza, but I did want to touch the painting. Who doesn't want to touch an expensive painting? As Candace Loon led us into her dining room, I lagged behind (nobody would ever notice) and considered touching it. But I was holding Toby's seltzer, and my hands were wet with condensation, so I figured it probably wasn't a good idea. Instead, I dragged one wet hand along the credenza as I left the room, leaving behind a thin trail of water.

Candace Loon's dining room table had been constructed from a redwood tree that was struck by lightning in 1955. "Isn't it gorgeous?" she said. "We actually used it in my *Vogue* shoot, back in 2013." She got on top of the table and stretched her arms above her head like she was posing for a shoot. "Anyway, they let me have it afterward."

You've seen the *Vogue* cover—everyone has. It's the one where Candace Loon is naked on the table, her arms pulled across her chest, with this wild bouquet of flowers in between her legs. That was over a decade ago, but she looked just as elegant and carefree, all stretched out and poised, as she had back then. I felt certain that everyone in the room was imagining her naked.

Toby looked at me from across the table and held his hand to his mouth as if he were drinking from an invisible water bottle. This was my cue. I walked around the table and handed him his seltzer. He took a few big gulps, then gave it back to me.

"I'll show you our piano," she said, hopping off the table. I wondered where her boyfriend was. I knew what he looked like, but I'd forgotten his name. He had that attractive skinny look about him, with wild, curly hair.

She took us into the living room and sat down at her Yamaha digital grand piano in polished ebony. "We use this to live stream Elton playing from Vegas, and you can actually see the keys moving as he presses the keys on his own piano."

She pressed some of the keys. "I stopped dating musicians before I could learn to play."

I did touch the piano. As Candace Loon led everyone upstairs to what she called "the children's floor," I swept my fingers across the piano keys and imagined what it might be like to go to a party at her house—the piano in the corner by the window, playing itself as caterers walked around with trays of miniature crab cakes while Adam Levine snorted coke off her custom coffee table. Everyone dressed in designer clothing loose in all the right places.

Upstairs on the children's floor, Candace Loon was showing the crew the wallpaper, hand-painted with monkeys swinging from magnolia trees by some South African artist. An original Space Mountain roller-coaster car from Disney World hung by stainless steel wires from the ceiling above the staircase.

"I won it at auction," she said, pointing to it proudly.

I was in awe of her—her skin, her confidence, the way she spoke with her hands. I wanted to have a glass of whiskey with her poolside. I'd even go out with her fucked-up son with the neck tattoos. I could be the one to bring out the good in him. Then maybe she'd let us live in her pool house.

"You're staring," Toby whispered and nudged my shoulder. "Chill the fuck out."

"Sorry," I said quietly.

"Seltzer."

I handed him his seltzer. He took a small sip, then handed it back to me.

Candace Loon took us into her youngest kid's room, where she showed us his custom chestnut jungle gym and a bronze replica of his baby feet, mounted on white marble.

"It's fifty pounds." She smacked the marble. "I wanted it to be heavy enough that he wouldn't knock it over. He's got ADHD, you know. Hence the jungle gym."

I was drawn to the feet. They seemed, to me, like a trophy—an assertive, gaudy ornament of Candace Loon's greatest achievement. There was something a little unhinged about them, like, I wouldn't have been surprised if they came alive and started dancing on their marble platform. On our way out of the kid's room, I pressed my thumb against the cold, bronze toes. The metal felt good against my fingers, and I got this bizarre urge to sniff it. Once everyone had filed out of the room, I leaned over and sniffed the toes. They smelled exactly like nothing. I needed more from them, but I wasn't sure what, or how to get it. I stuck my tongue out and licked the big toe. I tried to do it casually, not to make a big deal out of it, so if someone were to walk back into the room and see me, they might even think I was doing a totally normal thing. The toe was cold and metallic— exactly what you'd expect a bronze statue to taste like. Somehow, this was disappointing. I wiped the wet spot away with my sleeve.

On the third floor, everything had a pink hue. Candace Loon pointed to the skylights, which were made of rose-tinted glass.

"The idea was, I sleep up here," she said. "I wanted the lighting to reflect the dream state. I swear I've been sleeping better since I had this glass installed."

She stopped outside her bedroom door, which was shut, and placed her hand on the glass knob hesitantly. It was pretty common for the celebrities not to want to show us their bedrooms. A lot of them put it in their contracts, in case we were thinking of trying something sneaky. But Candace Loon had agreed to it.

Toby was standing next to me, and I could feel him looking at me, so I held his seltzer in front of his chest. When he didn't take it, I glanced up at him to see what the hell his deal was and noticed he was staring at me, eyebrows raised, as though I, of all people, should say something to encourage

Candace Loon to let us into her bedroom. This was more responsibility than I was used to, so much more that I almost forgot to speak. Then Toby cleared his throat, and I said just about the stupidest thing I've ever heard.

"I promise not to touch anything."

"Oh, no. It's not that. I just didn't have time to make my bed this morning."

"Even better," Toby said, for some insane reason. Candace Loon gave him a weird look. "What I mean is, our viewers will be able to relate."

She looked back and forth from Toby to me, me to Toby, almost like she wanted me to lean over and whisper the right answer into her ear. It's remarkable how quickly a celebrity will trust you when you're the least threatening person in the room.

"He's right," I said. "I can't remember the last time I made my bed."

All of a sudden, she laughed. I felt compelled to laugh with her. So we laughed together, just the two of us, inside a private joke that only she understood. It was stupid, but it was really something. Then she opened her bedroom door.

Her bedroom was huge, with its own en suite kitchen complete with river-stone hot-burner plates for brewing tea. She got all her tea from India or China.

"I don't trust Western tea," she said. "We fuck everything up with microplastics."

Her idea of an unmade bed was one whose duvet cover was slightly rustled on one side. Every part of it was white— the headboard was made of antique raffia that had been painted oyster white, which was apparently different from linen white, the color of her linens. Her bed had only four pillows, also linen white.

"I don't like too many pillows," she said. "These are actually stuffed with a combination of goose feathers and preserved peony petals. They put you right to sleep."

I stared at her bed. I imagined her sleeping entirely still on her back, her hands folded across her chest like a beautiful corpse. Toby cleared his throat, and I handed him his seltzer.

Candace Loon's bathroom had a soaking tub, a high-tech rain shower, a sauna, and a vanity made of reclaimed wood from the piers of Venice, Italy, that stretched the entire length of one wall. She showed us the section of the vanity where she did her skin-care routine: dozens of glass droppers lined up along the mirror, each containing a different kind of cold-pressed serum meant to brighten or tighten.

"And this"—she picked up a small, flat slab of rose quartz with rounded edges—"is my *gua sha*. I would die without it." She held the slab to her face and wiggled it along her jawline. "Great for lymphatic drainage." She looked right at me. I searched for a message in her eyes, something like *There are no secrets between us*, but I couldn't find one. "I bought it on Amazon. Eight ninety-nine."

Toby wanted to film her sitting in the soaking tub so viewers could see how big it was relative to the size of a human. Reluctantly, she stepped into the tub, sat down, and rested her head against the porcelain. She looked more annoyed than uncomfortable, but it was a good shot—you could have fit five more people in there with her.

"Let's get you stepping into the bathtub one more time," Toby said. "But this time, try to be more authentic about it. More spontaneous."

As Candace Loon repositioned herself, her back turned to me, I placed my hand on the vanity, and it landed on top of her rose-quartz *gua sha*. It was warm and familiar, and a little oily against my fingers. I didn't want to let go. Actually, letting go was impossible. While everyone's eyes were on Candace, I slowly dragged my hand toward the edge of the vanity and slipped the *gua sha* into my back pocket.

It was that easy. Nobody saw me do it. And after I'd done it, I didn't feel the rush you're supposed to feel when you steal something. I felt more like I had found something I'd lost, moved a misplaced object back to its home. I imagined that, even if Candace Loon had seen me do it, she would have tossed her hands in the air and laughed, then showed me her hand-poured candles from the Amalfi Coast, or whatever.

She got out of the tub and stretched her arms above her head. "Well, now I need a real bath. So it's time for you guys to get out of here."

We followed her down the two flights of stairs to the lemon-scented foyer.

"Thanks a lot," Toby said, once we were in her doorway. He sounded distracted, not grateful.

"Sure," Candace said. She looked at me again. My ears burned a little, but I felt safe, light, as though my neck had been rolled thin like a string of dough and parted in the middle, gently releasing my head from the rest of my body.

"You should start making your bed," she said, smiling.

"Oh, yeah. Definitely."

We walked to the van. The crew packed up their gear. I loaded the cooler into the trunk. I opened the side door and crawled back to the third row of seats. As I sat down, I felt Candace Loon's rose quartz pull against my pocket.

After we dropped the crew off at the office, Toby asked me to park the van in the lot. This was the second big part of my job: driving the van to the lot.

"Actually, I'll just come with you," he said, moving into the passenger seat. I took his spot in the driver's seat and drove us down. For the first few minutes, we were both silent. We never had much to say to each other. Even when Toby did want to communicate with me, it was usually through hand motions, signaling what he needed and how quickly he needed it.

He turned to me. "Good job with Candace today."

I wondered if he knew what I'd done, had somehow sensed that I'd disrupted something sacred.

"Sure. I didn't really do anything."

"That's not true." He picked up the packet of gum in the cup holder and took out a piece for himself, then offered the pack to me. I waved it away. "You provide a sense of comfort. You're the safety net. These people, they don't always take to me. They don't always feel comfortable with so many cameras in their home. It's good to have someone whose presence says, 'We come in peace.'"

"We come in peace." I kept my back pressed firmly against the seat in case the rose quartz was tempted to slip out of my pocket. I felt it there, patiently waiting.

"Exactly. Do you think you're capable of that?"

"Of peace? Sure." I pulled into the lot, parked the van next to a line of identical vans.

"That's what I thought. I want you to know you have a purpose. I like to check in about this stuff. You know, you remind me so much of my kid. And she was sort of a loose cannon."

Something tragic had happened to his daughter. It was a fluke. She might have fallen through a glass balcony, or something like that.

"I'm not really your kid. I'm a whole different person."

He was quiet for a moment, just sitting and staring straight ahead. He was beginning to bald on the sides of his head, and the way the afternoon light hit his face cast a deep shadow under his eyes.

"Well." He took a deep breath and held it. "Anyway."

★　★　★

At home later, I arranged my face and body lotions along my bathroom sink like Candace Loon's. I leaned the *gua sha* against the tile, took a step back, and stared at the scene. For the first time in a while, I felt important.

★　★　★

Our next shoot was at Sandra Woodbrook's Los Feliz Victorian home. I knew it was going to be a freaky one. Sandra Woodbrook was the kind of designer who styled her clients in dresses made from shards of glass collected from landfills, coats made entirely out of roadkill fur. For a while, nobody even knew what she looked like because whenever she was out in public she wore a horse's skull over her face. A real one. The rumor was that the skull had belonged to her childhood horse, but nobody ever confirmed that.

When Sandra Woodbrook opened the door to her home, the first thing I noticed was the taxidermic Bengal tiger in the center of her parlor. It was standing on its hind legs and wearing a silk bow tie.

"Sai, here, was gifted to me by the Buddhist monk I was lucky enough to study with in Jaipur, who has now passed." She tickled the tiger's chin. "This poor boy was murdered by poachers, and in some small way, we've brought him back to life."

She was wearing a white, floor-length dress with bell sleeves and cuffs made of real red roses. As she led us into her sitting room, petals fell from the cuffs of her sleeves to the marble floor, and we had to be extra-careful not to step on them as we followed her. I felt the urge to collect them, a trail of candy left specifically for me, but I thought the whole thing might have been intentional, the loose petals now an integral part of the house's decor.

The walls in Sandra Woodbrook's sitting room were painted a forest green, except for one wall entirely covered in white feathers. I thought it was disgusting, but I also kind of wanted to pet it.

"They're a combination of snowy owl and whooping crane," Sandra Woodbrook said. "All ethically sourced, of course. After all, out of death blooms art."

"Very cool," Toby said, but he was looking at me. He raised his eyebrows, which meant he was thirsty. I handed him his Diet Coke.

In her living room, more taxidermy. An entire colony of Victorian-era taxidermic birds, each wearing a customized silk peacoat. They were arranged on her coffee table in a Socratic circle, as if they were contemplating their untimely deaths. Sandra Woodbrook plucked one from its place in the circle and held it in the palm of her hand.

"Another friend of mine, an Australian designer, crafted these little peacoats. Aren't they precious?"

She petted the bird's head with her forefinger. Toby had the cameramen zoom in on the bird. Its beak was slightly parted, and it looked bloated, like it had died full of worms. I thought it was repulsive. I yearned for Candace Loon's house, its lemony, rose-tinted air and glossed floors. Everything in this house had eyeballs. Sandra Woodbrook showed us more rooms, more stuff. It was all art. It was all from somewhere else. It was all a gift from someone who loved her, whose name she'd forgotten.

She led us to the kitchen, where we took a moment to appreciate her bespoke British-racing-green stove with copper-dipped burner plates.

"I've always thought of a stove as more of an aesthetic item than a functional one." She twisted one of the knobs. "I have no idea how to use this thing."

I thought she probably had a personal chef who knew how to use it. You could tell she wanted us to feel impressed by all her eccentricities. She let go of the knob and kept walking. Toby looked at me with panic in his eyes and nodded toward the stove. This was my moment, the one where I save the day. We might all die of gas poisoning in this freaky house, if not for me. I reached out and twisted the knob to off. Ta-da. Toby gave me a thumbs-up, a wink of recognition for the heroic task I'd just performed. My job was so stupid. I hoped he'd give me a raise.

Once everyone had followed Sandra Woodbrook out of the kitchen, I grabbed the knob again and turned it just slightly to the left, maybe half an inch. I didn't hear the hiss of gas. I didn't hear anything at all. I tugged on the knob gently, and it came loose from the stove. I stuck it in my pocket and walked out of the room.

★ ★ ★

After that, something inside me came undone. I felt like a balloon whose knot had been untied, and which was now flying all berserk around a small, tight room. I went into more celebrities' homes. I stole more things.

From Dakota Johnson, I took the gold-framed four-leaf clover that she'd picked with her ex-boyfriend at the Cliffs of Moher.

At Kendall Jenner's house, I took a set of Native American drumsticks.

I stole eggs from Margot Robbie's chicken coop.

I took Robert Downey Jr.'s Hindu prayer beads.

Peacock feathers from the vase in the center of Blake Lively's dining room table.

Ariana Grande's cashmere socks.

Alicia Keys's aromatic oils.

Harry Styles's razor.

Adele's eighteenth-century hand-carved flute.

Kristen Bell's clay figurine.

A fork and a knife from Zendaya's utensil drawer.

I kept everything in the cabinets under my bathroom sink. I hardly ever looked at any of it. I just liked knowing that it was there—a collection of trophies.

★　★　★

The morning of Arlo Banks's home video, I was feeling a little ambitious, a little invincible, and I made the bold decision to switch the Diet Coke in the cooler for Coke Zero.

"Interesting," Toby said, digging a can from the cooler and examining it. "Is there any seltzer?"

"They ran out," I said. I didn't want to deal with Toby. I wanted to be inside Arlo Banks's home. His last movie was a shitty modern rendition of *Don Quixote*, in which he played a young, hot fitness-instructor version of Don Quixote on a days-long acid trip. The movie was so bad everyone had to see it, and apparently he'd had a little meltdown because of it. He disappeared to Europe for a while and then returned, even hotter and in love with some Spanish girl he'd picked up from one of the Spanish islands. People were into them. They posted a lot of videos and photos on social media, kissing under a waterfall, picnicking at the idyllic base of a Swiss mountain. None of this had anything to do with interior design.

"Did you try the Whole Foods?" Toby was staring at me like I'd betrayed his trust in some monumental way that would be impossible to recover from. It filled me with rage, and I felt afraid, for a moment, of what I might do next.

"I didn't. I'm sorry."

"Hm." He looked around the property, eyes squinted, searching for something. "I wonder if there's a Whole Foods nearby."

"There isn't."

"Well"—he settled his gaze back on me—"I guess there are more important things to worry about."

"I guess so."

He opened the Coke Zero and took a sip. He looked satisfied. Then he handed the can to me. "You're feeling okay today?"

"I feel fine. I feel great."

He hesitated, put his hands on his hips, and pursed his lips. "Kind of has a weird aftertaste. Like metal, or something."

I stared at the can.

He pulled a pack of gum from his pocket and popped one piece into his mouth. "This day is off to a weird start."

"Sorry."

"I'm counting on you."

I nodded. "We come in peace."

Toby glanced at Arlo Banks's home. It was very square, except for his front door, which was shaped like a triangle.

"Let's go wide on the door," Toby shouted to the cameramen, and walked away from me. "I don't want to lose the contrast."

Arlo Banks was waiting on the other side of the door for his cue, and when Toby signaled it, the door opened.

"Hey, guys," Arlo said almost apathetically. "Welcome to my house."

He was shorter than I'd imagined him, but you could practically see his ab muscles through his T-shirt. I was surprised by how attracted to him I was.

"Good shit." Toby motioned to the cameramen. "Take us inside."

The inside of Arlo Banks's home was an interior designer's nightmare. The foyer and living room were open concept with hardwood floors and floor-to-ceiling windows with views of the Pacific throughout. Thick wood beams stretched across the ceiling in a lattice design, giving the place a bohemian, accidentally chic vibe. It could have been a really beautiful home, all beachy and airy and light. But there was a massive television the size of a home theater screen taking up one whole wall, and a black leather couch spanned the opposite wall. On the glass coffee table between them, the magazine had placed one of their signature stone vases stuffed with massive, obtrusive branches. The whole thing looked mismatched in a way that made me feel physically uncomfortable.

"This is the living room," Arlo said, leading the cameramen toward his leather couch. He stared awkwardly at the branches in the vase. "And these are my branches."

I laughed. I couldn't help myself. Arlo looked at me and smiled. It was a gentle, earnest smile, not the big toothy smile you'd expect from a massive celebrity. I could tell he hadn't replaced his natural teeth with veneers, and I started to like him.

"Nothing like a good old-fashioned bachelor pad," Toby said.

Arlo looked confused. This made him even more attractive. "My girlfriend lives here, too."

"Of course." Toby nodded nervously. "Is she home?"

Arlo fell silent and stared at his feet. His eyes became wide and vacant, and he appeared to have drifted into his head, where some big, sad thoughts were happening. The longer I looked at him, the more I wanted to wrap my arms around him. I imagined him resting his chin on my head, his tears gliding down his face and into my hair. *There, there*, I'd say, rubbing his back.

"She's out," Arlo said, refocusing his gaze on Toby. Then Arlo smirked, as if he'd told himself a private joke. "I never know where she goes."

I looked around the room—it was hard to believe a woman lived here with him. There were no blankets anywhere, for one. A large trapezoidal mirror hung on the foyer wall above a narrow entry table, which was completely naked except for Arlo's car keys, tossed absently in the center. A green electric guitar stood on a stand in a corner of the living room, next to the leather sofa. On the other side of the sofa, two empty wicker baskets were stacked on top of each other.

Everyone was silent for a beat, which somehow matched the room's empty yet chaotic energy. I felt unsure of what to do with my eyes, my hands, but compelled to do *something* with them, so I lifted Toby's Coke Zero to my mouth and took a sip. When I lowered the drink, he was staring at me, eyes narrowed. I held his gaze and took another sip.

"Can we see upstairs?" I asked. I wanted to know what Arlo's bedroom looked like, what bizarre choices he'd made in there. Maybe that was where he kept all the exotic things his fancy friends had given him.

He kind of raised his eyebrows at me, like he was impressed I could speak. "Sure."

He led us up the stairs to a lofted bedroom. A cowhide rug was splayed across the wood floor under his bed. And his bed was made, the duvet tucked tightly into the frame the way they do it in hotels. I wondered if he'd done that himself or if a housekeeper did it for him. The bed faced the west window with views of the ocean, which was a nice touch. It was flanked by two wooden side tables. A matching wooden dresser stood in the corner. Other than that, the room was bare, the whole thing resembling a stock photo of a Malibu bedroom. I looked around for something, anything, to grasp on to, but I was utterly bored.

"I like to sleep with the windows open," Arlo said. "I like the sound of the ocean." It sounded like a line he'd memorized in preparation for our visit.

"Let's get a shot of the view," Toby said, and the cameramen moved into position. As they panned the room, I focused on Arlo, who was gazing sadly at the water.

"I can't explain it," he said softly, like he didn't want anyone to hear him.

"What's that?" Toby asked.

Arlo blinked and shook whatever dark thought he was having out of his head. "I mean the ocean, why I like it."

Toby seemed satisfied with this answer, but I knew Arlo was lying. I knew it because I was also a liar. He had let something inside him slip out, and now he had to cover it up.

"Do you want to see the kitchen?" Arlo said, snapping into character, suddenly chipper. "The kitchen is sick."

He walked downstairs and back through the living room toward a door that looked like it opened to a closet. We followed him, and he opened the door to reveal, instead, an entire kitchen—smaller than you'd expect a celebrity's kitchen to be, but remodeled. It had a big white-marble island in the center with six white leather stools, each draped with a sheepskin rug. The cabinets were also white, the built-in refrigerator disguised as one of them. But nobody was looking at any of that.

Above the island, a rack hung from the ceiling—the kind you'd hang pots and pans from. But there were no pots and pans. Instead, four large cured ham legs dangled from the rack's four corners, each tied by a wire that wrapped around the ham's dead little hoof. Their fatty, yellow exteriors looked slick to the touch, giving the whole kitchen the feeling of a bright, white operating room. The hams were hanging low enough that you could reach up and grab them.

"My girlfriend is from Spain." Arlo pointed to the hams. "She has a whole curing chamber in the garage."

Everyone looked up at the hams. Toby cleared his throat. I ignored him.

"So you eat these?" Toby asked.

Arlo shook his head. "I'm a vegetarian. I think they just remind her of home."

"They're decoration, then?"

Arlo shrugged. "Sure, I guess."

I couldn't take my eyes off the hams, all fatty and slimy and dead. They were so opposite Arlo's clean, freshly shaven face, his bright, glimmering eyes. I was impressed by his ability to share a home with something that ugly. I thought he must have been a pretty good boyfriend.

He showed us the inside of his refrigerator, which was filled with mostly drinks—cartons of coconut water, cans of iced coffee, bottles of mineral water imported from Spain— and a few bunches of spinach. But everyone, including Arlo, seemed disinterested with these ingredients.

"We mostly eat out," he said.

"I'd like to see the curing room," Toby said, still hung up on the whole ham thing. "I don't think we've ever filmed one of those before."

"Curing chamber," Arlo said. "I don't know what kind of state it's in."

"That's what editing is for."

Arlo shrugged again. I could tell he was still distracted by his thoughts, and I got the feeling that we'd interrupted something. We had caught him in a moment of vulnerability that he wasn't used to showing people.

On the other side of the kitchen, two French doors opened to the patio. Arlo pointed in their direction and started walking.

"Garage," he said, like he was trying to remember where it was.

Everyone followed him out the doors and onto the patio. I was the last of us. I was giddy with impatience, trying with all my strength not to run over and touch the hams before everyone had left the room. I stood in the doorway and waited for everyone to disappear down a tree-lined path on the other side of the patio that presumably led to the garage. Toby turned around.

"Are you okay?" He sort of mouthed it so as not to draw attention to himself.

The interruption, and the delay it created, felt like a thousand years.

"I have to pee, Toby. Am I allowed to pee alone or would you prefer to wait outside the bathroom door."

Toby froze. He looked embarrassed, and also shocked. I'd expected to feel some kind of relief, talking to him like that, but instead I felt guilty, like I'd just kicked an animal. He turned around and continued walking down the path. I watched him vanish into the trees. Some combination of freedom and fear filled my stomach, like I was out in the world on my own for the very first time. I closed the French doors and walked back to the hanging hams, moving almost robotically. A block of chef's knives sat on the center of the island behind the sink, and I leaned over and grabbed the biggest one. I hadn't decided yet whether I wanted to eat the ham, but I knew I wanted a piece of it. I reached up with my free hand to hold the ham still and tried slicing into the side of it with the knife. It was tougher and oilier than I imagined it would be, and with little leverage, I couldn't gather enough force to slice off a big piece. A few scraggly pieces of fat fell onto the marble countertop. I put the knife down and wiped them to the floor, then took a step back and contemplated my options.

The thing was, I really needed the ham. It was my only opportunity to take a piece of Arlo Banks home with me, the only thing in his house that had any intrigue. I had this idea in my head that, once I was holding the ham, I'd understand whatever part of himself he was hiding.

I hoisted myself up onto the island and examined the wire tied around the hoof. I could untwine it fairly easily, so I squatted on my tiptoes and did exactly that. The hoof came loose and the ham dropped onto the counter in front of me. It looked, somehow, less dead this way, lying on its side on the marble countertop. Or maybe it looked like it had never been alive. I slid off the island and picked it up, cradling it in my arms. It must have been ten pounds. Behind me, I heard the French doors open.

I turned around to see Arlo standing in the doorway. His gaze landed on the ham. I followed it to the knife, then to the empty space above the island where the ham had been. He didn't look alarmed or even confused. In fact, I couldn't tell what he was thinking at all.

"It fell," I lied.

Arlo walked into the kitchen and around to the other side of the island. He opened a drawer and rummaged around in it.

"Forgot the garage keys," he said, plucking the keys from the drawer and holding them up for me to see. We stared at each other. His eyes really grabbed you—once they'd caught you it was basically impossible to look away. I realized this was his superpower, and I was about to lose what little control of the situation I had. He nodded to the ham. "What are you going to do with that?"

He spoke so casually, as if he'd almost expected to walk in and find me here, compromised. I felt a strong connection to him. We shared some strange desire, or impulse, maybe, tucked beneath our innocuous exteriors.

"I'm not sure. I think I wanted a piece."

"Why?"

The look on his face, so steady and clear, told me he already knew why. He just wanted to hear me say it.

"Proof."

He put the keys in his pocket, walked over to me, and held his hands out. I gave him the ham, and he placed it on the island. The whole time he didn't break eye contact. I wondered if that was an acting move. I thought he should do more horror movies. He would've made an excellent villain—so pretty and unassuming until, well.

He picked up the knife and held it out in front of him. He examined it as though he'd never used it before, as though he didn't even know it lived in his kitchen.

"My girlfriend is gone," he said to the knife.

I didn't know what to say, so I said nothing.

"We got into a fight. I don't know where she is. I haven't seen her in two days."

"I'm sorry."

"It's my fault." He spoke directly to the knife. "Nobody knows."

"I won't tell anyone."

He looked at me. He smiled, and his face became friendly again. It was true talent, and I felt briefly sad for him for getting sucked into so many goofy roles—the prep school kid, the dopey sidekick, the hot, dumb lifeguard.

He pointed the knife at my face jokingly. "Now we each have a secret to keep."

He placed his other hand firmly on top of the ham, then stuck the knife into its side and began slicing through it. It took longer than I thought it would, and he appeared to be working pretty hard to get the knife through the ham. His arm glided violently back and forth, his face wincing as he worked. I thought about offering to help, but I didn't want to interrupt the moment. It was a shame Toby and the others were outside, waiting like morons for nothing. They would've loved to get this on camera.

Finally, he managed to slice off a hunk of ham about the size of a small wallet. He put the knife down, picked up the piece of ham, and gave it to me. I held it and felt proud.

"Are you going to eat it?" he asked.

"I don't think so. I don't want it to disappear."

He nodded.

"I should get back out there." He looked around at the ham scene. "Do you mind?"

"Oh, sure. I'll clean up."

"Thanks." He dug into his pocket for the garage keys and walked back through the French doors. He closed the doors gently behind him. For some reason, this made me want to cry. I held the ham to my chest. It was totally disgusting. It smelled like a foot. Eventually, it would grow stale and harden, a statue of something that had once been alive, a gift from one friend to another.

Okay, Okay, Okay

Posie and I are going to Mexico because we don't have anything better to do. It's easy to get there from where we live in San Diego—certain people do it all the time. Others are too afraid. They think when you go to Mexico, you die.

Racists, Posie calls them. But last week they found the bodies of two girls in a king suite at one of those time-share resorts. Carbon monoxide poisoning. We aren't going to that resort. We're going to the one next door.

On the phone, Posie tells me she's packing her sheer black dress. "I'll only wear it if the moment presents itself. With black underwear."

She's getting married in a month. She's the last of my friends to get married, except for me and one other girl who moved to New Hampshire to be closer to her nephews and doesn't talk to me anymore. But I've known Posie my whole life, and there's no version of the world in which we aren't friends, even once she's married. We went to high school together, moved West together. For a while we lived together in a garage down in Ocean Beach—this old guy, some beach bum, owned the house, and we were pretty sure he was dealing crack. (He asked us if we wanted any crack, which was how we knew.) We paid him five hundred a month to live in the garage. It had a toilet and a sink but no kitchen or anything, but we could climb up on the roof and watch the sun set over the ocean. It's crazy how much garbage you'll put up with for an ocean view.

Posie met the guy she's marrying out here. He's a surfer and a financial analyst. All men fall in love with Posie because she's got good boobs and perfect teeth. I think she looks like Scarlett Johansson, but with a better face. Back when we used to go out a lot, we never went a night without some guy trying to take her home with him. She always showed them a good time. She'd let them buy her shots and tell her how pretty she was, how smart. I don't know why they always thought she was so smart. Sometimes she'd take her bra off in the bathroom and watch their faces as they tried to keep eye contact the rest of the night. But she always came home with me—until she met Carl, the guy she's marrying.

I like Carl. He's kind and has lots of money. He brings her flowers and takes the trash out. He lets her use his credit card. Plus, she loves him. I can tell she loves him a lot. She makes him dinner. She says things like "We've been watching that new show" and "We're thinking of moving to L.A." They moved in together—this beautiful apartment in La

Jolla with a deck that overlooks the water—only a few months before he proposed. They invite me over for dinner all the time. She cooks, he cleans. It's all very romantic and wholesome. If she moves to L.A., I don't know what I'll do with myself.

★ ★ ★

Posie refuses to call Mexico her bachelorette party. Probably because it's just the two of us, and that looks pretty sad.

"Bachelorettes are so embarrassing," she told me when she booked it. "It's like, you need an excuse to go away with your friends? Lame."

Posie and Carl are having this big, fancy wedding up in Santa Barbara. She wants disco balls and champagne coupes and a shiny black-and-white dance floor. She wants her hair to look like Brigitte Bardot's, all piled perfectly loose on top of her head.

I don't have any sheer black dresses to bring to Mexico. All I have are baggy T-shirts and loose pants to hide how fat I've gotten.

"You aren't fat," Posie says on the phone. "You're totally proportionate. Your head is the right size for your neck is the right size for your tits. It's all perfect."

She says stuff like this to make me feel better, I know, but it sounds like *You were born to be this fat.*

"And you have to stop worrying about gaining weight. Guys don't care. Nobody cares."

"I care."

"What I'm saying is, you shouldn't."

This is easy for her to say.

"Carl wants me to bring a carbon monoxide detector," she whispers into the phone. Then she laughs. "Can you believe him? I told him, sure, no problem, I'll get one. Ha!"

"It's sweet he wants you to live."

"That's all you can really ask for."

★ ★ ★

Oh, sure, I've had boyfriends. But they were always quitting their jobs to backpack across Costa Rica or selling pre-rolled joints to teenagers by the pier. And none of them liked me enough to stick around.

★ ★ ★

The flight to Mexico is only two hours, so Posie and I split headphones and watch some rom-com from the early 2000s about a girl who's had sex with too many people. Then she falls in love with her handyman, who convinces her she hasn't had sex with too many people, after all. Throughout all of this sex, she lives alone in a two-bedroom apartment in Manhattan.

"Can you believe they used to make movies like this?" Posie says. "Do you even know how many people you've had sex with?"

She doesn't mean it as an insult, but it feels like one.

When we arrive in Mexico, the woman at reception offers us margaritas and a two-hour-long presentation in order to get "exclusive discounts."

"A presentation about what?" I ask her. But Posie kicks my ankle and shakes her head.

"Gracias, pero solamente estamos aquí por tres días, y no tenemos tiempo que perder," Posie says to the woman.

"You can still speak Spanish?"

In high school, Posie got straight A's. Our Spanish teacher was some twenty-three-year-old just out of college. We ran into him at the deli/liquor store one night and he bought us a case of Natural Light.

"We live in *San Diego*," she says, as if that explains it. "I'm better when I'm drunk."

It's so hot in Mexico we can barely go outside. We've been in California for so long it's easy to forget how hot it gets everywhere else. We spend the entire day in the ocean, which is crystal clear and still as a tub, nothing like the seaweed-tangled rip currents we're used to. We float on our backs, dive down and touch the sand. Colorful fish squirm around our feet, and Posie tries to catch them. When you live at the beach, you learn to feel comfortable in the water. You don't have any other choice. Occasionally, Posie gets out to order beer and piña coladas from the servers. Every time she emerges from the water onto the shore, she walks like a *Sports Illustrated* model, adjusting the strings of her bikini bottoms so that they sit above her hips. I don't think she's trying to impress anyone—she doesn't know any other way to be. At the end of the day she says, "I've peed in this ocean twenty-three times."

All along the shore, there are Mexican vendors selling activities. It's difficult to tell how old they are, they're wearing white from head to toe so not an inch of their skin is exposed to the sun. Some of them are wearing two baseball hats on top of each other, one facing the front, the other facing the back to cover their neck. They want to take us jet skiing, snorkeling, banana boating. They want us to buy handblown glass pipes and bandanas that say NICE CUNT in neon script.

"Hola, ladies," they say as we get out of the water. "You want to have fun?"

"Maybe tomorrow," I tell them.

"Hey, girl," one guy says. He puts his hand out in front of us to stop us from walking any farther. The sand is hot on the bottoms of my feet. "You are beautiful."

It's hard to tell which of us he's looking at because I can't see his eyes through his sunglasses.

Posie looks at me and smiles. "She is beautiful, isn't she?"

"What's your name?" the man says.

"Rhea."

"Rhea? That's my favorite name."

Posie rolls her eyes. "Uh-huh, sure it is."

"Do you two want to have some fun?"

"We're not doing any activities today," Posie says.

"Fuck the activities," he says, smiling wide under all his sun gear. "What are you doing tonight? I have joints, cervezas, cocaine. You pick."

"Maybe tomorrow," I tell him, feeling cute. "We're getting tacos." I can sense him smiling at me as we trot away.

★　★　★

At night, we find a taco stand somewhere in town and Posie orders in Spanish. We sit at a table with plastic chairs on the sidewalk and slip limes into our beers.

"I love being in another country," Posie says. "I can't explain it. I just feel safe. I feel like nobody is judging me."

"Nobody is ever judging you."

"At home, there are so many expectations, you know? So many responsibilities. The second you land in another country, everyone expects so little of you. They're like, 'Oh, you naive little tourists, how cute.' It's so easy to blow everyone's minds."

"I guess."

Posie shoves the end of a taco into her mouth, takes a sip of beer, and burps. "I have to tell you something."

"Please don't move to L.A."

"No, not that."

"What?"

She's silent for a second, like she's trying to figure out which words to use, translating the idea into something digestible. "I'm pretty sure I'm pregnant."

"What do you mean 'pretty sure'? Did you take a test?"

"Not yet. But my tits." She squeezes them and makes a face. "They're sore as shit."

"That could just be your period coming."

"No." She folds her arms across her chest and sticks her hands into her armpits. "It started on the sides."

"What are you going to do?" As soon as I ask, I know the answer.

"We want to have kids. I've wanted to be a mom my whole life. I think that's, like, the thing I could be really good at. I just didn't think it would happen right now."

"You're really good at Spanish."

"My whole life I've been wondering what I'm supposed to *do*, you know? You have writing. That's what you do. That's what makes you happy every day, or at least not unhappy. I don't have anything like that. Sometimes I feel like I'm wandering around all loosey-goosey, waiting for something to pick me up and carry me away. I was always a little worried that drugs might do it. But I think a baby could be the thing to hold me down. In a good way, I mean."

I feel a heavy sadness solidifying in my stomach. It's hard to explain, but it feels like we've been disconnected, suddenly, messily, like a wishbone snapped not quite in half.

"Should you be drinking?"

She takes another sip of beer. "That's why I didn't take a test. I wanted to wait till after Mexico. If this baby is anything like me, it can handle a few drinks."

"That's for sure."

She stares down at her stomach and points at it. "I need you to give me this weekend, okay? I need this one weekend. After that, it's all about you. I promise."

"I want to cry." The words come out without permission.

"Me, too." She smiles softly at the basket of tacos between us. I hold the tears back because I feel stupid for having them in the first place.

★ ★ ★

On the walk home, Posie says, "That guy was cute, from earlier."

"Was he?"

"He had a nice voice."

Posie is always noticing things about men that I never see. She likes the cartilage on their ears, the way their hair curls on their calves, how their eyebrows move when they talk. I guess when you're as beautiful as she is, you know where to find beauty in the details of other people.

"It was so smooth," she says. "His words moved together like they were dancing."

★ ★ ★

Like the dead girls next door, we have a king suite.

Posie pulls the carbon monoxide detector out of her suitcase and laughs at it. "I don't have any batteries."

She turns off the lights and slides into bed next to me and pulls the covers over us both. Her head is on the same pillow as mine.

"Read us one of your stories," she says.

"I don't have any with me."

"Read that one you've memorized. About the woman who chews her food and spits it out down the garbage disposal, and then her daughter has to call the plumber to remove all the chicken bones. That one cracks me up."

"You're the one who's memorized it." The room is so dark I can't tell if my eyes are open or closed.

"How does it start? Oh, right—hey, it's a sad story, isn't it?"

"It's a little bit of both."

"You're so good at that."

"I forget how it starts."

"'When Louisa's mom stopped eating, Louisa started eating double . . .'"

★ ★ ★

The next morning, we sit down at the resort's beach café for breakfast, and Posie orders us two mimosas and a bowl of fruit. It's too hot outside to eat, so we take our mimosas straight into the ocean. The shoreline is quiet this early in the morning, the vendors yet to arrive, the college kids still sleeping off last night's tequila. We have the water to ourselves save for one extremely sunburned family trying to get a holiday photo on the shoreline and a few other families with young kids who splash around in floaties. I try not to look at them, but I can tell Posie is eyeing a father and daughter who are running away from the tide as it rolls in, then running toward it as it recedes. The kid squeals every time her feet get wet.

"Rhea," I hear someone call from the shore. A man who looks about my age is wading into the water. "Have you thought about what I said?"

As he gets closer, I recognize him as the guy from yesterday, but he looks different without all the layers. He has a big, round, shaved head and pretty green eyes. And then he's next to me, his body fully submerged in the water. I can see Posie swimming toward us from the corner of my eye.

"Have I thought about what?"

"Want to have some fun today?"

Posie's head pops out of the water next to us. "Do we know your name?" she asks.

"Mario," he says, still looking at me.

"I'm Posie." She sticks out her hand to shake his, and he takes it.

"Come snorkeling with me today," he says. "I'll bring beer, tequila. I'll bring my friend." He nods to another man pulling a set of paddleboards into the water. He's much skinnier and more athletic looking than Mario, with curly dark hair that falls at his shoulders. "You'll have fun."

"What's his name?" Posie asks, pointing at the other guy.

"His name is Jean Carlos, but we call him Panna."

"Panna?"

"It means, like, 'brother.'"

"How come you want to go snorkeling with us so badly?" Posie asks with a smirk. She doesn't know how to talk to boys without flirting with them.

"Have you seen the people on this beach? Everyone is insane. They want us to bring them champagne. They want us to fan them. They want someone to rub lotion on their fake tits. When I see people who look like a good time, I want to choose them. I want to have fun, too, you know?"

Posie doesn't seem convinced, but she was right about his voice. I like listening to him talk.

"How much for snorkeling?" she asks.

"No." He shakes his head. "Nothing for you. Let's go out and have fun on the boat. There's a beach all the way out there, another one, with a rock you can jump from. You know, like diving? There are turtles swimming out there."

Posie just shrugs and looks at me. "Sounds fun to me."

"You're sure?" I can't help but feel like she's suddenly disabled, incapable of performing the way she usually does. She'd hate it if she knew I felt this way.

"Shut up," she says. "Of course I'm sure."

★　★　★

The boat is small and motorized with a square pane of plexiglass on the bottom so you can see the fish swimming below—only the glass is so dirty and scratched you can't see much at all. The boys bring a cooler filled with beer and one bottle of tequila and some limes. Jean Carlos drives the boat. Mario sits down next to me, and Posie squeezes in between us.

"Rhea," Mario says. "Your name goes well with mine."

We drink the beer. It turns out Jean Carlos speaks no English, only Spanish and Italian. Posie is ecstatic.

"I'm so good at Spanish when I'm drunk," she says, and takes a big gulp of beer. "Panna, tell me about *tu familia*."

They speak in broken Spanish and English, each practicing their skills on the other. Every word that comes out of her mouth makes him fall more and more in love. She knows exactly what to do with his adoration—squeeze every last bit of it out of him until she's all plumped up, then she'll flash her engagement ring and break his poor little heart. As he speaks, every so often she furrows her eyebrows in confusion, and he stops his rambling and holds up one hand and says, "Okay, okay, okay," then continues talking exactly the same.

I feel Mario's hand brush my hair from my neck. The whole time, I'm thinking these boys could kidnap us no problem. Here we are, two unassuming American girls, two drunk idiots in the middle of the ocean with two strange men. And one of us—one of us is *pregnant*. Anyone would say it's a bad idea. But I can't help but feel like we're the more dangerous ones.

Somewhere in the middle of the ocean, Posie leans over and whispers in my ear, "This man has quite the story. He's married, you know. But his wife lives in Oaxaca and they don't speak anymore. Or maybe they speak, but only as friends."

"You understood all of that?"

But she just smiles and goes back to talking.

"Your friend is very confident." Mario seems impressed, or surprised. "Most girls aren't."

"I don't think that's true anymore."

"It's true." He shakes his head all disheartened. I feel like he's disappointed in me.

★   ★   ★

The water at the island is even bluer and clearer than it is at the resort. The waves roll the boat into shore and rock it back and forth as we try to step off one at a time. Jean Carlos goes first and holds his hand out to help Posie and me as we stand on the boat's ledge. I take his hand and he catches me in his arms, just like in a movie, except more slippery and awkward. Posie doesn't take his hand—she just jumps off the side of the boat into the water.

Lots of people are on this island, snorkelers, other tourists who want to jump off the rock. Posie and I put our snorkeling masks on.

"You are probably too drunk to swim," Mario says to me.

We laugh at him, then run out into the ocean.

I don't care about fish very much. I don't mind them scurrying around below me, but I don't care to pay attention to them. What's fascinating, though, is how deep the ocean is below us, how far down I can see until the water becomes a dark, impenetrable blue. I dive down to see how far I can make it, how long I can hold my breath. I feel sort of insignificant down here, sort of small and useless.

When I come up for air, the boys are there, swimming in circles around Posie.

"They found us," she says, giggling. She points to the giant rock jutting out of the middle of the cove. "Let's go to the rock."

★　★　★

When we get there, we take our masks off, hoist ourselves onto the rock, and climb on our hands and feet all the way to the top. It's about fifteen feet high. I pretend to be a little afraid, and Mario reaches out to hold my hand.

"We'll go together," he says.

As we jump, I can feel the entire weight of my body falling heavily toward the surface. There's so much of me, so much more than there used to be, and yet I feel like half of myself. The sadness from last night is suspended in my gut, slowly floating up my throat against the pull of gravity. When I land, Mario releases my hand, and I plummet down, down, down. Down there in the dark silence, it escapes from my mouth—the sadness—and as I float back up to the surface, I'm crying a big, ugly cry.

"Are you hurt?" Mario swims to me and wraps his arms around my waist. It feels good to be held, but unfamiliar.

"I don't know." I wrap my legs around him.

"What hurts?" His eyes are scanning my body, examining for wounds.

"I'm just drunk."

I look up at the rock for Posie, but she's not there. Neither is Jean Carlos. I glance around the water for them, but I don't see them anywhere.

"Where's Posie?" I ask, as if Mario will inherently know better than I could. He pulls me closer to him and raises an eyebrow.

"Where is she?" I say again.

"They're probably together somewhere." He puts his hand on the back of my head and pushes it toward his face, and his lips latch on to mine. They're wet and salty, his tongue like a live fish in my mouth.

I pull away. "She wouldn't do that. Really, where is she?"

"You don't think your friend can look out for herself?"

"She's pregnant," I say, louder than I intend. I don't know what I expect him to do with this information. The look he gives me makes me think he's never seen a pregnant girl before. And in a blink I realize that boys know nothing. Mario glances around the water awkwardly, then nods to the rock. When I squint, I can see wispy blonde hair just peeking out over the top of it, blowing in the wind.

"We have to go over there."

"What if they're, you know . . ."

"They aren't."

I pull away from him and swim toward the rock and around it to the other side. As I get closer, I can hear Jean Carlos's voice.

"Okay, okay, okay."

He's sitting near the top of the rock next to Posie. They're facing each other, sitting all slanted with their knees bent into their chests. Both of his hands are placed delicately on her shoulders, his arms extended. When she sees me, she smiles and waves me up, but I stay where I am.

"He wants to buy me a house overlooking the ocean," she says. "He says he'll plant olive trees."

"That sounds nice," I say. "Did you accept?"

"I said if Carl leaves me, I would consider it."

Jean Carlos opens his mouth like he's about to say something that's taken a lot of strength to muster. "If you are happy"—he squeezes Posie's shoulders—"I am happy."

She puts her hands on top of his and places them in his lap. "I'm happy."

He nods and hangs his head, and I can see the sadness weigh down the back of his neck. I want to give him a hug. "Okay, okay, okay."

"Are you guys going to jump, or what?"

"I don't think so." Posie folds her arms around her shins and rests her head on her knees. "I'm not really in the mood anymore."

I tell her to go feetfirst. I tell her the baby will be okay. I remember, now, that word is the same in Spanish. *Bebé.*

"Right," she says. "I know."

Allowing herself no time to think, she stands up, turns around, and leaps off the rock, the golden tips of her hair the last to disappear behind the edge. On the other side, there's a splash.

Lopsided

After my kidney transplant, I wanted to break up with my boyfriend. Rand was tall and stiff with a neatly trimmed beard at all times. He reminded me of the manicured hedges wealthy people plant around the perimeter of their yards to shield their houses from everyone else's dirt. I wanted to break up with him for a handful of reasons. While I was in recovery at the hospital, I wrote each reason down on the back of a Get Well Soon card my aunt sent me:

1. Rand plays fantasy football.
2. He bought me U2 tickets for Christmas one year.
3. He takes too many pictures (e.g., me in the dialysis room, puffed up and wearing my glasses, stuck with needles and tubes).
4. He once said that if he'd been alive at the time, he might have voted for Nixon.

5. He paid $260 to have a Ray Lewis jersey pressed, framed, and hung on the wall above our stove.
6. If we ever got a dog, he would buy it sweaters and bootees to wear in the winter.
7. Then he would want us to pose with the dog, in the sweater and bootees, for a picture to send out to friends as our Family Christmas Card.
8. He doesn't understand why we can't get a dog.
9. One time, while he was on the toilet, I heard him grunt through the bathroom door, followed by a plop in the water.
10. Sex takes too long.

I have always been sick, the way other people have always been Yankees fans or dog lovers or wearers of pantyhose. I've learned the waiting rooms and acoustic hallways of every nearby hospital like a child learns a new language—living inside it until it creates a permanent space for itself in the brain. Mount Pleasant's emergency room smells like piss. It smells like everyone waiting needs a new kidney, a new liver, new deodorant. The doctors at St. Joseph's once diagnosed my gallbladder infection as gas pains. They diagnosed my gas pains as appendicitis and my appendicitis as period cramps. At Rosewood, the nurses are always on the lookout for domestic abusers. They watch too much *Law & Order* in the break room. They'd scan me for bruises and stare at Rand with flat mouths and squinted eyes, like they might intimidate him into confessing to crimes he didn't commit. Once I was there for a sinus infection and they wouldn't let him in the room.

"Do you want to be alone?" they asked. Sometimes I did.

During dialysis I did. But there was always somebody else at the dialysis center, or somebodies, sick bodies, crammed together in clunky rows of cushioned chairs, pinned down by needles. I avoided eye contact. I distracted myself with magazines, like I was getting a pedicure instead of a kidney treatment. I would have preferred to be alone, to sit inside my pretend pedicure, where nobody could point to the blood-filled tubes and ask me how I felt. I felt like a flooded septic tank. I felt full of shit. I didn't want to talk about it.

"How'd it go?" Rand would ask when he picked me up, as if each time he was expecting I'd tell him I'd been cured, or made a new friend, or found a fun recipe for eggplant parm that we had to try. I had been sick when we met, three years beforehand, but not this sick, not dialysis-three-days-a-week sick, and Rand's cavalier coping mechanisms were beginning to rot my patience. So I said whatever lies I could think of that would deter him from asking me that question again: *We lost Lauren today* or *They couldn't seem to find the vein. It took them eight tries. Blood everywhere.* Other times, I would walk straight through him to the car without a word.

★　★　★

I brought the breakup list home with me after the transplant. But under my own flannel sheets, my head cleared of its medicated fog, I decided to make a few logistical edits. Six and seven were hypotheticals, so to be fair I took them out. I also had to rethink number nine. Pooping is nobody's fault. Besides, Rand hadn't known I was listening. When I think of the noises I've made when nobody is listening, a grunt isn't so bad. In fact, the grunt was kind of endearing. It reminded me of the sound babies make when they try to stand for the first time. The real issue was that I had heard that grunt before—short, deep, breathy with relief. Rand made that same grunt in bed. After I heard the toilet grunt, sex with Rand felt dirty. Not the sexy sort of dirty. The bacterial sort of dirty, like holding a kid's hand after he's sucked his thumb. In the end, I rewrote number nine:

9. Rand's shitting grunt is the same as his fucking grunt.

But Rand loved me, failing organs and all, and none of my reasons for wanting to break up with him held up on their own. So I tore the Get Well card into pieces and stuffed it down the garbage disposal. I flicked the disposal on and listened to all my reasons grind to dust. Then, on the back of a different Get Well card—this one from an old professor—I wrote down the reasons that Rand and I should be together:

1. Rand has no sisters.
2. We like all the same TV shows, except *Entourage*. Rand has such a hard-on for *Entourage*.
3. Whenever I get a speeding ticket in the mail, Rand pays it without telling me.
4. Neither of us believes in God anymore.
5. Rand gave me his kidney.

Lupus is a hot topic right now. Lots of celebrities have it. They also need new kidneys, some of them. They'll post photos of themselves to raise awareness, sick and thin with translucent skin and dark eyes. I can relate to those photos. I have similar photos of myself. Rand took them. Before Rand gave me his kidney, I was depressed. I was ninety-five pounds and wobbly at best. I was sick of being taken care of. I was sick of complaining. For a while I didn't think Rand understood how sick I was. He saved my hospital bracelets in the bedside table as if they were souvenirs from romantic trips we'd never taken together. He said ridiculous things like *You look great today* or *There's my girl* when I didn't look at all great or even like a girl. He made dinner reservations at restaurants with tasting menus. He even tried to plan a ski weekend. It wasn't until he offered me the kidney that I realized he knew exactly how sick I had been. He was only trying to distract us from it.

After they get new kidneys, lupus celebrities say things like *I've been given a second chance at life* or *My scars remind me not to take life for granted.* They talk about their new exercise regimen, the joys of acupuncture, how they've rediscovered religion. They post photos of themselves with their kidney donors over the years: in diapers, in Halloween costumes, in hospital beds. They say, *Without so-and-so, I wouldn't be alive* or *There are no words to describe how thankful I am that so-and-so gave me a piece of so-and-so's self* or *So-and-so will forever be a part of me.*

Sometimes I feel that way about Rand. Sometimes I look at him while he's getting dressed for work and think, *You made me whole again.* Other times I think, *What's yours is mine is ours.* But most of the time I think that he gave me the kidney so that I wouldn't leave him.

When we found out that Rand was a match, he told me he would do anything for me, then signed the paperwork without hesitation. We didn't have a conversation about it.

We didn't weigh the pros and cons. He made up his mind without me, and all I had to do was follow along. In a way, it felt like a marriage proposal, only instead of a diamond ring, I got an organ. It was as if he had gotten down on one knee and said, *Take this kidney and love me forever, or die.*

What was I supposed to do?

★   ★   ★

One morning I woke up in bed next to Rand, his body nuzzled against my back, his arm slung over me. I felt him moving against me, subtly, like he was in a dream, and when I opened my eyes fully, I noticed his arm was tucked up under my sleep shirt and gripping my left tit. He mumbled something incomprehensible in his sleep and rocked his hips slightly against my back.

Rand once described a sex dream he'd had, a sex dream about me, in which we held hands throughout the whole thing and I ended up pregnant and gave birth to twins conjoined at the hand, so they would be forced to hold hands throughout their lives. I didn't want to know what kind of fucked-up wholesome sex dream Rand was having now, so I had to be creative about the way I woke him up. If I did it gently, peeled his hand from my tit and kissed his forehead, he'd wake up all turned on and ready for the real thing. I was so uninterested in sex—all the motions and angles and heavy panting it required. Even worse was the thought of having to explain to Rand why I couldn't have sex with him, after he was already so pumped up, and having to sit there and watch him deflate while I blamed my junky organs when really I just didn't want to hear that ugly shit-grunt.

The only way to wake up Rand and ensure that sex was off the table was to cause him some sort of trauma. That way, he'd be in too much pain to remember his dreamy orgasm. I snuck my leg out from in between his and bent it in front of me. Then on beat with the jive of his hips, I kicked back and jammed my heel into his thigh. His whole body jerked and he gasped awake.

"Ow," he said into my ear. "I think you just kicked me in your sleep."

"I don't think so," I said with my eyes closed.

He kissed the side of my head and sat up. He seemed confused. He leaned over me and grabbed something out of the nightstand.

"Turn around for a second," he said.

It occurred to me I could have gotten out of bed from the start and avoided the whole situation.

I turned over and looked up at Rand. He'd grabbed a small ointment tube from the nightstand, and when he held it up to my face, I saw that it was scar cream. Grinning, he lifted my shirt just above my belly button to reveal the scar, deep and purple. He squeezed some ointment onto his finger and rubbed it into my skin.

"Now you do me." He lifted his own shirt up and over his head. His scar was fatter and more raised than mine. It looked like a wormy parasite. The thought of rubbing it made my throat ache. I would rather have had sex.

I said the first thing that came to mind. "I want to get something pierced."

"What?"

"Pierced."

I wanted to pop holes in myself and force the pressure out. Rand frowned. "Pierce what?"

"I don't know." I looked down at my chest, at the spot where his hand had been. "Maybe my nipples."

A lot of celebrities also have nipple piercings. I wanted to be on trend inside and out.

"But I like your nipples the way they are."

I made a mental note: *11. Rand likes everything the way it is.*

"Tell me the truth," I said. "Are you a Republican?"

"What does that have to do with anything?"

"We're supposed to be on the same page about these things."

Rand cradled his face in his hands. "I'm not even sure what we're talking about anymore."

"I'm getting my nipples pierced."

"But what about infections?" Rand's voice was climbing. "I don't think your doctors would want you to poke yourself with needles right now."

"It's been almost eight weeks," I said. And then, because I didn't want it to go unsaid, "I'm fine."

The words felt foreign to me. I realized I couldn't remember the last time I'd said them.

Rand slipped his shirt on. He looked deflated, finally, and I relaxed. Without the scar shoved in my face like a flashing payment reminder, I liked him again. I liked the way he looked when he wasn't trying so hard.

"Do you want to come with me?"

★ ★ ★

The tattoo parlor was open twenty-four hours, but we went in the morning to avoid any drunk girls who might want their gums tattooed on a whim. It was a small, dusty place with dim lighting. The man behind the glass counter was tall and beefy and wearing denim overalls. Tattoo murals crawled up his arms and stopped just below his neck, creating the illusion that he was wearing a skintight shirt. He wasn't wearing any shirt. He shook Rand's hand first and then mine. His hands were dry and swollen. They looked like they needed to be popped with a needle.

A twinge of fear pricked my chest. I was used to the fluorescent lighting and bright white walls of operating rooms, the sterile air and stiff sheets. Every time I'd been cut into I'd been surrounded by flower arrangements and blue latex. The men who did the cutting wore ties beneath their scrubs. I could smell the disinfectant on their skin. Always, they knocked me out.

I hadn't showered that morning and heat was gathering under my arms and in the space between my shirt and my stomach. My smell matched the smell of the air in the tattoo parlor—musty, like iron.

The tattooed man said his name was Kingsley.

"Lila," I said. "Do you pierce nipples?"

Rand cleared his throat.

Kingsley bent down and opened the sliding door to the glass counter. Inside the counter were all types of small rods and hoops, some with pearls or diamonds, others with spikes or neon tips. Kingsley grabbed a tray of brass and silver jewelry and placed it on the countertop.

"Nipple bars come in three sizes," he said. "Small, medium, and large."

I looked at the tray of jewelry. A row of thin metal bars, each about an inch long, were stuffed in the "small" column.

Next to those were the mediums, about a half inch longer. The larges were at the end, a little shorter than my pinkie.

I had no idea what size my nipples were. I had never thought about it before. But I guessed they had about the same diameter as a bottle cap.

"Medium?" I said.

"This is insane," Rand said.

"It's eighty-five dollars a nipple."

I took out my wallet and handed Kingsley my credit card. He handed me some papers to sign, and I scribbled my name at the bottom without reading them. In the medium section of the jewelry tray, I saw two sterling-silver rods with small pearls at each end. They looked like batons for a chipmunk. I picked them up and handed them to Kingsley. The whole time Rand was standing behind me, shifting on his feet, clearing his throat like he had something to say.

"Rad," said Kingsley, taking the little bars from my hand. He looked at Rand. "You, too?"

Rand looked up, startled. "Not me," he said, shaking his head.

"Not yet, anyway. This shit is contagious. Next thing you know, you'll be back here together asking for snake bites on your spines."

I almost laughed. It was Saturday but Rand was wearing his work clothes anyway: fitted khaki pants and a white collared shirt buttoned to the second from the top, tucked in with a brown leather belt, and the Italian leather shoes he bought during his semester abroad. He looked like a cop. On a Tuesday this might have been sexy. If he came home from work looking this way, buttoned-up and flustered, I'd probably be into it. But here in the dingy tattoo parlor on a

Saturday morning, I was embarrassed. I wished that Rand were a smoker, a bookie, a recovering addict—anyone slightly more suited to make conversation with a shirtless tattoo artist. But he couldn't play the part. Rand was unabashedly himself: clean, safe, the kind of person who apologized for thoughts he had but never said out loud.

"*Snake* bites?" Rand asked.

"It's a type of piercing." Kingsley held two fingers in the air and bent them to look like fangs. He hissed.

Rand looked at me and then at the cushioned leather table where Kingsley pierced people. The leather was cracked along the surface, and you could see the foam poking through some of the tears.

"So you'll be the one to . . ." Rand said to Kingsley. He pinched the air with his pointer finger and thumb and moved his hand back and forth, a mime popping an invisible balloon with an invisible needle. They seemed to be building their own impromptu version of sign language.

Kingsley winked at Rand. "I'm a professional."

I had the sudden urge to take my top off. "Over there?" I pointed to the leather table.

Kingsley nodded. I noticed that his bottom lip puffed out as if something was packed between the outside of his teeth and the inside of his lip. Then I saw the plastic cup on the countertop. He leaned over it and spit something slimy and brown.

"Let's rock and roll," he said.

I'd never cheated on Rand, but if I was going to, I'd have done it with someone like Kingsley.

I lay down on the frayed piercing table and stared at the ceiling. Kingsley sat down on the stool beside me, and Rand stayed standing, hovering above my head like a lit bulb hanging from a wire.

"Shirt off," Kingsley said.

There are two ways to take your shirt off. The first is the way you do it when you're alone, about to step into the shower or standing in the bright, cramped changing room of a discount clothing store. You slide one arm back up the sleeve and into the body of the shirt. Then you do the same thing with the other arm, so both your sleeves are empty and both your arms are against your sides. For a minute, while your shirt is still on and your arms are stuffed inside, you look like a Roman statue or a CPR dummy—stiff, armless. Then you use your arms and elbows to force the shirt over your head.

The second way to take your shirt off is the way you do it when you're about to have sex with someone new. You cross your arms in front of your body and lift the hem of the shirt up, revealing your skin inch by inch, until the shirt is up around your head so that all the other person can see is your headless body. With your arms stretched above your head, everything that normally sags is lifted and elongated. You stay that way for a second—headless, stretched out—then you pop the shirt off your head, your hair tousled, ready to go.

I hadn't taken my shirt off like that in years. But in the tattoo parlor, flanked on either side by my boyfriend and the nipple piercer, I crossed my arms and pulled up.

"Bra, too," said Kingsley.

I reached behind and unclasped my bra and let it hang limp around my shoulders. I slipped it off by the straps and it dropped to the ground. Not sure which man to make eye contact with, and not really wanting to look at either of them, I lay back on the leather table. Cool air wafted against my chest and I suddenly felt cold. As I stared at the ceiling, my right tit slid toward my right arm and nestled into my armpit. The left tit went left. It was like they were trying to escape each other.

"Who's first?" Kingsley tore open the paper packet of an alcohol wipe. "Right or left?"

"Left," I said without thinking.

Kingsley unfolded the alcohol wipe and pressed it against my left nipple. It was cold and made my skin tingle. I liked it.

"No, right," I said.

He turned the wipe over and pressed it against my right nipple. He leaned over and spit into his cup.

I could feel Rand looming there, clasping his hands behind him, then folding his arms across his chest, then resting both hands on top of his head so his elbows stuck out like wings, trying for whatever reason not to stare at my chest.

"Do you want me to hold your hand?" he asked.

"Sure."

Rand reached out and took my left hand and squeezed. On my other side, Kingsley blew into his own hands and rubbed them together, as if trying to warm them up. Then he cupped one warmed hand around the circumference of my right nipple. He held it firmly, the way you might hold a can of soup you were about to open, so the whole thing wouldn't slip back into my armpit. Rand squeezed my left hand tighter. Kingsley adjusted his grip. I felt like, at any moment, either one of them might lean over and try to kiss me.

In his free hand Kingsley held a long, thick needle. The little bar I'd chosen was stuck to the end of the needle like an extension.

"It goes in just like that?" Rand asked, staring at the needle. I couldn't tell if he was nervous or curious.

"Oh, sure," said Kingsley. "The areola is like tissue paper. Very sensitive."

"Will it hurt?" Rand asked.

"Why would you ask that right now?" I said.

Kingsley glanced from Rand to me to my nipple. I could tell he was trying to decide whether to answer the question. I half expected him to sign something cryptic to Rand with his hands.

"I'm ready," I said.

"You want a countdown?" Kingsley asked my tits.

I said no. Without counting, Kingsley jammed the needle through the center of my nipple and the bar slid in behind it. I watched. It stung a little, like a pinch. It didn't bleed. Then he twisted the two tiny pearls onto each end of the bar so it wouldn't fall out one way or the other. He leaned back on the stool and tilted his head to the side like he was studying a painting.

"Sick scar." He nodded to the raised purple place where they'd replaced my fucked-up kidney with Rand's sparkly one. Because of the transplant, that section of my torso was swollen and looked sort of like a tumor or a fetus growing sideways.

"Sorry," Rand mumbled under his breath. I wondered what thought he was trying to suppress. He was still holding my hand, and sweat was beginning to pool between our palms. His sweat. When I looked up at him, his eyes were clenched shut as if he were the one bracing to be hurt.

I wanted to cry. I felt no pain (my right nipple was going numb), but the space behind my eyes still tingled.

I had wanted to watch Rand squirm, and now that I had, I felt icky.

Kingsley wiped my right nipple with a wet gauze pad. It burned. Suddenly a trickle of hot blood seeped out. I watched it pool around the piercing and tint the little pearls orange. I had seen my own blood hundreds of times before, but always in the context of my disease: needles jabbed into my veins, burnt-red droplets in my urine. I hadn't seen my blood doing what it was supposed to do in a long time.

"One's good enough." I sat up and shook my hand loose from Rand's.

"You sure? You paid for two," Kingsley said.

"I'm sure." I grabbed my T-shirt and flung it over my body. I didn't bother with the bra.

"Might look a little lopsided. I'll give you a receipt. That way if you change your mind, you can come back for the other nipple, no charge."

Kingsley told me to clean the nipple with salt water only. If I cleaned it with anything but salt water, it would burn, maybe get infected.

"That piercing is a foreign body," he said. "Real bodies have a way of rejecting foreign ones."

"Not mine."

I walked out the door, bra in hand, and waited for Rand to follow. But he wasn't behind me, and when I turned back toward the tattoo parlor, I saw him through the door, saying something to Kingsley that I couldn't hear. Afterward they shook hands and Rand walked out toward me.

"What was that?" I tried to fold my arms across my chest, but my forearm brushed against my pierced nipple and a sharp, stinging pain spread through my right side.

"Ouch, dammit." I let my arms hang loose at my side.

"I asked him what he uses in his beard." Rand touched his own manicured scruff. "It looks so soft."

I imagined Rand with a thick thatch of wiry, spongy facial hair that began at his ears and extended past his chin, so you couldn't see where his cheekbones ended and his neck began.

"I like your beard the way it is." I reached out and rested my hand on his cheek. I smudged my thumb back and forth like I was trying to get rid of something, but I wasn't.

Rand pointed to my left nipple.

"Are you sure you don't want the other . . ."

"I don't know. Maybe after the next surgery."

Rand frowned.

"I'm kidding." I wasn't. There would be more surgeries. More parts removed, more pieces donated. Maybe not for a while, but eventually the hospital bracelets would accumulate again like coupons. I knew that. Rand knew it, too. But for now I was okay with pretending that neither of us understood who I was.

As we walked back to the car, my breasts thwacked against my body with each step. The right one hurt. I cupped my hand underneath it to keep it in place, but my nipple throbbed as all the blood in my veins rushed to heal it. I thought about taking the piercing out to make the job easier, but decided against it.

Once we were both in the car, Rand put the key into the ignition and said, "Kingsley was cool."

I didn't know what to think about that. Now that the whole thing was over, Rand was suddenly cool about sharing my tits with whoever wanted to hold them. We shared ownership of all of that now, had dual custody over each other's machinery. Rand's body was my body, my body was his body, and it didn't matter who did what with any of it.

"We should get some Neosporin for that." He nodded toward my chest.

"Salt water only."

"Don't you want to make sure it heals?"

"Just stop."

I wanted him to yell at me, to confirm the sick thoughts that had been sprouting all over my brain like weeds: We were irreversibly entwined now, each a fraying tip of the same string. But Rand didn't say anything. He adjusted his seat. He flicked on the blinker, turned left.

★ ★ ★

At home, Rand fried two grilled cheese sandwiches in a pan for lunch, and I fished out a shot glass from the back of a kitchen cabinet. On the front of the glass was a picture of a lemon slice, and underneath that the words WHEN LIFE GIVES YOU LEMONS, ADD TEQUILA AND SALT. I dug through the spice rack for salt.

"What are you doing?" Rand stared at the glass, alarmed.

I didn't say anything. I grabbed the salt and dumped two pinches into the shot glass. Then I went over to the sink and turned on the tap. Rand watched me while I waited for the water to warm. I stuffed my arms inside my shirt and shoved it up and over my head. I stood there, tits out like disco balls, the right one inflamed and pulsing, with my hand held under the tap until my fingers started to burn.

Rand's grilled cheese began to blacken and smoke. He pursed his lips and blew on it. I watched him. I dipped the shot glass under the water, then used my finger to swirl the salt and water together. I cradled my tit and lifted the shot glass to my nipple and quickly turned it face down, so the rim hugged my skin tightly and the water sloshed around the piercing, trapped between my skin and the glass.

I shrugged.

Rand started to laugh. He turned off the heat, and I peeled the glass away from my skin and let the water pour down my stomach. He grabbed me, one hand on my hip, the other clutched around the back of my neck. He kissed my skin like he was in love with my body—my swollen, tweaked body—starting at the base of my neck and working his way down. He kissed the hard space in between my breasts. He kissed the piercing, then opened his mouth and filled it with my nipple and sucked in hard. It burned. I thought it might bleed again. It was like he wanted to suck the poison out. I wobbled, held on to his shoulders to keep from falling. His tongue slid down my skin toward my stomach. He kissed the spaces between each rib, the soft skin of my hips. His tongue inched closer and closer to my scar. It waited there on the side of my body like a roadblock. I knew, soon enough, he wouldn't be able to avoid it. I wondered if he would even try. Something wicked blistered inside me. It was growing fatter, redder, more tender. I dug my nails into Rand's shoulders and hoped that, one day, somebody would remove it.

The Actor Naked

The first time I saw the actor naked was by accident. We didn't have that kind of relationship. I was walking from my office—a small room off the kitchen that also functioned as a training area for the actor's Labrador puppy—down the long marble hallway that led to the living room. The gas fireplace was broken and I had to mess with the switch to fix it. Also, the actor was going to have a new painting hung above the mantel, and I needed to take the measurements. At the end of the hallway, beyond the living room, the door to his bedroom was open. It was eleven o'clock in the morning, which was around the time he finished using his rowing machine in the gym. He could have been in there still, rowing away. But he wasn't. He walked straight into the doorframe, ass naked, his ass facing me while he stared out the window at the Empire State Building.

I had been the actor's assistant for six months and already knew almost everything about him. He was a small man— five foot five inches, my height exactly. He was fifty-two years old with frail arms and legs and a little patch of basal cell carcinoma on the top of his head where he was beginning to bald. He rubbed medicated cream on the patch every night. (I picked it up from the fancy pharmacy on the corner of 57th and Sixth.) His face was long and horsey (the bags under his eyes had nailed him a lot of villain roles) and well suited for his infatuation with Greek philosophy. He wore a size eight shoe, which almost looked too big on him, especially when he was wearing his vintage cowboy boots.

Now I could see that his ass was bony and drooped toward the floor a bit, almost like an older woman's. It was small and pale like the rest of him, exactly what I would have expected, except for a large red birthmark shaped like Long Island in the center of the left cheek.

I had to think quickly. If I kept walking like business as usual, he'd hear my shoes against the marble and turn around. The thought of coming face-to-face with the actor naked was sort of unbearable. He was known to spring into accents when uncomfortable (a month beforehand, when I'd asked him for a raise, he'd said, "Ask me again in three months, m'lady," in a distinctly Scottish accent), and if I had to listen to him panic in a French accent or something while staring at his dick, I didn't think I'd be able to recover. The only way to get out of this situation unscathed, I figured, was to slip my shoes off and tiptoe back to my office.

I knelt down slowly and began to untie my laces, making sure their plastic tips didn't tap the marble floor once they were loose. When I looked up, the actor's ass was still there, his birthmark staring me down. I wondered, briefly, if he'd left his bedroom door open on purpose. Maybe he wanted to feel the cheap thrill of public nudity without any of the consequences. I held the heel of my left shoe in place and wiggled my foot out while pressing my right hand against the wall to keep from falling over. My foot slipped free and I switched sides, steadying myself with my left hand against the left wall. The whole time I was in a staring contest with the actor's ass. I was trying to stay alert, to keep an eye out in case the ass made any sharp, unexpected movements. I tried to wiggle my foot out of my shoe, but the marble floor was more slippery against my sock than I'd accounted for. My foot slipped and I lost my balance. Instinctively, I slammed my hand against the wall to keep from falling over. The actor turned around.

His dick was about the size of a man's thumb. His balls sagged below it, and tufts of dark pubic hair surrounded all of it like a creepy, wiry wreath.

"Oh, no," he said. Then he jumped back into the corner of the room where I couldn't see him.

I stood there, with one shoe off, staring at the empty space where the actor's naked body had been. Not only had I seen his ass, dick, and balls, but he'd noticed me, practically undressing myself as if I were going to walk over there and join him at the window. Why had I needed to take my shoes off, anyway? And why had I been staring so intently? I felt like I'd been hypnotized, knocked senseless by something glowing and all-powerful. Not just an ass, but a famous ass. A famous ass whose bills I paid, whose lunches I ordered, whose medications I picked up, and whose credit card numbers I'd memorized.

And then there were the famous dick and balls to consider. What was I supposed to do with those? Forget them? Continue booking their first-class airfare and screening their calls and walking their dog as if they hadn't revealed some top-secret information to me in a moment of weakness?

I thought about quitting, leaving silently to rid us all of the shame. But for some reason I stayed. I picked up my shoe, limped back to my piss-stained office, sat in my chair, and waited.

We would be flying to Pensacola the following morning to shoot a movie called *Pyramid Scheme*, about a pyramid scheme. It was an indie produced and directed by a guy who was once a regular on *CSI: Miami*. Production was putting the actor up in a rancher on set, in which they'd installed a rowing machine and a wine refrigerator, stocked the living room with Tolstoy novels, and replaced the regular showerhead with a rainfall showerhead, all per my request, per the actor's preferences. After all, he was number one on the call sheet, the film's fearless leader. And I was his assistant, guard of the iPhone and deliverer of LaCroix. They were putting me up in the spare bed in the *CSI: Miami* guy's attic. He was married with two kids, one of the PAs told me in an email, so there wasn't anything creepy about it.

But now, things were different. The nudity had rearranged the molecular makeup of our relationship. Would the actor even want me in Pensacola? Certainly he'd feel uncomfortable asking the girl who'd just stared down his balls to take charge of his iPhone, to pack his suitcase.

Back in my office, I swiveled side to side in my chair. I put my shoe on. I blinked and saw the Long Island birthmark etched across the back of my eyelids. I decided to stop blinking, officially. I checked my email. Amie from Costume wanted to know the actor's hat size. Ryan, his manager, asked if he had read the script yet, the one about the giant killer snake.

If they don't hear from us soon, they're passing to Fassbender, he wrote. This was Ryan's third email about the killer-snake script this week. I'd been ignoring him. The actor had been offered the role of Jack Todd, an American assassin in Tokyo hired to take out a mysterious giant boa constrictor that was ravaging the city. Here's how it ended:

> JACK TODD mounts the snake's tail as it thrashes through the city, destroying buildings and eating people. He scurries up the body of the snake as the swallowed human bodies rumble beneath his feet. He carries a huge steak knife in his right hand. He reaches the snake's head and loses balance momentarily, but finds his footing. The knife nearly falls from his grip. The snake opens its mouth with a hiss. As his adrenaline builds, JACK TODD raises his arm and jams the steak knife into the snake's eye. The snake writhes, then collapses. JACK TODD removes the knife and wipes it on his shirt to clean it of the snake's blood. He makes eye contact with the camera.
>
> JACK TODD: I hope you like your snake rare.

It wasn't my job to determine which scripts were good and which were bad. My job was to schedule the actor's yoga lessons, order his chicken tacos on gluten-free tortillas at noon daily, run lines with him on the terrace, walk the dog, answer the phone, call the car, schedule the housekeeping, and, in his words, "keep shit from blowing up." But I couldn't bring myself to remind him about the killer-snake script. I wanted to believe that he was superior to that type of role, that he was a serious artist above all else.

He'd made a living playing sinister characters in dark movies—he was the heroin addict in *Bluest Dawn*, the murderous outlaw in *Of the Plains*. He'd made a fantastic death row prisoner, a killer crooked politician, and a pretty convincing homicidal Vietnam vet. The truth was he was ridiculously talented, but recently I'd started to question his judgment. *Pyramid Scheme* was the first lead role he'd accepted in a while, but the film was low budget, risky, and spearheaded by a bunch of first-timers—probably an embarrassing flop. If he got involved with the killer-snake people, too, I'd have to rethink everything. I could only feel good about my job if I had confidence in his, so I deleted Ryan's email and replied to Amie from Costume that the actor's head was a size seven and a half.

Sometime later, my intercom beeped.

"Can you come to my office?" The actor's voice was strained, like he was lifting something heavy.

"Be right there." As I shuffled down the hallway, I prepared myself for the possibility that he'd still be naked. Maybe, now that the seal had been broken, he'd be naked all the time. I could handle that—I'd just have to normalize his dick in my mind as though it were a more ordinary body part, an earlobe.

I walked through the living room, around the corner, and stopped outside his office door, which was closed. I held my ear to it as if I'd be able to hear whether he was clothed.

"*Agh!*" he screamed.

When I opened the door, he was doing a headstand against the floor-to-ceiling window, his legs pressed up against the glass to steady himself. He was not naked. He wore jeans and his cowboy boots and a floral-patterned oxford shirt tucked in with a belt so it didn't fall over his head. His face was flushed, his eyes concentrated on the stack of Knausgaard memoirs under his desk.

"Am I straight?" he asked.

"No."

"Dammit." He tensed his legs so they hovered near the window but didn't touch it. "What about now?"

"Sort of?"

"Fuck. Can you straighten me? I need to know what straight feels like."

I stood over him so my feet sort of straddled his face. As I grabbed his boots and pulled them farther away from the wall, all his weight fell on me. I adjusted my feet and leaned into him to keep from falling backward. His shins pressed against my chest. His crotch grazed my left thigh. There were enough layers of denim between my thigh and his dick that I could barely feel it, but I sensed it there. And I knew exactly what it looked like, behind all that denim.

The actor shifted his weight on his hands, and his crotch swiveled against my leg. He didn't seem to notice.

"Do you have me?" he said, panting.

"Yeah, one sec." I grabbed his knees and pushed them straight, and his legs lifted warily off my body. I walked backward slowly with my hands braced in case he fell. "You're straight."

"Okay, start counting. I need to hold this for one minute."

I counted in my head, nodding with each second. He grunted. His body shook. When I got to sixteen, his hips gave out and he fell forward.

"Goddamn it," he said, slumped on the floor. "I need to get this by Thursday. It's a pivotal scene—it's how he comes up with the idea, you know, for the scheme." He paused, trying to remember a line. " 'The weight of your body upon your scalp eliminates the weight of the world from your shoulders.' "

Stupid.

"I know," I said. "I read the script."

"Do they have a headstand guy down there?"

"Apparently the line producer is a yoga instructor. He does retreats and stuff."

"Make sure you warn them that I don't have it yet."

I watched his cheeks fade from red to pale as the blood drained from his face. Sweat pricked my armpits. I didn't expect a grand speech, but was he really not going to mention it?

"What time is the flight tomorrow?"

"Eight."

"And you called the car?"

"Yep."

"And the dog sitter?"

"She'll be here at six A.M."

He smiled at me like I was his newborn baby, like he was thrilled that I simply existed.

"Best assistant I ever had."

I walked out of his office, unsure if we'd come to an understanding. I called in his tacos.

"Two chicken tinga tacos," I said to the woman who picked up the phone. "Extra serrano peppers, no guacamole. And can you use those carb-free tortillas?"

★ ★ ★

When we arrived in Pensacola the next morning, the director-producer, Troy, and his family were waiting for us at the airport. Troy was a big guy with a meaty neck and sloped shoulders. He wore a tight orange T-shirt and cargo shorts. I recognized him from *CSI: Miami*. He looked like he'd spent a lot of time in the gym since then. His wife was petite and blonde, athletic looking. She was carrying a baby in a sling wrapped around her torso, smoothing the baby's head with one hand and holding their toddler's wrist with the other.

"Fuckin' A," Troy said. He wrapped his arms around the actor and slapped him on the back. "No turning back now."

I stood behind the actor and waited to be acknowledged. Troy's wife poked her head out from behind her husband. I noticed she was wearing blue eye shadow.

"Hi, I'm Tracy." She raised her daughter's wrist in the air and shook it. "This is Silvia, and this little lump of lard is Daniel."

"Tinsie," I said.

"So this is the killer who screens all my calls," Troy said, pointing at me.

"Hi." I fought the urge to curtsy. "Sorry."

"I should give you a raise for putting up with this fucker," the actor said to me. His eyes were beaming, like he'd just been inducted into an exclusive club he'd always wanted to join. It didn't make any sense to me—he was a Juilliard-trained star. He had two Golden Globes. Troy looked like a transformer who lived off beef jerky.

"Let's give my star the tour," Troy said.

The majority of the movie would be filmed in a trailer park near the bay that separated Florida from Alabama. The rancher that production had rented for the actor was down the street from the park. As Troy drove, pointing out which scenes we'd shoot where, the actor gazed out the car window.

"Magnificent," he said, pointing at a leathery-tan man sitting in a lawn chair, his feet propped up on the plastic rim of a kiddie pool.

"You forget what America is like, up there in your fancy city," Troy said.

"Sure do," said the actor.

Troy stopped the car to let a woman in denim shorts and a sports bra drag a propane tank across the gravel road in front of us.

"You see?" the actor said, nudging me, as if everyone outside the car were also an actor, putting on a show specifically for us. His shoulder, pressed up against mine, felt more familial than anything. Maybe this was what our relationship would be like, now that I'd seen him naked. But the more I thought about this, the creepier I felt.

The woman got halfway across the road, then dropped the tank, kicked it, and stomped off in frustration. My stomach ached. I realized I'd forgotten to pack the actor's Imodium.

When we got to the rancher, Troy put the car in park and carried the actor's luggage to the door—one suitcase under each hefty arm. The actor hopped out of the car and followed cautiously. He didn't nudge my shoulder again or say goodbye. In the seat behind me, the toddler sneezed into her hands.

"Good girl," Tracy said, staring at the kid through the rearview mirror. She made eye contact with me briefly and I tried to smile, but now alone in the back seat, I felt a little uneasy, like I'd lost my armor. Without the actor next to me, there was nothing to distance me from Troy and Tracy but a few feet of stale air. As Troy got back into the car, the urge to cry crept up my throat.

"Back to the mother ship," he said, and pulled out of the driveway.

★   ★   ★

Troy's house was small but gaudy, a miniature concrete mansion with a terra-cotta roof and two sphinx statues guarding the front door. Inside was fully carpeted with mostly white pleather furniture, glass tabletops decorated with glass figurines, and framed photos of the family all wearing the same tribal-patterned clothing. Tracy showed me around the house while Troy blended margaritas in the kitchen. She led me to the corner of the living room where another smaller, wooden room had been built into the wall beside the couch.

"Our sauna." She opened the door, walked into the tiny room, and sat down on the built-in bench. "I come in here to hide from the kids. It locks from the inside. Sometimes I don't even turn the infrared lights on. I just sit here in the dark."

She closed her eyes, leaned her head back against the wood. The edge of carpet surrounding the sauna was stiff and stained a murky brown, like an old, dried-out sponge.

"Do me a favor," she said, "leave me in here a minute." She kept her eyes closed and rested her hands on her stomach.

"Do you want me to close this?"

"Just for a minute."

I shut the door. Behind me, Troy was walking out of the kitchen with a margarita in each hand.

"Cheers," he said, handing me one. He sat down on the couch. Some of his drink spilled over the rim of the glass into his lap.

"So what can you tell me about the old man?" he asked. "What's he like on set?"

"Oh, you know"—I hovered by the couch's arm—"he likes to look at his takes."

"I'm a very hands-on director."

I had a bad feeling about them, about Pensacola and the whole thing. I imagined Troy drunk and bloated on set, stuffing his face with Cheez Whiz and crackers that Tracy had packed for him as a midday snack.

"He's a micromanager." Tracy's voice was muffled from inside the sauna.

"Sauna kicks ass," Troy said, lifting his drink in its direction.

We each drank two margaritas while Tracy made dinner, which was tilapia slathered in mayo and baked in the oven for twenty minutes. After, Troy disappeared to the garage and Tracy showed me to the attic. There was no bed up there, just a blow-up mattress lying deflated on the dusty wood floor.

"I'm so sorry," Tracy said. "I thought I made this up."

She plugged the cord into the wall and we both watched as the motor vroomed and inflated the mattress. Tracy put the sheets on, then pulled a comforter from its plastic bag and threw it over the bed.

"I'm sure you're used to a more luxurious setup," she said, staring at the bed. "But you know how these independent films are."

"It's okay. Last time they put me in a Super 8 and the toilet was clogged."

"That's terrible." She held her hand over her mouth dramatically as if holding in a gasp. She looked like she was auditioning for a commercial, like if she showed enough faces maybe someone would notice and stick her in the movie.

"It all depends on the production," I said.

In the room below us, the baby began to cry.

"Well, okay then," she said, then walked back downstairs.

That night, I dreamed about the actor naked. He was yelling at me for buying the wrong type of Brie cheese. The whole time he was scratching his balls, telling me to look him in the eye and apologize. I started crying, and when I woke up, I was sweating and panting. I felt grimy and blamed it on the humidity, the synthetic smell of air freshener wafting up from the floor below. As I watched the dusty orange light peek through the window, I wondered how long I'd be able to stand it there.

★   ★   ★

On set the next morning, the actor was in the makeup trailer, scrolling through dehumidifiers on his iPad.

"Here." He handed me the iPad. "Just get the best one. This humidity is making me soggy."

I took the iPad and his iPhone and the watch he'd forgotten to remove from his wrist and put them all in my bag.

I stood behind him and watched the makeup artist trim his fake beard.

"Not too neat." The actor stared at me through the mirror. "I've been meaning to talk to you about something."

"Okay." I stood up a little straighter to prove that I was mature enough to handle an uncomfortable conversation about nudity, privacy, the raw nature of artistic expression, or whatever. I wished the makeup artist would leave us to have this conversation alone, but she just stood there like she was deaf, gluing a tuft of scraggly hair to his sideburn.

"I don't mean this to come off as insensitive as it might sound. My Sancho—maybe you know him, or know of him?"

Sancho was the name he'd adopted on set for whoever was number two on the call sheet—an odd power move that usually went right over actors' heads, which he'd laugh about in private later on.

I'd read the call sheet a thousand times, highlighting the actor's call times and setting alarms in my phone. But I hadn't looked at anyone else's name.

"I don't know," I said.

"Well, he's a kid. Not a *kid* kid. But you know, your age. And I get the sense that this set isn't *exciting* enough for him. When we spoke this morning, he kept talking about Atlanta. 'In Atlanta we did this, in Atlanta we did that.' He was shooting *Hercules*, or something."

"Okay," I said, suddenly feeling a little lost. I looked at the makeup artist, but she kept her eyes on the actor's cheek.

"It's never good to work with an unhappy actor," he said.

"Right."

"I was thinking I could loan you to him, for the day."

He paused.

"What I mean is, you could assist him, instead of me, just for the time being. You're both young. Maybe you could keep him entertained."

"Entertained?"

"Yeah, you know. Talk to him. Go out on the town. I think he's used to more of a scene."

I pulled the call sheet up on my phone and zoomed in on the second name: Arlo Banks. I knew who he was. When I was a teenager, I'd had his *Teen Bop* magazine poster plastered to the wall above my bed. I'd stand on my pillows and press my face against the glossy plastic so our lips gently touched. But after a while, the paper of his lips turned hard and wrinkly, which made him look like he had cold sores, so I threw the poster in the garbage.

"Arlo Banks is on this movie?" I said, sort of accidentally. He'd starred in three big studio films in the last year. All of them were terrible. That was sort of his thing. He'd built a reputation for taking his shirt off and cracking quippy one-liners in movies that often lost millions at the box office. If Arlo Banks was doing *Pyramid Scheme*, the film's fate was pretty much sealed.

"Oh, you know how these kids do it. One minute they're serious about their career, the next they're off spearfishing in Guatemala."

I had no idea what he was talking about.

"Anyway, you'll do it? I need him to be ready to roll. Can't have him blowing the film."

"Sure. I'll talk to him."

"That's fantastic. Just make him feel like he should be happy to be here. And if my phone rings, take the message. Or come find me if it's important. And make sure they have that pamplemousse sparkling water."

I walked out of the trailer and sat down on its stoop. I was so confused about everything. What was I supposed to do with Arlo Banks? Take him to bingo night? Was this the actor's way of letting me go gently, pawning me off onto some other star so he could quietly disappear behind his naked shame?

I looked up Arlo Banks on my phone. He was just as attractive, all grown-up. He had a short, scruffy beard and neatly trimmed hair. He looked tan. I found a video of him skiing down a tall, snowy mountain, and another of him jumping into a lake from a rope tied to a tree. He was shirtless in that one, and you could see all six of his abs, the indent of his hips. Something inside of me began to dance. I had a crush on him, still—only now it felt more real, like I was scanning his online dating profile. I went back to the makeup trailer and put on some blush and mascara and ChapStick.

★　★　★

About an hour later, I found Arlo Banks in his chair beneath the tent production had set up at the first location: a rusty, lopsided trailer that was meant to be the main character's home pre-scheme, pre-millions. The actor was inside the trailer, shooting his first scene. Arlo Banks was on his phone, paying no attention to me. I walked up to him and said, "It's hot."

"As balls," he said to his phone. I thought of the actor's balls.

"I'm Tinsie." I sat down in the unmarked chair next to him.

"Like Tinseltown."

"I guess so." I stared straight ahead at the trailer, but I could feel him looking at me now, trying to figure out where I'd come from.

"Are you a PA?"

"Yeah," I lied. I suddenly felt ashamed of my job. At least the production assistants had big filmmaking dreams. They were there to advance their careers, to learn their way around a camera or a boom mic. I had landed this job because I was good at paying attention to details and buying gifts for people, and I stayed in it because standing next to a famous person made me feel important. In the world of celebrity personal assisting, I could only hope to graduate, one day, to a bigger and better actor. I could imagine myself carting a laundry bag of Brad Pitt's denim jackets to the dry cleaner, or ironing Oprah's crispy white shirts. But I felt pathetic in the presence of someone as carelessly famous as Arlo Banks. I wanted him to believe, or at least consider, that I might be a vaguely special, talented person.

The actor's voice echoed from inside the trailer: "Fuck! Why can't I remember that line?"

"That dude is so intense," Arlo Banks said. "He makes me feel like a bad actor."

"You aren't a bad actor."

"You don't have to do that. I know what kind of actor I am. I won a Kids' Choice Award."

"Oh." I wondered what kind of actor he thought he was.

He pulled a vape pen from his shirt pocket. "Do you smoke?"

Some nights, after six o'clock, the actor would have the housekeeper pour me a glass of red wine and bring it to my desk. But that only happened if I'd done something especially useful, like when I landed him a reservation at the two-tabled, Michelin-star sashimi house in Tribeca, or when I found his Soviet-era gold watch wedged in the body of the baby grand piano.

"Sure, yeah."

"I don't think you do," Arlo Banks said. "Not really."

"Oh." I felt I lacked the appropriate kind of experience to continue the conversation.

"I don't really, either." He placed the pen between his lips, inhaled, then opened his mouth and released a cloud of vapor. He blew it away from me.

From inside the trailer, I heard Troy's voice: "Let's get that again!"

Arlo Banks put the pen back in his mouth and, lungs full, said, "I should probably be watching."

"Oh, right." I stood up. "I'm sorry, I didn't mean to distract you."

"You aren't distracting me."

"Okay." I hovered, unsure if I should disappear forever.

"I wrap at four today."

I got this feeling that he wanted me to follow him around. Or maybe he wanted to be followed by someone, it didn't matter who. I thought about this possibility for a few moments and then decided I was probably secondhand high.

While I was standing there, stupidly contemplating my potential new role in Arlo Banks's life, the actor's phone vibrated in my bag. I dug it out and read the message from Ryan:

Need ansr re: jake todd by tmrw. Did u read? Call me.

When I looked up from the message, Arlo Banks was walking away.

★　★　★

For the rest of the day, I conspicuously followed Arlo Banks from scene to scene. A few times, I offered him a sparkling water.

"No thanks," he said, and the last time he looked at me funny, like he wasn't sure if I was a paid employee or a crazy fan who'd somehow sneaked onto set to stalk him and maybe poison his drink.

That afternoon, the actor prepped for his big headstand scene against the giant drinks cooler inside the tent—the bald spot of his head pressed into the dirt, his legs wobbling above him. I found Arlo back in his chair, hunched over his phone. I stood behind him again, pretending to be invested in the iPad.

Troy rushed past us. The collar of his shirt was dark with sweat.

"You need Willy?" he asked. "He can center your chakra."

"I got it," the actor said, upside down. He blinked at me, then blinked away.

"Whenever you're ready," Troy said.

The actor slowly lowered his feet to the ground, stood upright, and shook the dirt out of his hair. He raised his arms above his head and stretched from side to side. Then he casually kicked off his shoes, unbuttoned his shirt and tossed it to the side, and unzipped his pants and shimmied out of them. His checkered boxer briefs hung loose around his thighs, as if they'd been stretched from too much wear. He nudged their waistband down, and they fell right to the ground.

Nobody seemed shocked. Nobody stared at his naked body. Arlo Banks remained slouched in his chair, his head hung over his phone. He glanced up at the actor lazily, then carried on scrolling, as if this were all just part of the script, which it wasn't, I was sure. But this kind of thing happened all the time, didn't it? Directors made last-minute changes. Actors went rogue with improvisation. Certainly, this decision had nothing to do with me.

The actor walked out to the road, positioned himself in front of the cameras, and knelt down and put his head in the dirt. He struggled for a second to rest his knees on his elbows—his ass spread wide and trembling as he worked his legs against his arms, his birthmark gleaming in the Florida sun—but eventually he was straight.

"Bingo," Troy said.

I was so focused on looking away from the actor that I hadn't realized Arlo Banks had turned and was staring right at me.

"You look like you're going to puke," he whispered.

"Oh. Sorry. I mean, I'm okay."

He dug his pen from his pocket and handed it to me. "It'll help."

I took the pen, placed it between my lips, and inhaled slowly. I felt my throat clog and I tried not to cough. I heard the actor topple to the ground.

"Cut!" Troy said.

"Fuck me," the actor said. "Fuck, fuck, fuck." I felt his voice growing nearer, and before I could hand Arlo's pen back to him, the actor was upon us, standing with his feet turned out and his hands on his hips.

"Can I have the iPad," he said, looking at the pen in my hand.

I threw the pen into Arlo's lap and dug into my bag for the actor's iPad. I unlocked it, handed it to him. He swiped his finger back and forth, up and down, on the screen. I tried to imagine what he was doing but couldn't think of anything so urgent he had to address it mid-scene. His eyes were unfocused, frantically following his finger all over the screen, biding time.

"Tighten your abs," Arlo said, glancing up from his phone. "If you keep your core strong, you won't fall."

The actor nodded. He handed the iPad back to me. For a minute, he didn't move, just stood there in front of me with his dick out like he was waiting for something. He adjusted his stance, craned his neck to the left, then to the right. I could practically hear his dick talking at me: *Look. Are we good?*

For the briefest second, I looked.

He turned and walked back to the road and positioned himself in front of the camera. I stared at the ground, unsure of what to do with myself. I felt like I had been caught, but I wasn't sure what for.

Arlo stared off at the camera. "It's way past four." He stood up from his chair and stretched his arms above his head. "Let's go."

He started walking—away from the scene, the tent, the actor's ass as he toppled over into the dirt again. I took the actor's phone out of my bag, placed it on the chair with the iPad, and followed him.

He stopped outside a double-wide trailer with two lawn chairs sitting crooked by the front door. A dusty umbrella lay on its side between them.

"This is my trailer." He pointed to it. "We can go inside or we can sit out here on these chairs."

"Okay."

"Okay, you want to go inside? Or you want to sit in the chairs?"

I had no idea. I'd been on a movie set before, but I'd never felt this stupid and out of place. I couldn't stop thinking about the actor's dick, all confident and confrontational, trying to scare me away. Suddenly it occurred to me, as I dug my foot into the dirt, that I was being invited into the home of my childhood celebrity crush. How many times had I practiced kissing his two-dimensional lips? How often had I sat in front of my TV gazing into his icy eyes as he pranced around the screen? Now, here we were: two adults stranded together in a strange, swampy land. It didn't feel the way I'd imagined it.

"Inside," I said.

He opened the door to the trailer, and I followed him in. There was nothing special about the inside—no personalized bookshelves, no mini wine fridge. There was a scratchy-looking couch and a small kitchen and vinyl-paneled walls disguised as wood. I noticed an Xbox had been hooked up to the TV.

"Do you have an assistant?" I asked.

"Fuck no." He opened the refrigerator and grabbed two bottles of beer. "I've always said the day I need an assistant is the day I need to quit Hollywood. It's like, once you've got one, you stop seeing the humanity in people. I've seen it happen a million times—actors treating their assistants like mules. I might quit, anyway."

I thought of the time the actor made me drive three and a half hours to his beach house in Montauk to fetch him the tie he'd forgotten in his closet. Only now, in the memory, he was naked. I couldn't resist the image—his body all bony and droopy, despite the amount of time he spent on his rowing machine. I wondered if I'd ever be able to imagine him clothed again, or if his nudity had engulfed him completely, and now every time I thought of him I'd have to see his little thumb-dick and that freaky Long Island birthmark.

"You shouldn't quit," I said. "You're good."

I didn't know if I meant he was a good actor, which he wasn't, or a good person, which I had no idea about. Maybe I just wanted to say "good" out loud to speak the feeling into existence.

Arlo handed me the beer.

"Cheers." He smirked as he watched me lift the beer to my mouth. I felt my face get hot. A few silent moments passed. Then he said, "I don't mean for this to sound creepy, but can you take your hair down?"

"My hair?" I touched the hair tie at the base of my neck.

"I don't know why. It just makes me feel more relaxed."

I yanked the tie out of my hair and ran my hands along my scalp to shake out the knots. "Good?"

Good, I thought. *This is good. I am good. We are good.*

"Yeah," he said, walking toward me. He reached out and touched my hair. I stood very still and waited for him to let go or say something, but he did neither. He lifted the tips of my hair to his face and brushed them against his cheek.

"I'm sorry," he said, but he didn't let go. "Sometimes I do weird shit. It's like, whenever I'm filming, I feel so out of my body. Or maybe I feel in my body but out of my mind, like my brain is occupied by someone else and I just have to sit here and wait until they give it back to me."

"Who's in your brain right now?" The way his fingers tugged at the longer strands of my hair felt almost like a massage.

"I think it's me. But me from a long time ago, before I was anybody. Like I'm looking at you and thinking you're my fourth-grade math teacher. Miss Raines, or something. I feel like I felt in Miss Raines's class. Like I'm about to be humiliated."

"I'm not going to humiliate you."

He let go of my hair, took a step back. "This is going to be a shit movie, isn't it?"

I wasn't sure what he wanted to hear.

"Oh, I don't know. It could be artsy."

"I don't do artsy."

"Well." I didn't know what else to say.

"Just tell me it's going to be shit."

It felt sort of nice, being told what to say. For the first time in a while, I didn't have to think so hard.

"It's going to be shit."

He nodded, then shifted on his feet. He looked uncomfortable. "Tell me it's going to be all my fault. I'm a trash actor, a fraud. Something like that."

"Um, it's all your fault."

He stepped toward me again, stuffed his face into my hair. I didn't know if I should feel afraid or excited. I could smell the beer on his breath and a hot Florida day's worth of sweat on his neck.

"You smell like my fucking childhood," he said into my hair.

I wasn't sure what to do with that information.

"Say it again. Tell me I'm trash."

My phone buzzed in my back pocket. "One second," I said, pulling away from him. I took out my phone and read the message.

Need Imodium.

I put the phone on the counter behind me.

"Sorry," Arlo Banks said, looking embarrassed. "That was a weird thing to do."

"It's okay." I felt like I'd started to make a wrong decision, and now the only option was to follow through with it. It wasn't a bad feeling.

"You're trash," I said.

"I am."

"You're the worst actor I've ever met."

He drove his hand up my shirt. My phone vibrated on the counter. I turned to look at the message.

What is killer snake script?

He slid my shirt up and over my head, unhooked my bra, and tossed it to the floor.

"Tell me I'm disgusting," he said.

"You're disgusting."

I felt magnificent. I had nothing on my mind. It was as if I were reading from a script, mindlessly filling in a role for someone else.

My phone started to ring, vibrating steadily against the countertop. I ignored the call as Arlo Banks slid his tongue down my chest.

Call me now.

"Tell me I'm dog shit."

"You're dog shit."

He lifted me up onto the kitchen counter, gathered a clump of my hair in his fist, and pulled it backward, so my chin was pointed up at the ceiling. My phone vibrated violently beside us.

Arlo Banks let go of my hair and rested his hand at the base of my neck. He squeezed like he was trying to gently force something out of my throat. I felt an intense need to escalate things, to establish dominance or at least to prove that I wasn't afraid, so I placed my hand on top of his and squeezed harder. It was difficult to breathe, but I stared right into his eyes and waited for something to happen. And then, just as my head started to drift away, he let go of my neck. I gasped, but before I could catch my breath, he grabbed my hand in his and put my pointer finger in his mouth. I steadied my breath and watched him suck on my finger, slowly pulling away until all that was left inside his mouth was the tip of my nail. He smirked at me as he bit down and tore it off.

I yanked my hand away.

"What the fuck." I stared at my finger, the nail torn and jagged.

Arlo Banks swallowed. I imagined my nail scraping the inside of his throat.

"Are you okay?" I genuinely wanted to know.

He didn't say anything, just stared at me, a faint smile spread across his lips.

I stared at my hands and tried to be smart. "Do you want to do the others?"

He nodded.

I stuck my hand in his face. He put my fingers in his mouth one by one, bit the nails off, and swallowed them.

"You're all so fucking nuts," I said as he closed his lips around my pinkie.

He looked right through me. He bit down on my nail and slowly ripped at it until it came off. It pulled a little skin with it, and I could feel the sting of blood rising to the surface. He spit my finger out of his mouth. I hopped off the counter and put on my bra and T-shirt.

"Should I leave?"

For a moment, I thought I saw something apologetic in his eyes—that glassy inward gaze of regret. But then, as if on autopilot, he shimmied his pants and underwear down to his ankles and lay face down on the counter where I'd just been sitting, his legs jutting out straight behind him into the kitchen space. He tucked one hand under his pelvis and adjusted himself, and the next thing I knew, his dick was poking out from in between his thighs, almost like a tail.

"I'm sorry," he said into the laminate countertop, his voice muffled. "You can touch it."

★   ★   ★

It wasn't until he'd closed the door behind me and I'd walked about a half mile down the dirt road that I realized I'd left my phone behind. I considered going back, knocking on the door, waiting for Arlo to open it or otherwise pretend he couldn't hear me. But the thought of seeing him again made my stomach ache. So instead, I walked the four miles back to Troy's house. When I got there, two hours later, Troy and Tracy were sitting on their shiny white couch watching *Wheel of Fortune*. Their toddler was sitting on the floor, wiping something sticky and purple on the carpet.

"What happened to you?" Troy said. He kept his eyes on the TV. I folded my arms across my chest. "Your boss was looking for you. He's been calling."

"I'm getting fired," I said, staring at the TV.

Tracy blinked away from the TV and looked at me. She glanced at my neck, and I wondered if Arlo Banks had left a mark there.

"You should use the sauna." She nodded to the corner of the room where the wooden structure stood. "Believe me, after a tough day, it's just what the doctor ordered."

"Oh, shit," Troy said. "You gotta try the sauna. There's a shitload of creative energy in there. You know that's where I came up with this script. I passed out for, like, two hours. Had this wild, lucid dream about a knight riding into the mobile home park on a horse, screaming about how the Chinese were coming for us."

"What does that have to do with the script," Tracy said.

"Same basic theme." He yawned.

The idea of locking myself in a dark room didn't sound like the worst thing. I opened the door and peered inside. It smelled sour and stale.

"There's a hook in there for your clothes, and it locks from the inside," Tracy said. "But don't worry. We'll come knocking if you've been in there for too long." She put her feet in Troy's lap and stared blankly at the TV. I watched their eyes glow with the television's reflection as Troy gripped her foot in his hands and squeezed.

"It's Clint Eastwood," Troy said, pointing at the screen. "It's gotta be. See the double O?"

"Reese Witherspoon," Tracy said.

The *Wheel of Fortune* bell dinged. I lifted my shirt over my head and tossed it to the ground. Then I unbuttoned my jeans and kicked them to the side. Neither of them looked at me as I slid my underwear to the floor. I stood under the yellow light of the standing lamp, naked and exposed in the corner of their lives, waiting for a reaction I wasn't even sure I wanted.

"Who the fuck is Evan Rachel Wood?"

After enough time, I opened the door and stepped into the darkness.

High School Junkie Girlfriend

Tonight I'm playing hide-and-seek with Zac Efron. He finds me in his bedroom, topless beneath the sheets, strapped into the pair of Velcro sandals I used to wear as a kid. Last night I was on the beach with Adam Driver. It doesn't matter which beach. The water was turquoise. We ate baguettes and held hands and I asked him to lift me like one of the tiny actresses in his movies. He scooped me up (he's so strong, really, just like you'd expect) and carried me into the sea. Before that, I was at sleepaway camp with Ashton Kutcher—not the current Ashton Kutcher but the boyish, shaggy-haired 2003 version of him. He sneaked into my cabin at lights-out and kissed me in front of all my bunk-mates. There was something between me and Emma Stone one night, in the kitchen of some ballroom hosting some charity event for some cause. I remember cold steel against my skin, the smell of frying oil mixed with Calvin Klein perfume. Ryan Gosling's tongue is rough. Or maybe that was the other Ryan or maybe it was both.

When morning comes, I wake up next to nobody.

"Do you have breakfast?" nobody says. He gets up and struts naked to the kitchen and pulls a bag of stale popcorn from the cabinet. He brings the popcorn to my room and eats it in my bed, sprinkling salty kernels everywhere.

"Last night," he says. "I can do better than that."

He ducks beneath the sheets, enthusiastic, determined, like a kid who's just learned a new sport. He puts his face between my legs, presses his lips to the wrong spot, and starts to hum what might be the alphabet or "The Star-Spangled Banner." I close my eyes and think about last night. Zac Efron had calloused hands, probably from all the rock climbing.

"Success," nobody says, at the end of his song. He's established new parameters for success. I remember he works in sales—something technical. IT software or pharmaceutical equipment. As he gets out of bed and looks for his boxers, my phone dings on the bedside table. He stares at it insecurely. I reach for it. There's an email from Amy.

tues studio city, it says. *will send scenes and dets.*

Amy is my agent. She doesn't have a lot of love in her heart but she always responds to my emails. I haven't heard her voice in almost a year. Every time I read one of her messages I imagine her as a small, portable speaker. A virtual agent. This might be a bad sign, but so far she has landed me a few commercials, one episode of *SVU*, and an indie horror film produced by a man named Damian who went on to produce high-tech hotel showerheads. My role was GROCERY STORE WOMAN TWO. I had two lines: *I thought these beans were on sale* and *[terrified wail]*. I rehearsed the terrified wail in my car so none of my neighbors would hear and think I was being murdered or worse. On set, we did five wail takes. I screamed so hard I lost my voice. The film never went to theaters, but the terrified wail made it into the trailer.

Before all that, before Amy, I did an infomercial for a pair of padded underwear. I was the girl who couldn't sit down comfortably on hard surfaces. In my scene, I attempt to sit down at a picnic table, and when my ass touches the wooden bench, I shoot back up with a face like, *Fuck, that's hard!* Everyone else sitting at the picnic table looks up at me with concern. A nice older man approaches me with his wife. He motions with his finger, like, *Spin around, honey.* So she spins and shows me her ass, which is plump for a woman of her age. Then the husband and I take turns palming the woman's plump ass, looking impressed. Everyone at the picnic table watches and also looks impressed. The woman beams at us proudly. In the next scene, I'm standing beside the same picnic table, this time wearing a pair of ass-plumping underwear beneath my jeans. You can tell because my ass looks twice its normal size. I sit down at the table and reach for a hot dog, laughing and laughing, finally comfortable.

The infomercial was a mistake. Online, they turned my face into a joke. You can type *fuck that's hard girl* or *hard ass infomercial girl* into any search bar and you'll see my wincing face, usually pasted onto something pornographic. People have gotten creative. You can watch whole celebrity sex tapes with my face photoshopped onto their naked bodies. You don't even have to pay for them because my face renders them anonymous. I've seen them all. The whole thing is embarrassing, professionally speaking. Still, I search for myself. Staring at my face attached to a famous body sparks something inside me that I can only describe as motivation.

"Everything okay?" nobody says. His name is something like Calvin. He's standing with his knees slightly bent, ready to save the day. He's giddy thinking about all the support he could give. I'm drawn to him, and other guys like him—Gavins, Dustins, Austins with money to blow. They all want in, according to their names. I tell them I'm an actor and they treat me like a little creative genius in the hopes that I'll give them their own personal show.

"I have an audition." I refresh my email.

"Hey, that's great!" he says. "Should we get pancakes?"

"Sure."

But when we get to the restaurant, he can't decide between pancakes and egg whites.

"I'll start with a green juice," he says to the server. "And a mimosa. Two mimosas. This one just got an audition." He points to me, proud. We hardly know each other. The server stares at me competitively.

"Two mimosas," I say. Last night, in my dreams, I drank champagne from the bottle. I refresh my email again.

Over pancakes and egg whites and mimosas and green juice, the formerly naked man tells me he can't hear so well out of one ear.

"Cauliflower ear." He touches the lumpy flesh. "From wrestling."

He tells me he grew up in Virginia and misses his mom. He likes hiking and wrestling and watching sports on TV. I guess these are all normal things for people to like. He just bought a house in Valley Village, which doesn't excite me the way that he seems to think it should.

"It's the garbage pickup that gets me," he says. "I can never remember to put it out at the right time. Monday night, Monday night, Monday night." He presses his finger to his temple over and over. Then, in a turn of events, he tells me his sister is dead. Overdose, about a year ago. He has spent the last year processing, coming to terms. His friends have been helpful. They call him Griff, which is short for Griffin.

"What about you?"

I tell him that I have always believed, in some tiny pocket of my brain, that I am destined for greatness. Or, at least, that I am destined for fame. Or, at least, that I am destined to be around great or famous people. I'm not claiming to be unique or anything. I'm one of about a hundred million. But I can feel it—not in my gut, more like at the back of my throat, a little itch—something cosmic is going to happen to me. I'm not embarrassed to say it. This audition could be the one that saves my life.

"So are you, like, psychic?" he says.

"Sure. That's exactly it."

He pays the check while I'm in the bathroom, refreshing my email.

The role is HIGH SCHOOL JUNKIE GIRLFRIEND. Three scenes, twenty-one lines—more than I've ever done. HIGH SCHOOL JUNKIE GIRLFRIEND does a lot of yelling and begging. She skips class. She steals money from her brother's piggy bank and breaks into her neighbor's car. There is nothing in this piece of the script about what she looks like or sounds like or what type of drugs she's on, except for this one line that says most of her clothes are too big. On the first page of the last scene, Amy has handwritten the word *breakout* in the white space, which means, in virtual-agent lingo, that this is the scene that could hit big. The scene that could change a person's life. In this breakout scene, HIGH SCHOOL JUNKIE GIRLFRIEND convinces her boyfriend (also a junkie, but a more salvageable one, the one whose sober adulthood the film will follow) to hit her until she passes out. This sort of acting is best practiced on an empty stomach, not one full of pancakes. I will need the rest of the day to digest. Griffin wants to digest with me. He has nothing better to do because it's Sunday, which is a day of rest for people with money to blow.

"I have work," I say.

"Work?" He looks confused, like he suspects I've been lying to him this whole time.

I tell him I work at the hot tub showroom in Pasadena. "We also sell Jet Skis."

"I love Jet Skis."

He says he'll text me. He says he had a really nice time. He says he still thinks he can do better, if I'll give him another shot. The way he talks to me makes me feel powerful.

"We'll see," I say.

★ ★ ★

When I get to the showroom, my boss is in the back, "crunching numbers." This means he's watching YouTube videos. His name is Dash and he looks exactly like a drawing of a person named Dash, except that he's about twenty pounds overweight and is too high to go anywhere in a hurry. He always comments on my untucked shirt and my lunch, which means, I'm pretty sure, that he wants to sleep with me. I don't hate him, but his presence in my life makes me hate myself a little.

"Howdy," he says. He's bleached his hair overnight, and the skin around his hairline is pink and irritated. "Got a batch of floating cup holders we need to get rid of this week." He points to the cardboard box filled with inflatable cup holders next to his desk. "People go crazy over this shit."

"Do they, really?" I nudge the box with my foot.

"Yeah, they really do. What's with the attitude?"

"I'm doing a character."

"Hard Ass?" He imitates the infomercial wince, except when he does it he looks like he's trying to poop. "That shit was great."

"No, a different character. And you look constipated."

He laughs and a dribble of spit slides down his chin. He wipes it away. "Okay, okay. Just, can you tuck in your shirt at least?"

I salute the dead space between us. "Right away, Captain Boss Man Sir."

"Weird character."

All afternoon I roam the floor and try to embody HIGH SCHOOL JUNKIE GIRLFRIEND. I let my hair hang over my face, rub my eyes so the skin around them is irritated. I pace frantically across the room, looking for something—a needle or whatever it is junkies look for. I sit in one of the hot tubs and slump my shoulders and put my feet up on the rim. It's all coming pretty naturally, but it's the hardcore stuff

I'm worried about. The drugs and the slapping and the passing out. That's the stuff that gets you noticed, one way or another.

Dash watches me from the office doorway. "What are you supposed to be, a goblin?"

"Junkie." I slouch lower in the tub.

"Customer," he says. A woman comes through the front door and I hop out of the tub, tuck my hair behind my ears. She asks if she can test out the hot tubs.

"They're all empty." I point to the empty hot tubs.

She blinks at me. She's wearing a bathing suit underneath a sheer button-up blouse. I suddenly feel embarrassed.

"What if the jets aren't powerful enough?" she asks. "Isn't that something I should know before I buy one?"

She looks so disappointed in me. She's a woman whose life has mostly gone her way. I can tell from her diamond earrings and the fresh shock on her face. She isn't waiting around for anything cosmic to happen to her. I want to know how she made all her dreams come true.

"Would you like to sit in one of the empty hot tubs and use your imagination?"

She shakes her head. "My husband is so picky. Like, we've tried all those new mattress brands. The ones that come in the box to your house and then, poof! You know, when you open the box. We've had to send them all back. So now I just like to test everything before we spend the money. It's not the worst problem. I shouldn't complain about it. People have worse problems."

"I'm sorry." I don't want her to remember me as the girl who made her life difficult. "Do you have a pool?"

"Salt water."

I offer her a free floating cup holder as an apology.

"I'll need two. One for my husband."

I give her two floating cup holders and she gives me her husband's business card, asks me to call if anything changes with the hot tubs. According to the business card, her husband's name is Robert Darling, which is just about the most romantic name I've ever heard. I imagine her on the velvet chaise lounge in her parlor, draped in a satin robe and waving a glass of aged Scotch in the hazy, cigar-scented air. *Robert, darling, play us a song.*

I jam the business card into my pocket, thinking maybe I will call Robert Darling. Maybe I'll ask him to meet me at the Beverly Hills Hotel, the Rodeo Suite. I'll wear my wrap dress with the slit and brush my hair long.

"You're paying for those floaters," Dash says to me from his office, once the woman is gone. He walks out with a box of inflatable cup holders. He drops the box by my feet and stares at me with his arms crossed. There's an orange bleach stain on the collar of his shirt. I point to it.

"What size is that?"

He looks down at himself. "Why? Medium. I don't know. Why?"

"Can I have that size?"

"Ew, no." He makes a face like I've just farted in front of him. "This will be ginormous on you."

"I need it for my audition. I need clothes that are too big."

"When's the audition? Are you quitting?"

"Hopefully."

"Huh?"

"Can I just have the shirt? I won't wear it to work."

"Sure, whatever."

He lingers like he's expecting me to thank him for something. I'm about one bad day away from sleeping with him. Each time he gives me that stupid expectant look, the scene comes more and more into focus. It won't be sexy, if it does happen. It will be grim, almost creepy. The way I imagine it, we aren't even naked. We're two desperate nobodies, fully clothed with our hands down each other's khaki uniform pants, using minimal effort to achieve something average. The thought makes me want to cry. I pull my phone from my back pocket and dial Griffin's number.

"I'm free tonight," I say when he answers.

"Whoa, you really are psychic. I was just about to text you. Apparently the new Christopher Nolan is a real mind fuck."

Dash holds one hand to his ear like a phone and then jerks it away while mouthing, *Hang up.* When I don't, he holds his hand to his ear again, then again rips it away, this time with more vigor. He does this a few times, each time getting himself more and more worked up.

"I'll pick you up at seven," Griffin says.

"Great." I hang up.

"What the fuck," Dash says.

I reach into the cardboard box and remove a cup holder, pinch the valve, and hold it to my mouth and blow. It inflates into a miniature inner tube. Dash watches me like he has something to say.

"What?" I say.

"Nothing. I'm taking lunch." He starts to walk away. Then he stops, turns back, hesitates. "Look, do you want half of my tuna sandwich, or what?"

"I'm not eating today."

He huffs away like I've ruined a special moment. Like I've ruined his entire day.

★   ★   ★

The movie is all dark shadows and ominous tones. About halfway in, Griffin reaches over the armrest and puts his hand on my thigh. His eyes are laser focused on the film. He looks like someone whose mind is being fucked. I focus on Christian Bale, who is on-screen, flipping something like time or space upside down. I bet he does all his own stunts. I bet he had a trainer who taught him how to do back hand-springs, how to flip a monster truck tire up a steep hill. All the twisting and somersaulting makes me feel dizzy, and before I know it, my eyelids grow heavy, gravity pulls my head toward my chest.

I am HIGH SCHOOL JUNKIE GIRLFRIEND and Christian Bale is CONCERNED FATHER, which is not hot but maybe helpful professionally. CONCERNED FATHER Christian holds me in his arms and tells me he loves me, that he'd do anything for me. I'm high (high on what? I should find out) but it still feels good to hear. It feels good to be looked after. I'm so hooked on this feeling that I can't remember my line. CONCERNED FATHER Christian looks at me sideways, like, *Get it together.* But I can't remember what comes next. I grab his face in a panic and bring it to mine. I make out with my concerned celebrity father. He drops me on the floor.

When I wake up, Griffin is poking my shoulder. The credits are rolling.

"You fell asleep."

"Just for a minute."

I'm a little sweaty, a little freaked-out. It suddenly feels important to rush home and run my lines. I ask Griffin if he wants to run lines with me, but he says it might be triggering, dead sister and that whole thing. He says he might cry. He agrees to drive me home and make up his mind on the way.

"I'm most concerned about the slapping scene," I tell him in the car. "I've never been slapped."

"Most people would consider that a good thing."

"Have you ever been slapped?"

He thinks about this, then shakes his head. "My sister spit on me once. I think she was trying to be funny, but it was actually pretty gross."

"Was she high?"

"I don't know. Maybe." Griffin turns onto my street and pulls over beneath the streetlamp outside my apartment.

"What was she like when she was high?"

I don't know much about high people. At least, not the chronically high ones. I just imagine them all in mental institutions, frantically scratching their scalps and offering blow jobs to all the nurses in exchange for thimble-size cups of pills. I know this can't be completely true.

"Um." He rubs his eyes with his palms. "It was like she wasn't really there. Like she was only pretending to be there."

I have no idea what this means. "Like acting?"

"Kind of, yeah. Bad acting."

We sit silently in the car for a moment, staring through the windshield at the lit pavement. It occurs to me that we are under a kind of spotlight.

"Did she ever get violent?" I ask. "Like, did she throw things or scratch people?"

"What?" He stares at me.

I remember that he is partially deaf. I take his head in my hands and turn his good ear toward me. "Did she ever scratch people?" I say more slowly.

"No, she never scratched anyone. She was a normal person."

"Normal like you?"

He seems annoyed with me now, like he thinks I'm making fun of him. "I don't want to talk about my sister."

"I'm just trying to figure out this role. For instance, if I knew more about your sister, I could embody her in some way, sort of like a tribute to her."

He blinks at me like that doesn't change anything.

"Think of it as spreading awareness. I just need to know what she was like. Was she tired all the time? Did she ever talk to herself? Did the drugs make her breath smell weird? That kind of stuff."

"Surely you don't need to know all of this just for an audition," he says, as if he knows.

"Of course I do. They could make me do anything. That's the whole point. I have to be prepared for anything. At the very least, I need to know the basics."

"I have to roll the trash out," he says, like he's just remembered. He unbuckles my seat belt and waits for me to get out of his car. When I don't move, he says, "I'll call you tomorrow on my way home from work."

"Sure, whatever." I shove the car door open and get out. "Go sell something." I mean this to be an insult, but it comes out more like a question.

"I'm an accountant," he says, then drives away.

★ ★ ★

All night I run lines in the mirror, but it doesn't feel right. My eyes are too calm, and I can't make my voice sound high or distant enough.

"'I want to feel my blood rush to the surface,'" I say to the mirror, who is actually my junkie boyfriend. "'I want to feel the moment everything stops.'"

It's all sounding too present, too dramatic. It needs to feel lighter, more like a game—or like I think it's a game while also convincing the audience that it's not a game at all. The problem is that I have never been addicted to drugs. I have no idea how to do this "there but not there" thing. I should find a high person and ask them to show me. Or even get high and see for myself. The only high person I know is Dash, so in the morning, I drive to the showroom even though Monday is my day off.

"What kind of drugs?" he asks, when I tell him my plan. His shirt is not tucked in, but I don't say anything because I want him to help me.

"Pills?" I have no idea, but I know that's what Griffin's sister was into. "But I think anything will do."

"Fuck." Dash leans back in his desk chair and runs his hands through his fake-blond hair. "I didn't know you were into that shit."

"I'm not. It's for the role."

"Right." He makes air quotes with his fingers and winks at me. "'The role.'"

He's the biggest idiot I've ever met.

"I have some coke in my car. But if we do it, you have to stay and hang out with me. You can't just leave."

"Okay," I say, feeling like I'm making a great sacrifice in the name of art. Dash tells me to watch the store while he goes to his car, which is parked right out front. He sort of skips to his car, then skips back. I wonder if he has any friends or plans or dreams, or if this upcoming moment will be the greatest thing to ever happen to him. He locks the showroom door behind him and flips the sign to Closed. He glances around the room, then motions for me to follow him. He looks more like somebody pretending to have drugs than somebody who actually has drugs. He's a terrible actor, and I remind myself to tell him this next time he comments on my lunch.

Once we're in his office, Dash pulls from his pocket a little plastic bag filled with white powder. It looks like a sandwich bag for a mouse.

"Do you have any bills?" he asks.

I have only ever seen cocaine on TV. The characters always use credit cards or hotel keys to make white lines on mirrors or glass tables or expensive, framed artwork. Usually there's a gun or a man in a tank top nearby, like Matthew McConaughey or someone who looks like Matthew McConaughey.

"I have no money."

He looks around the room for a better answer, eyeing a hot tub pamphlet on his desk. He grabs the pamphlet, then opens the bag and spills some of the coke onto the desk so it forms a little mound. He uses the spine of the pamphlet to separate the mound into three thin lines, then tears a page out and coils it up into a straw.

I watch him closely, taking note of the way he stuffs the straw into his nostril and leans over the desk. He presses his pointer finger against his other nostril, then sniffs hard, and the straw vacuums up a whole line of cocaine. He stands up, pinches his nose. He holds the pamphlet straw in my direction.

I stare at it. "I've never done this."

"Yeah, yeah." He thinks I'm joking. He thinks I'm like him.

"I mean it."

Dash lets go of his nose and stares at me. "Really?"

"Really."

"The best thing about coke"—he bounces up and down on his toes—"it makes you smarter."

I want to laugh but my life sort of depends on him right now. Whatever happens to me next is his fault—for example, if I start foaming at the mouth or drop dead. I don't like the idea of sudden death in the hot tub showroom, but actors have to rack up experiences like medals. Leonardo DiCaprio, for example, once crawled inside a bear carcass. He told me about it himself, one night, over caviar. And he won an Oscar for that role.

I take the straw and flip it so that the end that was inside Dash's nose is now against the table. I copy all of Dash's steps. The cocaine burns my nose. A warm glob drips down the back of my throat. My eyes feel leaky.

Dash takes the straw back and snorts up the last line, then he walks over to the surplus box of floating cup holders in the corner and blows one up.

"I'm going to be a famous actress," I tell him, suddenly concerned that he does not understand how talented I am. I'm on the brink of being discovered. Just put me onstage and watch me glow.

"Yeah." Dash's face is turning pink from blowing up cup holders. "And I'm a banker."

He's so stupid it hurts me to look at him. I want to punch him in the face, and I feel like I could probably do it and not get fired or even hurt my hand too badly. But that's not why I'm here.

"I need you to run lines with me. And maybe film it so I can watch after."

"We just did lines." He tosses the cup holder to the ground and picks up another. "We should monogram these things. Like, personalize them somehow. This whole place should feel more personal. Hot tub seats that mold specifically to your butt."

His eyes get really wide. I don't have the patience to explain what it means to run lines. I can already feel HIGH SCHOOL JUNKIE GIRLFRIEND crawling into my skin, creeping up my throat.

"'I want to feel my blood rush to the surface.'" I smile wildly and rub my arms as if calling on my own blood. "'I want to feel the moment everything stops.'"

"What the fuck." Dash stares at me, his eyes frantic and glazed. "What are you talking about?"

It seems like he's gearing up to run away, so I walk toward him and put my hands on the wall on either side of his body and trap him there, which feels like a very junkie thing to do.

"'I need this.'"

"Need what?" He pulls at the freaky blond tips of his hair with his fists. "More coke? I have more coke."

He reaches into his pocket, but all of a sudden there's a knock on the showroom door. I jump and run to the opposite corner of the office and stand there on my toes. Dash leans his head into the office doorway.

"Fuck," he says. "This is why you can't give people free shit. They always come back for more."

There's another knock, and a woman says, "Hello? Are you really closed? It's eleven A.M. I see you."

"Go let her in," Dash says.

"I'm not wearing my uniform. I'm not even being paid right now."

"I just gave you drugs."

I can't argue with this logic, so I tiptoe quickly out of the office and unlock the front door.

"Thank you," says the woman. She's wearing the same diamond earrings as last time. A man gets out of a car in the parking lot and walks into the store behind her. He's wearing a slim-fit suit and runs a hand through his slicked hair as he looks around the room. He's tall and thin and younger than I imagined him, almost like a boy dressed up as a mid-century ad executive.

"I brought my husband." The woman motions to Robert Darling, the man himself.

"Hello," I say, with extra pep because I'm feeling worthier of their time than I felt before. "Welcome back."

The woman ignores my glow and instead directs her attention to her husband.

"You pick," she says, gesturing to the array of hot tubs. "I'm sick of making all the decisions."

Rob Darling sticks his hands in his pockets and saunters around the room. His shoes glisten under the store's fluorescent lights. His tie is a little crooked, as if he's already undone it once today. I tuck my hair behind my ears and follow him from tub to tub on my toes.

"This one." He points at a hot tub with purple lights. He knocks on the plastic rim with his fist.

"Do you want to sit in it?" I say. I hop onto the rim of the tub and put my feet inside, smacking them against the plastic like a tap dancer.

Robert Darling stares at me like I'm ridiculous in a cute animal sort of way, then gestures to his suit to show me his attire isn't fit for sitting in an empty hot tub. Silly me.

"Kidding," I say, jumping out of the tub. I ring them up at the register and tell them we can deliver in a week.

"A whole week?" Robert Darling says. The woman looks at me like she's waiting for something to explode.

"Maybe sooner," I lie.

Rob Darling gives me his credit card.

"Hey." He points at my nose. "You look just like someone. Honey, doesn't she look like someone from some show we like? What the fuck is that show called?"

I stand up a little straighter to give him a better view. I don't know why. I'm sure I'm not the girl, but maybe I am.

"Sorry," the woman says to me. "He always thinks everyone is someone."

"It's uncanny," he says, surveying me. "You look just like her. Whatever her name is."

"You're crazy," the wife says. "You're probably thinking about that Spanish girl. She's dating that famous actor and they live in Spain."

"Actually, I am an actor," I say, smoothing my hair against my scalp. I can't stop touching my hair. It feels important that my hair looks good right now, in case they decide to take a photo or invite me back to their villa in the Hills, or whatever.

They look at me with raised eyebrows.

"What have we seen you in?"

"*Law and Order,* maybe. I was the babysitter who let the kid drown in the bathtub."

The woman gasps. She thinks I'm a terrible person, in disguise.

"No," says Robert Darling. He rests his chin on his fist, looks intently at my face. Then, something like horror flickers across his. Yes, he has seen my face before. He has seen it wincing in hilarious pain, probably attached to something pornographic. Something he didn't want to pay for. I can see it in the way he blinks the memory away: He has jerked off to my face. Or at least to the body that came with it.

"What?" the wife says. She glances from his face to mine. "Is he right? Have we seen you?"

Robert Darling and I lock eyes. I consider doing the wince, holding a match to the little secret between us. But the idea makes my stomach twist, like if I give in to that role, my whole future could implode right here in the showroom. You don't get nominated for an Oscar for having a cameo in a few pornos. Better to nail a breakout role and wear something sheer and glittery to the premiere. So I smile instead to show him that I am prettier and more respectable than he remembers. A little snicker escapes from his mouth, and he chokes it back down, clears his throat to recover.

"No, no, you're right. I'm thinking of the Spanish girl." He reaches down and grabs his wife's hand. "Thanks. You'll call when it's on the way?"

"Sure."

His wife lays her head against his shoulder as I run his credit card. She looks relieved, like she's just broken him in, in some new way.

"He hates it when I'm right." She smiles. "But the thing is, I can't remember the last time I was wrong. Can you, babe?"

Her voice is high and sweet, the kind of voice you use when you want someone to think you're adorable. I don't think she's adorable. In fact, I think she's pretty dumb. Still, I'm jealous of her.

"Sure can't," he says, looking away from me. I wonder if he thinks she's adorably dumb, and what he thinks of me in comparison.

I watch them leave, hand in hand. *Robert, darling, take me to lunch, won't you?*

Dash skips into the office doorway. His face is totally red now, which makes his hair seem even whiter.

"That was close," he says. "What did they want?"

"A hot tub."

"Yeah, no duh. But they didn't see anything, right?"

"They didn't see anything." I walk over to the front door and lock it and turn the sign to Closed. "I need you to run lines with me."

"I don't know what you're talking about," he says slowly, like we're speaking two different languages.

"For my audition," I say, equally as slow. "I need to practice."

He stands up a little taller. He thinks I've tasked him with a secret mission and the world is depending on his execution of it. "Yeah. I can do that."

Back in his office, I print out my scenes. He goes to the printer and thumbs through them.

"Who am I?"

I tell him in this first scene I'm HIGH SCHOOL JUNKIE GIRLFRIEND, and he is BROTHER. All he has to do is say BROTHER's lines and do what BROTHER does and tell me if I've gotten any of my own lines wrong.

"Rad," he says. He pulls the mouse bag of coke from his pocket and spills more onto the desk.

"What are you doing? We already did that."

"Yeah, like, fifteen minutes ago." He makes lines again with the pamphlet. "You're supposed to be high, right?"

"Yeah."

"So?" He holds the pamphlet straw toward me.

I am better than Dash. Better than his creepy hair and his mouse drugs and his red face. But HIGH SCHOOL JUNKIE GIRLFRIEND is supposed to be desperate, strung out. In fact, she might be into Dash. She might feel comforted by his lack of ambition and eagerness to share his drugs. They might actually be a perfect match—two desperate nobodies just trying to pass the time, nothing cosmic headed their way.

I take the pamphlet straw and snort the line. Dash wiggles his arms and his legs, clears his throat, and looks down at the script.

" 'I need to borrow some money.' "

"That's my line," I say.

"Oh, then you say it."

" 'I need to borrow some money.' "

" 'Mom says I can't give you any money,' " he says, in a voice that's squeakier than his own.

" 'I don't care what Mom says.' "

He stares down at the script like he's trying to memorize all the lines in the next ten seconds.

"I need you to make eye contact with me," I say, breaking character. "Otherwise I might as well be alone."

"Right, sorry." He fixes his posture.

" 'I don't care what Mom says,' " I say again. I reach down and pick up a floating cup holder to use as a prop. Then I lift it above my head and slam it on the ground.

Dash giggles.

"What?"

"That's a cup holder."

"No, it's a piggy bank." I pick up the cup holder. "Again."

Dash says the lines and I throw the cup holder on the ground again, this time grunting a little, pretending it's heavier than it really is.

"Again."

I slam the cup holder on the ground over and over, and each time I scream louder. I don't feel like I'm acting, or like I'm there but not there. I feel like HIGH SCHOOL JUNKIE GIRLFRIEND, and I'm more present than ever. On the last smash, I get one tear.

"Whoa," Dash says. "How are you doing that?"

"I don't know. I've never done it before." I want to catch the tear in a jar and save it.

Dash takes the mouse bag out of his pocket along with his keys, opens it, and dips a key in and removes it with a tiny mound of cocaine on the tip. He lifts the key to his nose and stuffs the tip of it into his nostril, sniffs.

I have never seen cocaine done this way, and I suddenly feel proud of myself for coming here today. I feel like I made the right choice, professionally, and if I do get the part, I'll introduce this new key method into HIGH SCHOOL

JUNKIE GIRLFRIEND's portfolio, and I think everyone will be pretty impressed.

Dash hands me the bag. I stick the key in, stuff it into my nostril.

"Wait," he says. He stares at me with wide, glassy eyes, like he's just learned a new truth. Then he takes his shirt off. His chest is pale and virtually hairless. His stomach is doughy, almost like a toddler's.

"What the fuck." I step back. He tosses me his shirt and it lands on my head. It smells like an old burrito.

"For the role," he says.

I pull the shirt off my head and hold it at arm's length. "I can't have a new one?"

He looks down at the script. "So you think"—he points to the paper—"HIGH SCHOOL JUNKIE GIRLFRIEND would wear a crisp, brand-new polo shirt?"

I'm a little shocked by his logic. "No." I shake out the shirt. "Obviously I do not think that."

In the employee bathroom, I put the shirt on in front of the mirror and stare at myself. My hair is already tousled from all the movement, my eyes a little red and panicky. I smell stale, almost rotten.

"Look at you," I say to HIGH SCHOOL JUNKIE GIRLFRIEND. In the script, that's her full name. "Look at all the potential you're wasting."

Where are this poor girl's parents? They must be dead. They died before they could name her. And this boyfriend, the main junkie (whose name is SAM, by the way), where does he get off stealing the show? Why does he get to recover on camera while I stand here grinding my teeth to dust, begging to be slapped out of the movie? And why, why, why does nobody believe in me?

I should call Griffin and apologize. *I'm sorry I was inconsiderate about your sister*, I'll say. *I'm sorry your sister is dead.* No, I should call Amy and remind her who I am. *Hello, it's me, GROCERY STORE WOMAN TWO. GIRL WHO CAN'T SIT ON HARD SURFACES, just checking in. Is it my time yet?*

"Hey!" Dash screams at me from the other side of the door. "Are you taking a shit?"

When I walk back into the office, he's still topless, with his finger inside the empty mouse bag. He sticks the finger in his mouth and rubs his gums, then tosses the bag to the floor.

"You look like shit," he says.

"I need you to slap me."

"What? Fuck no. That's, like, corporate punishment. What if you sue me?"

"I'm not going to sue you. It's part of the scene. It's acting."

"No way."

I smooth out my hair and stare right into his glassy eyeballs. "Do it or I'll leave."

He glances around the room as if there might be a hidden camera somewhere. Then he takes a few deep breaths, bounces up and down on his toes. His belly jiggles.

"Okay, I'm ready."

I point to the script. "Third page. You're SAM."

"SAM, SAM, SAM." He licks his pointer finger and scans the script. "Okay. Scene."

I want to laugh at him, but instead I move closer and put my arms around his neck and sort of hang off him, because I am supposed to be in love with this person. His face contorts in confusion for a second, and then, it's unmistakable: pleasure. His eyes soften and a smile creeps up the corner of his mouth. He's dreamed about this before—about me, draped around his thick neck, begging for attention. It's all over his face. I'm making his dreams come true.

I want to remind him that this is the stage direction in the script, but I can't afford to break character right now.

" 'Slap me.' "

" 'I don't know,' " he says, glancing down at the script. His breath is hot and sour. " 'Maybe it's a bad idea.' " He puts his arms around my waist, which is not in the script.

" 'I'm full of bad ideas. Slap me. I need this.' " I run a hand through his freaky hair. " 'I want to feel my blood coming to the surface.' "

"*Rush.*"

"What?" I pull back.

"The line is 'I want to feel my blood rush to the surface.' "

"Fuck."

"Just say it again."

"Now I'm all mixed up." I let go of him and close my eyes. I search the backs of my eyelids for HIGH SCHOOL JUNKIE GIRLFRIEND.

"Just pick up right there," Dash says. " 'I want to feel my blood rush to the surface.' Come on, we were on a roll."

"Shut up. I'm thinking."

I can hear Dash's feet shuffling against the carpet. Then, out of nowhere, I feel a sharp smack against my cheek. The smack throws me off-balance and I stumble backward against Dash's desk. When I open my eyes, he's staring at his hand like it's holding a weapon. I touch my cheek. It's tingly, and a little numb. It doesn't hurt.

"I'm sorry," Dash says. "I don't know. I'm sorry."

"Do it again." I stand up and walk toward him.

"What? No. That was, like, totally crazy."

"Slap me."

I feel his hand hit my face, but not really. It's more like I see it coming and then it's over. I touch my cheek and it feels like someone else's skin.

"'I need this,'" I say. Only I'm almost screaming now.

Dash's hand strikes my cheek. My ears ring. I feel, suddenly, like I'm somewhere else. Like I'm watching myself. I don't look pretty or adorable, but I can feel the tickle in my throat that tells me I'm doing something significant. I scream the lines again and again, louder and louder, and Dash hits me two, three, four more times, until both our faces are red and warm with blood. The scene is wild and violent, but neither of us looks afraid. We look more like a team—two people rushing toward the same end, competing against some invisible force. As his hand comes swinging toward my face, I grab his wrist and we fall to the ground, dizzy and out of breath. We lie on our backs and stare up at the ceiling.

"Whoa," he says. His bare stomach rises and falls as he catches his breath. "I can't feel my hand."

"I can't feel my face." I grab my face in my hands and it's true, I can't feel it. I touch my lips and they're completely numb. I can't feel any part of myself, and I wonder if I'm even still me or if I've become someone else entirely.

"You're really good," he says. "I didn't think you would be, if I'm being honest. But you really could be an actor."

"I am an actor."

"Yeah, but you know what I mean. A real one."

My phone vibrates in my back pocket. I reach down and slide it out from under me. It's an email from Amy. It makes me feel good to know that she is thinking of me right now, like maybe I'm doing something right. I open the message.

Lead pushed a yr. no aud. chin up.

I read the email a few times. The words blur together like someone has smudged a dirty finger across them. Dash raises his hand in the air and rotates it, marveling at its abilities. His hand has a mind of its own. It reaches down and plays with the hem of my shirt. Technically, this is Dash's shirt. Technically, Dash's hand can do whatever it wants with his own shirt. I feel his knuckles against my hip as his hand fumbles around. Then, almost in slow motion, it slips beneath the shirt and crawls up my stomach. It pauses around my rib cage. I don't feel afraid of it.

The hand lands on my tit. It rests there for a second, then gives a little squeeze, a little *Hello, I am here, I feel you, can you feel me?*

A lot can happen in a year. I could become a whole new person. I could be famous by then.

ACKNOWLEDGMENTS

To my endlessly loving and supportive husband, Greg, thank you for encouraging me to write every time writing felt impossible and stupid. Thank you for being the dad who wants to hold the baby all the time. I'm enormously thankful to my agent, Madeline Wallace, for believing in these stories and bringing this book to life, and for being willing to drop everything to read a new draft, a new sentence, or even a long, rambling text that has nothing to do with anything. To the team at Bloomsbury, particularly Jillian Ramirez, my editor, thank you for your unwavering enthusiasm for these characters, your eye for the details, and your perspective, which helped transform these stories. I'm forever grateful for Jessica Anya Blau, for showing me how to be a writer, and Maddie Tavis, for the good times that created my voice. A massive thank-you to my family: my parents, Denis and Kindall Rende, for showing me that it's possible to build a career by doing the things you love as long as you have parents willing to pay for your vacations; and my siblings, Galen, Will, and Austen Rende. I'm so grateful to everyone at the Syracuse MFA program, particularly the people who taught me how to write, and most importantly, how to enjoy writing: Dana Spiotta, George Saunders, Jonathan Dee, and Arthur Flowers. And to my Syracuse fiction cohort, Neil Cooney, Rebecca Kurtz, Laura Moreno, Melissa Beneche, and Jackson Frons, thank you for sharing your talent, your feedback, and your friendship, especially during the winter; and an extra thank-you to Jackson Frons for your endless unsolicited fact-checking, without which this book would have dozens of inane inaccuracies. I'm so thankful for all my friends, particularly Molly Johnsen, for validating my obsession with reality TV and for eating Jell-O chocolate pudding with me every night while I was writing this collection; Molly Zager, for your camera skills and your stories; and Annell López—you've been the perfect pen pal. I couldn't have written this book if celebrities didn't exist, so I have to thank all the celebrities who gave me something to obsess over for twenty years. And finally, thank you, Scarlett, my beautiful, babbling kid, for giving me something better to obsess over. I love you. These stories are for you.

A NOTE ON THE AUTHOR

Sydney Rende has lived in New York City and Southern California, where she had her own odd brushes with celebrities. Her fiction has appeared in *Joyland*, *Carve Magazine*, and elsewhere, and she's dabbled in travel and fashion writing for *T: The New York Times Style Magazine* and *Who What Wear*. She has an MFA in fiction from Syracuse University.